MURDER AT THE SAVOY

MAJ SJÖWALL · PER WAHLÖÖ

Translated from the Swedish
by Amy and Ken Knoespel

VINTAGE BOOKS
A Division of Random House
New York

VINTAGE BOOKS EDITION, April 1977
Copyright © 1970 by Maj Sjöwall and Per Wahlöö
Copyright © 1971 by Random House, Inc.

Library of Congress Cataloging in Publication Data
Sjöwall, Maj, 1935-
   Murder at the Savoy.
   Translation of Polis, polis, potatismos!
   Reprint of the ed. published by Pantheon Books, New York
   I. Wahlöö, Per, 1926-1975, joint author.   II.   Title.
[PZ4.S61953Mu6]   [PT9876.29.J63]   839.7'3'74   76-42999
ISBN 0-394-72342-2

Manufactured in the United States of America

1

The day was hot and stifling, without a breath of air. There had been a haze quivering in the atmosphere, but now the sky was high and clear, its colors shifting from rose to dusky blue. The sun's red disk would soon disappear beyond the island of Ven. The evening breeze, which was already rippling the smooth mirror of the Sound, brought weak puffs of agreeable freshness to the streets of Malmö. With the gentle wind came fumes of the rotting garbage and seaweed that had been washed up on Ribersborg Beach and in through the mouth of the harbor into the canals.

The city doesn't resemble the rest of Sweden to a very great degree, largely because of its location. Malmö is closer to Rome than to the midnight sun, and the lights of the Danish coast twinkle along the horizon. And even if many winters are slushy and windblown, summers are just as often long and warm, filled with the song of the nightingale and scents from the lush vegetation of the expansive parks.

Which is exactly the way it was that fair summer evening early in July 1969. It was also quiet, calm and quite deserted. The tourists weren't noticeable to any extent—they hardly ever are. As for the roaming, unwashed hash-smokers, only the first bands had arrived, and not so many more would show up either, since most of them never get past Copenhagen.

It was rather quiet even in the big hotel across from the railroad station near the harbor. A few foreign businessmen were deliberating over their reservations at the reception desk. The checkroom attendant was reading one of the classics undisturbed in the depths of the cloakroom. The dimly lit bar contained only a couple of regular customers speaking in low voices and a bartender in a snow-white jacket.

In the large eighteenth-century dining room to the right

of the lobby there wasn't much going on either, even if it was somewhat livelier. A few tables were occupied, mostly by people who were sitting alone. The pianist was taking a break. In front of the swinging doors leading to the kitchen stood a waiter, hands behind his back, looking contemplatively out of the big open windows, probably lost in thoughts of the sand beaches not too far away.

A dinner party of seven, a well dressed and solemn gathering of varying sexes and ages, was sitting in the back of the dining room. Their table was cluttered with glasses and fancy dishes, surrounded by champagne coolers. The restaurant personnel had discreetly withdrawn, for the host had just risen to speak.

He was a tall man in late middle age, with a dark-blue shantung suit, iron gray hair and a deep suntan. He spoke calmly and skillfully, modulating his voice in subtly humorous phrases. The other six at the table sat watching him quietly; only one of them was smoking.

Through the open windows came the sounds of passing cars, trains switching tracks at the station across the canal, a switchyard that is the largest in northern Europe, the abrupt hoarse tooting of a boat from Copenhagen, and somewhere on the bank of the canal a girl giggling.

This was the scene that soft warm Wednesday in July, at approximately eight-thirty in the evening. It's essential to use the expression "approximately," for no one ever managed to pin down the exact time when it happened. On the other hand, what did happen is quite easy to describe.

A man came in through the main entrance, cast a glance at the reception desk with the foreign businessmen and the uniformed attendant, passed the checkroom and the long narrow lobby outside of the bar, and walked into the dining room calmly and resolutely, with steps that weren't notably rapid. There was nothing remarkable about this man so far. No one looked at him; he did not bother to look around either.

He passed the Hammond organ, the grand piano and the buffet with its array of glistening delicacies and continued past the two large pillars supporting the ceiling. With the same resolve he walked directly toward the party in the corner, where the host stood talking with his back turned to him. When the man was about five steps away, he thrust his right hand inside his suit coat. One of the women at the table looked at him, and the speaker half turned his head to see what was distracting her. He gave the approaching man a quick, indifferent glance, and started to turn back toward his guests, without a second's interruption in the comments he was making. At the same instant the newcomer pulled out a steel-blue object with a fluted butt and a long barrel, aimed carefully and shot the speaker in the head. The report was not shattering. It sounded more like the peaceful pop of a rifle in a shooting gallery at a fair.

The bullet struck the speaker just behind the left ear, and he fell forward onto the table, his left cheek in the crenelated mashed potatoes around an exquisite fish casserole à la Frans Suell.

Sticking the weapon into his pocket, the gunman turned sharply to the right, walked the few steps to the nearest open window, placed his left foot on the sill, swung himself over the low window, stepped into the flower box outside, hopped down onto the sidewalk and disappeared.

At the table three windows away a diner in his fifties became rigid and stared with amazement, a glass of whisky halfway to his mouth. In front of him was a book that he had been pretending to read.

The man with the suntan and the dark-blue shantung suit was not dead.

Stirring, he said, "Ow! It hurts."

Dead people don't usually complain. Besides, it didn't even look as if he were bleeding.

2

Per Månsson was sitting in his bachelor den on Regementsgatan, talking to his wife on the telephone. He was a Detective Inspector with the Malmö police force, and although he was married, he lived as a bachelor five days out of the week. For more than ten years he'd spent every free weekend with his wife—an arrangement which had so far satisfied both of them.

He cradled the receiver with his left shoulder while he mixed a Gripenberger with his right hand. It was his favorite drink, consisting simply of a jigger of gin, crushed ice and grape soda in a big tumbler.

His wife, who'd been to the movies, was telling him the plot of *Gone With the Wind*.

It took some time, but Månsson listened patiently, because as soon as she had finished the story he planned to ward off their usual weekend get-together with the excuse that he had to work. Which was a lie.

It was twenty minutes after nine in the evening.

Månsson was sweating in spite of his light clothing—a fishnet undershirt and checkered shorts. He had closed the balcony door at the beginning of the conversation so that he wouldn't be disturbed by the rumble of the traffic from the street. Although the sun had long ago sunk behind the roofs of the buildings across the street, it was very warm in the room.

He stirred his drink with a fork, which he was embarrassed to admit had been either stolen or taken by accident from a restaurant called "Översten." Månsson wondered if a person could take a fork by accident and said, "Yes, I see. It was Leslie Howard then who ... No, huh? Clark Gable? Uh-hmm ..."

Five minutes later she'd got to the end. He delivered his white lie and hung up.

The telephone rang. Månsson didn't answer immediately. He was off work and wanted to keep it that way. He slowly drained his Gripenberger. Watching the evening sky darken, he lifted the receiver and answered, "Månsson."

"This is Nilsson. That was a helluva long conversation. I've been trying to get you for half an hour."

Nilsson was an Assistant Detective, on duty that night at the central police station on Davidshall Square. Månsson sighed.

"Well?" he said. "What's up?"

"A man has been shot in the dining room at the Savoy. I'm afraid I'm going to have to ask you to get over there."

The glass was empty but still cold. Månsson picked it up and rolled it against his forehead with the palm of his hand.

"Is he dead?" he asked.

"Don't know," said Nilsson.

"Can't you send Skacke?"

"He's off. Impossible to get hold of. I'll keep looking for him. Backlund is there now, but you probably ought to ..."

Månsson gave a start and put down the glass.

"Backlund? Okay, I'll leave right away," he said.

He promptly called a taxi, then put the receiver on the table. While dressing, he listened to the rasping voice from the receiver mechanically repeating the words "Taxi Central, one moment please" until his call was finally put through to the operator.

Outside the Savoy Hotel several police cars were carelessly parked, and two patrolmen were blocking the entrance from a growing crowd of curious evening strollers jammed together at the bottom of the stairs.

Månsson took in the scene as he paid for the cab, put the receipt in his pocket, observed that one of the patrolmen was being rather brusque and reflected that it wouldn't be long before Malmö's police force had as bad a reputation as their colleagues in Stockholm.

He said nothing, however, only nodded as he walked past the uniformed patrolmen into the lobby. It was noisy there now. The hotel's entire staff had gathered and were chatting with each other and with some customers streaming out of the grill. Several policemen completed the picture. They seemed at a loss, unfamiliar with the surroundings. Evidently no one had told them how to act or what to expect.

Månsson was a big man in his fifties. He was dressed casually in dacron pants and sandals, with his shirt out. He took a toothpick from his breast pocket, pulled off the paper wrapper and stuck it in his mouth. As he chewed, he methodically took stock of the situation. The toothpick was American, menthol-flavored; he'd picked it up on the train ferry *Malmöhus*, which provides such things for its passengers.

Standing by the door leading to the large dining room

was a patrolman named Elofsson, whom Månsson thought was a little smarter than the others.

He walked over to him and said, "What's the story?"

"Looks like someone's been shot."

"Have you had any instructions?"

"Not a word."

"What's Backlund doing?"

"Questioning witnesses."

"Where's the man who was shot?"

"At the hospital, I guess."

Elofsson turned slightly red. Then he said, "The ambulance got here before the police, obviously."

Månsson sighed and went into the dining room.

Backlund was standing by the table with the gleaming silver tureens questioning a waiter. He was an elderly man with glasses and ordinary features. Somehow he'd managed to become a First Assistant Detective. He was holding his notebook open in his hand, busily taking notes. Månsson stopped within hearing distance, but said nothing.

"And at what time did this happen?"

"Uh, about eight-thirty."

"*About?*"

"Well, I don't know for sure."

"In other words, you don't know what time it was."

"No, I don't."

"Rather odd," said Backlund.

"What?"

"I said, it seems rather odd. You have a wrist watch, don't you?"

"Of course."

"And there is a clock on the wall over there, if I'm not mistaken."

"Yes, but . . ."

"But what?"

"Both of them are wrong. Anyway, I didn't think of looking at the clock."

Backlund appeared overwhelmed by the response. He put down the pad and pencil and began to clean his glasses. He took a deep breath, grabbed the notebook and started writing again.

"Even though you had two clocks at your disposal, you still didn't know what time it was."

"Well, kind of."

"We've got no use for 'kind of' answers."

"But the clocks aren't synchronized. Mine's fast, and the clock over there's slow."

Backlund consulted his Ultratron. "Odd," he said, writing something down.

Månsson wondered what.

"So, you were standing here when the criminal walked by?"

"Yes."

"Can you give me as full a description as possible?"

"I didn't really get a good look at him."

"You didn't see the gunman?" said Backlund, startled.

"Well, yes, when he climbed out the window."

"What did he look like?"

"I don't know. It was pretty far away, and that table was hidden by the pillar."

"You mean you don't know what he looked like?"

"Not really."

"How was he dressed then?"

"In a brown sport coat, I think."

"Think."

"Yeah. I only saw him for a second."

"What else did he have on? Try pants, for example."

"Sure, he had pants on."

"Are you certain?"

"Well, it sure would have seemed a little . . . like you said, odd, otherwise. If he hadn't had any pants on, I mean."

Backlund wrote furiously. Månsson started chewing on the other end of the toothpick and quietly said, "Say, Backlund?"

The other man turned around and glared.

"I'm in the middle of questioning an important witness . . ."

He broke off and said sullenly, "Oh, so it's you."

"What's going on?"

"A man was shot in here," said Backlund in great earnest. "And you know who?"

"No."

"Viktor Palmgren. The corporation president." Backlund laid heavy stress on the label.

"Oh, him," said Månsson. And thought, this'll be a helluva time. Aloud he said, "It happened over an hour ago and the gunman climbed out the window and got away."

"It may look that way."

Backlund never took anything for granted.

"Why are there six police cars outside?"

"I had them close off the area."

"The whole block?"

"The scene of the crime," said Backlund.

"Get rid of everybody in uniform," Månsson said wearily. "It can't be very pleasant for the hotel to have police swarming around in the foyer and out on the street. Besides, they must be needed more some place else. Then try to get up a description. There has to be a better witness than this guy."

"Naturally, we'll question everybody," said Backlund.

"All in due time," said Månsson. "But don't detain anyone who doesn't have something crucial to say. Just take names and addresses."

Backlund looked at him suspiciously and said, "What are you planning to do?"

"Make some telephone calls," said Månsson.

"Who to?"

"The newspapers, to find out what's happened."

"Was that supposed to be a joke?" said Backlund coldly.

"Right," said Månsson absentmindedly and looked around.

Journalists and photographers were roaming around in the dining room. Some of them must have been there long before the police, and one or more had been on the spot in the grill or the bar when the famous shot was fired. Probably. If Månsson's suspicions proved correct.

"But the manual requires . . . ," Backlund began.

Just then Benny Skacke hurried into the dining room. He was thirty years old, and already an Assistant Detective. Previously he had been with the National Homicide Squad in Stockholm, but had asked to be transferred after taking a rather foolish risk that had almost cost the life of one of his superiors. He was dedicated, conscientious, somewhat naive. Månsson liked him.

"Skacke can help you," he said.

"A Stockholmer," said Backlund skeptically.

"Right," said Månsson. "And don't forget that description. That's all that matters now."

He threw his shredded toothpick into an ashtray, went out into the lobby and headed for the telephone across from the reception desk.

Månsson made five calls in rapid succession. Then he shook his head and went into the bar.

"Well, look who's here!" said the bartender.

"How's it going?" Månsson said and sat down.

"What can we give you today? The usual?"

"No. Just a grape soda. I've got to think."

Sometimes everything gets messed up, Månsson thought. This case had really got off to a bad start. In the first place, Viktor Palmgren was important and well known. True, it was hard to tell exactly why, but one thing was certain—he had plenty of money, at least a million. The fact that he had been shot down in one of the most famous restaurants in Europe didn't help matters. This case would attract a lot of attention and could have far-reaching consequences. Immediately after the shooting, the hotel personnel had carried the wounded man out to a TV lounge and fixed a makeshift stretcher. They'd alerted the police and an ambulance at the same time. The ambulance had come very quickly, picked up the wounded man and taken him to General Hospital. For a while there had been no sign of the police. In spite of the fact that a patrol car had been parked at the railroad station—in other words, less than 200 yards from the scene of the crime. How had that happened? He had received the explanation now, but it wasn't especially flattering to the police. The call had been misinterpreted at first, the case judged to be less urgent than others. The two patrolmen at the train station had therefore spent their time picking up a completely harmless drunk. Only after the police had been alerted a second time had cars and uniformed men been dispatched to the hotel, with Backlund fearlessly in the lead. What had then been undertaken in the way of investigation seemed totally slipshod. Månsson himself had sat rehashing *Gone With the Wind* with his wife for more than forty minutes. Besides that, he'd had two drinks and been forced to wait for a taxi. When the first police-man arrived, half an hour had passed since the shot was fired. As to Viktor Palmgren's condition, the situation was equally unclear. He had been examined at the emergency ward in Malmö, then referred to a neurosurgeon in Lund, about fifteen miles away. At this very second the ambulance was still on its way. One of the most important witnesses, Palmgren's wife, was also in the ambulance. She'd probably sat across from him at the table and had been the person most likely to get a close look at the gunman.

An hour had already gone by. An hour wasted, and every second of it was precious.

Månsson shook his head again and glanced at the clock above the bar. Nine-thirty.

Backlund marched into the bar, followed closely by Skacke.

"And you just sit here?" Backlund said, quite surprised.

He strained his eyes to stare at Månsson.

"How's the description coming?" said Månsson. "We've got to get a move on."

Backlund fumbled with his notebook, put it on the bar, took off his glasses and began cleaning them.

"Listen," Skacke said quickly, "this is the best we can come up with right now. Medium tall, thin face, thin dark brown hair, combed back. Brown sport coat, pastel shirt, dark gray pants, black or brown shoes. Age about forty."

"Fine," said Månsson. "Send it out. Right away. Block all main roads, check out trains, planes and boats."

"Right," said Skacke.

"I want him to stay in town," said Månsson.

Skacke left.

Backlund put on his glasses, stared at Månsson and repeated his pertinent question, "And you just sit here?"

Then he looked at the glass, saying with even greater astonishment, "Drinking?"

Månsson didn't reply.

Backlund turned his attention to the clock over the bar, compared it with his watch and said, "That clock's wrong."

"Of course," the bartender said. "It's fast. A little service for guests who're in a hurry to catch a train or boat."

"Hmm," Backlund said. "We'll never get this figured out. How can we determine the correct time when we can't rely on the clock?"

"It won't be too easy," Månsson said absentmindedly.

Skacke came back.

"Well, that's done," he said.

"Probably too late," Månsson said.

"What in the world are you talking about?" Backlund said, seizing his notepad. "About this waiter . . ."

Dismissing him with a gesture, Månsson said, "Wait. We'll take that later. Benny, go call the police in Lund and ask them to send a man to the neurosurgeon at the hospital. The man they send should have a tape recorder with him so he can take down anything Palmgren says. If and when he regains consciousness. He'll have to question Mrs. Palmgren, too."

Skacke departed again.

"About this special waiter. I'd say he wouldn't have noticed a thing if Dracula himself had fluttered through the dining room," the bartender said.

Irritated, Backlund kept quiet. Månsson waited to say anything else until Skacke came back. Since Backlund was officially Skacke's superior, he carefully addressed his question to both of them.

"Who do you two think is the best witness?"

"A guy named Edvardsson," said Skacke. "He was sitting only three tables away. But . . ."

"But what?"

"He isn't sober."

"Liquor's a curse," Backlund said.

"Okay, we wait with him until tomorrow," said Månsson. "Who can drop me off at headquarters?"

"I can," said Skacke.

"I'll stay here," Backlund said stubbornly. "This is officially my case."

"Sure," said Månsson. "We'll be seeing you."

In the car he mumbled, "Trains and boats . . ."

"Do you think he's gotten out of here?" asked Skacke hesitantly.

"He could have left. Any way you look at it, we've got

a whole lot of people to call. And we can't worry about waking anybody up."

Skacke looked sideways at Månsson, who was taking out another toothpick. The car swung into the courtyard of the main police station.

"Planes," Månsson said to himself. "It could be a rough night."

The station seemed large, grim and very empty at this time of day. It was an impressive building. Their steps echoed desolately on the broad stone staircase.

By nature, Månsson was as slow-moving as he was tall. He detested rough nights, and besides, most of his career was behind him.

The opposite was true of Skacke. He was twenty years younger, thought about his career a lot and was eager and ambitious. But his previous experience as a policeman had made him careful, anxious to do what was expected.

So, in fact, they complemented each other quite well.

Inside his room Månsson immediately opened the window, which faced the station's asphalt courtyard. Then he sank down in his desk chair and sat silently for several minutes, reflectively spinning the platen on his old Underwood.

Finally he said, "Get all the radio messages and calls sent up here. Take them on your telephone."

Skacke had a room on the other side of the corridor, across from Månsson.

"You can leave the doors open," Månsson said.

And after several seconds he added with mild irony, "That way we'll have a real tracking center."

Skacke went into his room and began using the telephone. After a little while Månsson followed him. He stood with a toothpick in the corner of his mouth, one shoulder propped against the doorpost.

"Have you given this any thought, Benny?" he said.

"Not very much," said Skacke carefully. "It seems incredible, somehow."

"Incredible is the word for it," Månsson said.

"What I don't get is the motive."

"I don't think we should give a damn about the motive until we get the details straight."

The telephone rang. Skacke made a note.

"The person who shot Palmgren had only one chance in a thousand of making it out of the hotel dining room afterward. Up to the second the shot was fired, he acted like a fanatic."

"Something like an assassination?"

"Right. And afterward? What happens? Miraculously enough he escapes, and then he doesn't act like a fanatic any more, but panics."

"Is that why you think he's trying to leave town?"

"Partly. He walks in and shoots and doesn't care what happens afterward. But then, like most criminals, he panics. He simply gets frightened and only wants to get away from there, as far and as fast as possible."

That's one theory, Skacke thought. Seems rather loosely founded, though.

But he said nothing.

"Of course it's only a theory," Månsson said. "A good detective can't rely just on theories. But for the time being I don't see any other line we can work on."

The telephone rang.

Work, Månsson thought. What a helluva way to work. And he was supposed to have a day off!

It was a rough night in the sense that nothing really happened. Some people who more or less fitted the description were stopped on the highways leading out of the city and at the train station. None of them seemed to have anything to do with the case, but their names were taken.

At twenty to one the last train left the station.

At quarter to two the police in Lund sent the message that Palmgren was alive.

At three o'clock another message came from the same source. Mrs. Palmgren was in shock, and it was difficult to question her thoroughly. However, she had seen the gunman clearly and was sure she didn't recognize him.

"Seems on the job, that guy in Lund," said Månsson with a yawn.

Just after four the Lund police got in touch again. The team of doctors treating Palmgren had decided for the present not to operate. The bullet had penetrated behind his left ear; it was impossible to tell what damage had been caused. The condition of the patient was reported to be as good as could be expected.

Månsson's condition wasn't good. Tired, his throat very dry, he went out to the washroom time after time to fill up on water.

"Is it possible for someone to live with a bullet in his head?" asked Skacke.

"Yes," said Månsson, "it's been done before. Sometimes it's enclosed by the tissue, and the person recovers. If the doctors had tried to remove it, however, he probably would've died."

Backlund had evidently stuck to the Savoy for a long time, for at four-thirty he called to say that he had blockaded and sealed off an area in anticipation of the technical squad's investigation of the scene of the crime, which might take place in several hours, at the soonest.

"He wants to know if he's needed here," said Skacke, holding his hand over the receiver.

"The only place he could possibly be needed is at home in bed with his wife," said Månsson.

Skacke conveyed the message but modified the wording somewhat. Soon after this Skacke said, "I think we can rule out Bulltofta. The last plane left at five after eleven. Nobody on board answered the description. The next one takes off at six-thirty. It's been booked up since the day before yesterday, and there's nobody on the waiting list."

Månsson mulled over that for a while. "Hmm," he said finally. "Guess I'll call up somebody who sure isn't going to like being dragged out of bed."

"Who? The police chief?"

"No, he probably hasn't slept any more than we have. By the way, where were you hiding out last night?"

"At the movies," said Skacke. "You can't sit home and study every night."

"I've never sat home and studied," said Månsson. "One of those hydrofoils left Malmö for Copenhagen at nine o'clock. Try to find out which one it was."

That was an unexpectedly difficult task, and half an hour went by before Skacke could report, "It's called *Springeren,* and right now it's in Copenhagen. It's unbelievable how sore some people get when you call and get them out of bed."

"You can comfort yourself with the fact that I've got a much worse job now," said Månsson.

He went into his room, picked up the telephone, dialed Denmark, 00945, and then the home number of Police Captain Mogensen, Danish Bureau of Investigation. He counted seventeen buzzes before a thick voice said, "Mogensen."

"This is Per Månsson in Malmö."

"What the hell do you want?" said Mogensen. "Do you know what time it is?"

"Yes," said Månsson, "but this could be very important."

"It'd better be goddamned important," the Dane said threateningly.

"We had an attempted murder here in Malmö last night," said Månsson. "There's a chance that the gunman flew to Copenhagen. We have a description."

Then he related the whole story, and Mogensen said bitterly, "For chrissake, do you think I can work miracles?"

"Why not?" said Månsson. "Let us know if you find out anything."

"Go to hell," said Mogensen in a surprisingly clear voice and slammed down the receiver.

Månsson shook himself, yawning.

Nothing happened.

Backlund called later to say that they'd begun investigating the scene of the crime. It was then eight o'clock.

"Hell, he's really on the ball," Månsson said.

"Where do we go from here?" asked Skacke.

"Nowhere. Wait."

At twenty to nine Månsson's private line rang. He lifted the receiver, listened for a minute or two, broke off the conversation without saying so much as thanks or good-bye and yelled to Skacke, "Call Stockholm. Right away."

"What should I say?"

Månsson looked at the clock.

"That was Mogensen. He said a Swede who gave his name as Bengt Stensson bought a ticket from Kastrup to Stockholm last night and then waited stand-by for several hours. He finally got on an SAS flight that took off at eight twenty-five. The plane should have landed at Arlanda ten minutes ago at most. The guy might fit the description. I want the bus from the airport into the city stopped at the air terminal, and this man taken into custody."

Skacke rushed to the telephone.

"Okay," he said breathlessly half a minute later. "Stockholm will take care of it."

"Who did you talk to?"

"Gunvald Larsson."

"Oh, him."

They waited.

After half an hour Skacke's telephone rang. He yanked the receiver to his ear, listened and was left sitting with it in his hand. "They blew it," he said.

"Oh," Månsson said laconically.

But they'd had twenty minutes, he thought.

3

A similar expression was used in the main police station on Kungsholmsgatan in Stockholm.

"Well, they blew it," said Einar Rönn, sticking his sweaty red face through a crack in the door to Gunvald Larsson's room.

"Which one?" Gunvald Larsson asked absentmindedly.

He was thinking about something completely different, specifically three unusually brutal robberies in the subway the night before. Two rapes. Sixteen fights. This was Stockholm, quite a different place. Even though there were no murders last night, not even a homicide. Thank god. How many burglaries or thefts had been committed, he didn't know. Or how many addicts, sexual offenders, bootleggers and alcoholics the police had taken into custody. Or how many policemen had worked over presumably innocent people in patrol cars and local stations. Probably too many to count. He minded his own business.

Gunvald Larsson was a First Assistant Detective on the Assault and Battery Squad. Six foot three, strong as an ox, blond, blue-eyed, he was very snobbish for a policeman. This morning, for example, he was dressed in a pale gray, lightweight suit with matching tie, shoes and socks. He was an odd character; not many people liked him.

"You know, that bus to Haga air terminal," Rönn said.

"Well, what about it? They blew it?"

"The patrolmen who were supposed to check the passengers didn't get there soon enough. When they arrived the passengers had all got out and disappeared, and the bus had driven off."

Finally switching his thoughts to the subject at hand, Gunvald Larsson glared at Rönn with his blue eyes and said, "What? But that's impossible."

"Unfortunately not," said Rönn. "They just didn't get there on time."

"Have you gone crazy?"

"I'm not the one who is in charge of this," Rönn said. "I wasn't the one."

He was calm and good-natured, originally from Arjeplog in the north of Sweden. Although he had lived in Stockholm for a long time, he still used some dialect.

Gunvald Larsson had received Skacke's call quite by chance and considered checking this bus as a simple routine measure. He scowled angrily and said, "But goddammit, I called Solna promptly. The man on duty there said they had a patrol car on Karolinskavägen. It takes three minutes at most to drive to the air terminal from there. They had at least twenty minutes. What happened?"

"The guys in the car seem to have been detained on the way."

"Detained?"

"Yes, they had to issue a warning. And when they got there the bus had already left."

"A warning?"

Putting on his glasses, Rönn looked at the piece of paper he was holding in his hand. "Right. The bus's name is Beata. Usually it comes from Bromma."

"Beata? What kind of asshole has started giving names to busses?"

"Well, it's not my fault," Rönn said sedately.

"Do the geniuses in the patrol car have names, too?"

"Very likely. But I don't know what they are."

"Find out. For chrissake, if busses have names, patrolmen must have them too. Although really they should only have numbers."

"Or symbols."

"Symbols?"

"You know, like kids at nursery school. Like boats, cars, birds, mushrooms, bugs or dogs."

"I've never been in a nursery school," Gunvald Larsson said scornfully. "Now find out. That guy Månsson in Malmö is going to die laughing if there's no reasonable explanation."

Rönn left.

"Bugs or dogs," Gunvald Larsson said to himself. And added, "Everybody's crazy."

Then he went back to the robberies in the subway, picking his teeth with the letter-opener.

After ten minutes Rönn came back, glasses on his red nose, paper in hand. "I've got it now," he said. "Car three from the Solna police station. Patrolmen Karl Kristiansson and Kurt Kvant."

Gunvald Larsson jerked forward suddenly, nearly committing suicide with the letter-opener. "Christ, I should have known. I'm hounded by those two idiots. They're from Skåne, too. Get them over here on the double. We've got to straighten this thing out."

Kristiansson and Kvant had a lot of explaining to do. Their story was complicated and not at all easy. Besides, they were scared to death of Gunvald Larsson and managed to postpone their visit to the police station on Kungsholmsgatan for nearly two hours. That was a mistake, for in the meantime Gunvald Larsson made successful inquiries on his own.

Finally they were standing there anyway, uniformed, proper, caps in hand. They were six foot one, blond and broad-shouldered, and looked woodenly at Gunvald Larsson with dull blue eyes. They were wondering to themselves why Gunvald Larsson would be the one to break the unwritten but golden rule that police aren't supposed to criticize the actions of other policemen or to testify against each other.

"Good morning," said Gunvald Larsson in a friendly manner. "Nice that you could make it."

"Good morning," said Kristiansson hesitantly.

"Hi," said Kvant insolently.

Gunvald Larsson stared at him, sighed and said, "You were the ones who were supposed to check the passengers on that bus in Haga, weren't you?"

"Yes," said Kristiansson.

He reflected. Then he added, "But we got there late."

"We couldn't make it on time," Kvant improved.

"I've gathered that,"' said Gunvald Larsson. "I've also gathered that you were parked on Karolinskavägen when you got the call. Driving to the air terminal from there takes about two minutes, three at most. What make of car do you have?"

"A Plymouth," Kristiansson said, squirming.

"A perch does a mile and a half an hour," said Gunvald Larsson. "It's the slowest fish there is. But still it could've easily covered that stretch in a shorter time than you did."

He paused. Then roared, "Why the hell couldn't you get there on time?"

"We had to caution somebody on the way," said Kvant stiffly.

"A perch probably could have come up with a better explanation," Gunvald Larsson said with resignation. "Well, what was this caution about?"

"We . . . were called names," Kristiansson said feebly.

"Abuse of an officer of the law," said Kvant emphatically.

"And how did that happen?"

"A man riding by on a bicycle shouted insults at us."

Kvant was still acting the part while Kristiansson was standing saying nothing, but looking more and more uneasy.

"And that prevented you from carrying out the orders you'd just received?"

Kvant had the answer ready. "In an official statement, the National Chief of Police himself said that a complaint should definitely be brought against anyone who abuses an officer, especially an officer in uniform. A policeman can't be made a laughing stock."

"Is that so?" said Gunvald Larsson.

The two patrolmen glared at him unsympathetically.

He shrugged and went on: "Now I grant you that the

potentate you mention is famous for his official statements, but I doubt that even he could have said anything so utterly stupid, for chrissake. Well, how did those insults go?"

" 'Pig!' " Kvant said.

"And you think you didn't deserve that?"

"Absolutely not," Kvant said.

Gunvald Larsson looked searchingly at Kristiansson, who shifted his weight and mumbled, "Yes, I suppose so."

"Yeah," Kvant said. "And even if Siv would say . . ."

"What is Siv?" said Gunvald Larsson. "Is that a bus, too?"

"My wife," said Kvant.

Gunvald Larsson disentangled his fingers and put his enormous hairy hands on the desk top, palms down. "Here's how it happened," he said. "You were parked on Karolinskavägen. You had just gotten the alert. Then a man rode by on his bicycle and shouted 'Pig!' at you. You were obliged to caution him. And that's why you didn't make it to the air terminal on time."

"That's right," said Kvant.

"Yeeaah," said Kristiansson.

Gunvald Larsson watched them for a long time. Finally he said in a low voice, "Is that true?"

No one answered. Kvant began to look apprehensive. Kristiansson nervously fingered his pistol holster with one hand, wiping the sweat off his forehead with his cap.

Gunvald Larsson remained quiet for a long time, letting the silence deepen. Suddenly he raised his arms and slammed his palms down on the table, with a smack that made the whole room shake.

"It's a lie," he shouted. "Every single word is a lie; and you know it, too. You'd stopped at a drive-in. One of you was standing outside the car eating a hot dog. As you said, a man rode by on a bicycle and someone shouted something at you. But it wasn't the man who shouted, it was his son who was sitting in the kiddie carrier on the back of the bike. And he didn't yell 'Pig!' but 'Daddy, this little pig . . .' He is only three years old. He plays with his toes, for chrissake."

Gunvald Larsson broke off abruptly.

By now Kristiansson and Kvant were as red as beets.

At long last Kristiansson mumbled indistinctly, "How on earth did you know?"

Gunvald Larsson looked piercingly from one to the other. "All right, who was eating the hot dog?" he asked.

"Not me," said Kristiansson.

"You sonovabitch," Kvant whispered out of the corner of his mouth.

"Well, let me answer the question for you," Gunvald Larsson said tiredly. "The man on the bicycle simply wouldn't let two idiots in uniform bawl him out for more than fifteen minutes for something a three-year-old happened to say. So he called here to complain and had every right to do so. Especially since there were witnesses."

Kristiansson nodded glumly.

Kvant tried to make a final defense: "It's easy to hear the wrong thing when you've got your mouth full of . . ."

Gunvald Larsson cut him off by raising his right hand.

He pulled over his notepad, took a pencil out of his inside pocket and printed in large letters, "GO TO HELL!" He tore off the page and shoved it across the desk. Kristiansson took the sheet, glanced at it, turned a deeper shade of red and gave it to Kvant.

"I can't bear to say it one more time," Gunvald Larsson said.

Kristiansson and Kvant took the message and left.

4

Martin Beck didn't know anything about all that.

He was in his office at the South police station on Västberga Allé, working on quite different problems. He had pushed back his chair and was sitting with his legs outstretched and his feet on the lower desk drawer, which he'd drawn halfway out. He bit down on the filter tip of a newly-lit Florida, thrust his hands deep into his pants pockets and squinted out the window. He was thinking.

Since he was a Chief Inspector in the National Homicide Squad, it might be supposed that he was meditating on the ax murder on the South Side, which was still unsolved after a week. Or on the unidentified female corpse that had been fished up from Riddarfjärden the day before. But that wasn't the case.

He was brooding over what he should buy for his dinner party that night.

At the end of May, Martin Beck had found a two-room apartment on Köpmangatan and moved away from home. He and Inga had been married for eighteen years, but the marriage had been on the rocks for some time, and in January, when his daughter Ingrid had moved in with a friend, lock, stock and barrel, he'd talked to his wife about separating. At first she'd protested, but when the lease was ready, and she was faced with the facts, she accepted. Rolf, their fourteen-year-old, was her favorite, and Martin Beck suspected that she was actually pleased to be alone with the boy.

The apartment was cozy and large enough, and when he'd finally arranged the few things he'd taken with him from his and Inga's home out in the dismal suburb of Bagarmossen and bought what he still needed, he'd had an attack of recklessness and invited his three best friends for dinner. Considering that, at best, his knowledge of cooking consisted of boiling eggs and brewing tea, that was reckless to say the least; he realized that now. He tried to recollect what Inga used to serve when they had company, but managed only to evoke diffuse images of hearty dishes whose preparation and ingredients were totally foreign to him.

Martin Beck lit another cigarette and thought with confusion of Sole Walewska and filet of veal *à la Oscar*. Not to mention *cœur de filet provençale*. Furthermore, there was one more detail that he hadn't taken into consideration when he extended his unpremeditated invitation. He had never seen three people with appetites so voracious as those of the forthcoming guests.

Lennart Kollberg, who was the person he worked with most closely, was both a gourmet and a gourmand; he'd had the chance to observe this the times he'd ventured down to the lunchroom. In addition, Kollberg's size indicated a strong interest in the delicacies of the table—not even an ugly knife wound in the stomach about a year earlier had been able to remedy that peculiarity. Gun Kollberg didn't have her husband's figure, but did have quite a good appetite. Åsa Torell, now a colleague of his, too, since she had been placed on the Vice Squad after graduating from the Police Academy, was a real Gargantua.

He remembered very distinctly how small, thin and spindly she'd looked a year and a half earlier, when her husband, Martin Beck's youngest Assistant Detective, had been shot to death on a bus by a mass murderer. She'd got over the worst now, regained her appetite and even become a little rounder. Presumably she had an astounding metabolic rate.

Martin Beck considered asking Åsa to come earlier so she could help, but dismissed the thought.

A meaty fist rapped on the door, which was promptly opened, and Kollberg came into the room.

"What are you sitting here thinking about?" he said, throwing himself into the extra chair, which creaked precariously under his weight.

Nobody would suspect that Kollberg knew more about burglars' tricks and the science of self-defense than perhaps anyone else on the force.

Martin Beck took his feet down from the drawer and pushed the chair nearer the desk. He put out his cigarette carefully before answering.

"About that ax murder in Hjorthagen," he lied. "Nothing new's turned up?"

"Have you seen the autopsy report? It says that the guy died after the first blow. He had an unusually thin skull."

"Yes, I've seen it," Martin Beck said.

"We'll have to see when we can talk to his wife," Kollberg said. "She's still in deep shock, according to what they said at the hospital this morning. Maybe she bludgeoned him to death herself, who knows?"

He stood up and walked over to open the window.

"Close it," said Martin Beck.

Kollberg closed the window.

"How can you stand it?" he complained. "It's like an oven in here."

"I'd rather be baked than poisoned," Martin Beck said philosophically.

The South police station was located very near to Es-
singe Parkway, and when the traffic was heavy, like now, at
the beginning of vacation time, it was obvious how thick
the air was with exhaust fumes.

"You'll only have yourself to blame," Kollberg said and
lumbered over to the door. "Try to survive until tonight,
anyway. Did you say seven?"

"Yes, seven," Martin Beck said.

"I'm hungry already," said Kollberg provocatively.

"Glad you can come," Martin Beck said, but the door
had already slammed shut behind Kollberg.

A moment later the telephone began ringing and people
arrived with papers to sign, reports to read and questions
to answer, and he had to push aside all thoughts of the
evening's menu.

At quarter to four he left the police station and took
the subway to Hötorgshallen. There he walked around
shopping for such a long while that finally he had to take
a taxi home to Gamla Stan to have time to fix everything.

At five to seven he'd finished setting the table and
surveyed his work.

There was matjes herring on a bed of dill, sour cream
and chives. A dish of carp roe with a wreath of diced
onion, dill and lemon slices. Thin slices of smoked salmon
spread out on fragile lettuce leaves. Sliced hard-boiled
eggs. Smoked herring. Smoked flounder. Hungarian sala-
mi, Polish sausage, Finnish sausage and liver sausage from
Skåne. A large bowl of lettuce with lots of fresh shrimp.
He was especially proud of that, since he had made it
himself and to his surprise it even tasted good. Six different cheeses on a cutting board. Radishes and olives.
Pumpernickel, Hungarian country bread, and French
bread, hot and crusty. Country butter in a tub. Fresh
potatoes were simmering on the stove, sending out small
puffs of dill fragrance. In the refrigerator were four bottles of Piesporter Falkenberg, cans of Carlsberg Hof and a
bottle of Løjtens schnapps in the freezer compartment.

Martin Beck felt very satisfied with the results of his
efforts. Now only the guests were missing.

Åsa Torell arrived first. Martin Beck mixed two Cam-
pari sodas for them and she made a tour of inspection,
drink in hand.

The apartment consisted of a bedroom, living room, kitchen, bathroom and hall. The rooms were small, but easy to take care of and comfortable, too.

"I don't really have to ask if you like it here," Asa Torell said.

"Like most native Stockholmers, I've always dreamed of having an apartment in Gamla Stan," Martin Beck said. "It's great to get along on my own, too."

Asa nodded. She was leaning against the window frame, her ankles crossed, holding the glass with both hands. Small and delicate, she had big brown eyes, short dark hair and tanned skin, and she looked healthy, calm and relaxed. It made Martin Beck happy to see her so, for it had taken her a long time to get over Ake Stenström's death.

"How about you?" he asked. "You moved not very long ago, too."

"Come see me sometime and I'll show you around," said Asa.

After Stenström's death, Asa had lived with Gun and Lennart Kollberg for a while, and since she didn't want to return to the apartment where she'd lived with him, she'd exchanged it for a one-room apartment on Kungsholmsstrand. She had also quit her job at a travel agency and started studying at the Police Academy.

Dinner was a great success. Despite the fact that Martin Beck didn't eat much himself (he did so seldom, if ever), the food was disposed of rapidly. He wondered anxiously if he'd underestimated their appetites, but when the guests stood up from the table, they seemed full and content, and Kollberg discreetly unbuttoned the waistband of his pants. Asa and Gun preferred schnapps and beer to wine, and when the dinner was over, the Løjtens bottle was empty.

Martin Beck served cognac with coffee, raised his glass and said, "Now let's all get a real good hangover tomorrow, when we have time off on the same day for once."

"I don't have time off," Gun said. "Bodil comes and jumps on my stomach at five and wants breakfast."

Bodil was the Kollbergs' almost two-year-old daughter.

"Don't think about it," Kollberg said. "I'll take care of her tomorrow, hungover or not. And don't talk about work. If I'd been able to get a decent job, I'd have quit after that incident a year ago."

"Don't think about it now," Martin Beck said.

"It's damned hard not to," Kollberg said. "The whole police force here is going to fall apart sooner or later. Just look at those poor clods from the country, who meander around in their uniforms and don't know what to do with themselves. And what an administration!"

"Oh, well," Martin Beck said to divert him and grasped his cognac.

Even he was very worried, most of all by the way in which the force had been politicized and centralized after the recent reorganization. That the quality of the personnel on patrol was getting lower all the time hardly improved things. But this was hardly the proper occasion to discuss the matter.

"Oh, well," he repeated wistfully and lifted his glass.

After coffee Åsa and Gun wanted to wash the dishes. When Martin Beck protested, they explained that they loved to wash dishes anywhere but at home. He let them have their way and carried in whisky and water.

The telephone rang.

Kollberg looked at the clock.

"A quarter after ten," he said. "I'll be damned if it isn't Malm telling us that we have to work tomorrow anyway. I'm not here."

Malm was Chief Superintendent of Police and had succeeded Hammar, their previous chief, who had recently retired. Malm had come from nowhere, that is to say from the National Police Board, and his qualifications appeared to be exclusively political. Anyway, it seemed a bit mysterious.

Martin Beck picked up the receiver.

Then he grimaced eloquently.

Instead of Malm, it was the National Chief of Police, who said gratingly, "Something's happened. I have to ask you to go to Malmö first thing tomorrow morning."

Then he added, somewhat belatedly, "Please excuse me if I'm disturbing you."

Martin Beck didn't respond to that, but said, "To Malmö? What's happened?"

Kollberg, who'd just mixed a highball for himself, raised

his eyes and shook his head. Martin Beck gave him a look of defeat and pointed to his glass.

"Have you heard of Viktor Palmgren?" said the Chief of Police.

"The executive? The V.I.P.?"

"Yes."

"Of course I've heard of him, but I don't know much about him other than that he has a million different companies and he's loaded. Oh, yeah, he also has a beautiful young wife who was a model or something. What's wrong with him?"

"He's dead. He died tonight at the neurosurgical clinic in Lund after he was shot in the head by an unknown assailant in the dining room of the Savoy in Malmö. It happened last night. Don't you have newspapers out in Västberga?"

Martin Beck again refrained from replying. Instead he said, "Can't they take care of it themselves down in Malmö?"

He took the glass of whisky Kollberg offered him and took a drink.

"Isn't Per Månsson on duty?" he continued. "He surely ought to be capable of . . ."

The Chief of Police cut him off impatiently.

"Of course Månsson is on duty, but I want you to go down and help him. Or rather to take charge of the case. And I want you to leave as soon as you can."

Thanks a lot, thought Martin Beck. A plane did leave Bromma at a quarter to one in the morning, but he didn't plan to be on it.

"I want you to leave early tomorrow," the Chief of Police said.

Obviously he didn't know the schedule.

"This is an extremely complicated, sensitive matter. And we have to solve it without delay."

It was quiet for a moment. Martin Beck sipped his drink and waited. Finally the other man continued, "It's the wish of someone higher up that you take charge of this."

Martin Beck frowned and met Kollberg's questioning look.

"Was Palmgren that important?" he said.

"Obviously. There were strong vested interests in certain areas of his operations."

Can't you skip the clichés and come out with it? Martin Beck thought. Which interests and which certain areas of which operations?

Evidently it was important to be cryptic.

"Unfortunately I don't have a clear idea of what kind of operations he was engaged in," he said.

"You'll be informed about all that eventually," the Chief of Police said. "The most important thing is that you get to Malmö as quickly as possible. I've talked to Malm, and he's willing to release you. We have to do our utmost to apprehend this man. And be careful when you talk to the press. As you can well understand, there's going to be a good deal written about this. Well, when can you leave?"

"There's a plane at nine-fifty in the morning, I think," Martin Beck said hesitantly.

"Fine. Take it," said the Chief of Police and hung up.

5

Viktor Palmgren died at seven-thirty-three on Thursday evening. As recently as half an hour before the official declaration of death, the doctors involved in his case said that his constitution was strong and the much-discussed general condition not so serious.

On the whole, the only thing wrong with him was that he had a bullet in his head.

Present at the instant of death were his wife, two brain surgeons, two nurses and a first assistant detective from the police in Lund.

There had been general agreement that an operation would have been much too risky, which seemed fairly sensible, even to a layman. For the fact remained that Palmgren had been conscious from time to time and on one occasion in such good shape that they could communicate with him.

The detective, who felt more dead than alive by this time, had asked him a couple of questions: "Did you get a good look at the man who shot you?" And, "Did you recognize him?"

The answers had been unambiguous, positive to the first question and negative to the second. Palmgren had seen the would-be killer, but for the first and last time in his life.

That didn't exactly make it any more comprehensible. In Malmö Månsson's face was creased with heavy lines of misgiving, and he yearned for his bed, or at least for a clean shirt.

It was an unbearably hot day, and the main police station was by no means air-conditioned.

The only small lead he'd had to go on had been bungled.

Those Stockholmers, Månsson thought.

But he didn't say it, out of consideration for Skacke, who was sensitive.

Furthermore, how much had that lead been worth?

He didn't know.

Maybe nothing.

But still. The Danish police had questioned the staff of the hydrofoil *Springeren*, and one of the hostesses on board during the nine o'clock trip from Malmö to Copenhagen had noticed a man, primarily because he had insisted on standing on the afterdeck during the first part of the thirty-five-minute journey. His appearance, meaning mostly his clothing, corresponded somewhat to the scanty description.

Something actually seemed to fit together.

The fact is, you don't stand up on the deck of these hydrofoils, which in most respects resemble airplanes more than boats. It's even doubtful whether you would be permitted to stand out in the fresh air during the passage. Eventually the man had wandered down and sat in one of the armchairs. He hadn't purchased tax-free chocolate, liquor or cigarettes on board and thus hadn't left any written notes behind him. To buy anything, you have to fill out a printed order form.

Why had this person tried to remain on deck for as long as possible?

Perhaps to throw something into the water.

In that case, what?

The weapon.

If, in fact, the same person was involved. If, in which case, he wanted to get rid of the weapon.

If, in fact, the man in question hadn't been afraid of becoming seasick and had therefore preferred the fresh air.

"If, if, if," Månsson mumbled to himself and broke his last toothpick between his teeth.

It was an abominable day. In the first place, the heat, which was next to unbearable when you were forced to sit inside. Moreover, inside the windows, you were completely unprotected from the blazing afternoon sun. In the second place, this passive waiting. Waiting for information, waiting for witnesses who had to exist but didn't get in touch.

The examination of the scene of the crime was going badly. Hundreds of fingerprints had been found, but there was no reason to assume that any of them belonged to the man who had shot Viktor Palmgren. They'd placed their greatest hopes on the window, but the few prints on the glass were much too blurred to be identified.

Backlund was most irritated by not being able to find the empty shell.

He called several times about that.

"I don't understand where it could have gone," he said with annoyance.

Månsson thought that the answer to that question was so simple that even Backlund should be able to think it out for himself. Therefore he said with mild irony, "Let me know if you have a theory."

They couldn't find any footprints, either. Quite naturally, since so many people had tramped around in the dining room, and also because it's next to impossible to find any usable impressions on wall-to-wall carpeting. Outside the window the man had stepped into a window box before hopping down onto the sidewalk. To the great detriment of the flowers, but offering scarcely any information to the criminal technicians.

"This dinner," Skacke said.

"Yes, what about it?"

"It seems to have been some sort of business meeting rather than a private gathering."

"Maybe so," Månsson said. "Do you have the list of the people who were seated at the table?"

"Sure."

They studied it together.

Viktor Palmgren, executive, Malmö, 56
Charlotte Palmgren, housewife, Malmö, 32
Hampus Broberg, district manager, Stockholm, 43
Helena Hansson, executive secretary, Stockholm, 26
Ole Hoff-Jensen, district manager, Copenhagen, 48
Birthe Hoff-Jensen, housewife, Copenhagen, 43
Mats Linder, vice-president, Malmö, 30

"All of them must work for Palmgren's companies," said Månsson.

"It looks like it," said Skacke. "They'll have to be questioned thoroughly once more, of course."

Månsson sighed and thought about the geographical distribution. The Jensen couple had already returned to Denmark the previous evening. Hampus Broberg and Helena Hansson had taken the morning flight to Stockholm, and Charlotte Palmgren was at her husband's bedside at the clinic in Lund. Only Mats Linder was still in Malmö. And they couldn't even be really sure of that. As Palmgren's second in command, he traveled a lot.

Thus the day's misfortunes seemed to culminate in the message of death, which reached them at a quarter to eight and which at once transformed the case into murder.

But it was to get worse.

It was ten-thirty and they sat drinking coffee, hollow-eyed and weary. The telephone rang and Månsson answered.

"Yes, this is Detective Inspector Månsson."

And immediately afterwards:

"I see."

He repeated the phrase three times before he said good-bye and hung up.

He looked at Skacke and said, "This isn't our case any more. They're sending a man down from the National Homicide Squad."

"Not Kollberg," Skacke said anxiously.

"No, it'll be the one and only Beck. He's coming tomorrow morning."

"What'll we do now?"

"Go home to bed," said Månsson and stood up.

6

When the plane from Stockholm landed at Bulltofta, Martin Beck didn't feel very well.

He'd always had a distinct aversion to flying, and inasmuch as this Friday morning he was also suffering from the effects of the party the night before, the trip had been particularly unpleasant.

The hot, heavy air struck him when he came out of the relatively cool cabin, and he began to sweat even before he'd finished walking down the steps. The asphalt felt soft under his shoe soles as he walked toward the domestic arrivals building.

The air in the taxi was sweltering despite the open window, and the imitation leather covering on the back seat felt red-hot through the thin cloth of his shirt.

He knew that Månsson was waiting for him at the police station, but he decided to go to the hotel first to shower and change. This time he had reserved a room not at the St. Jörgen's, as he usually did, but at the Savoy.

The doorman greeted him so exuberantly that for an instant Martin Beck suspected that he was being confused with a long-lost guest of great importance.

The room was airy and cool, facing north. From the window he could see the canal and the railway station and beyond the harbor and Kockum's wharf, a white hydrofoil, which was just disappearing into the pale blue haze on its way over the Sound to Copenhagen.

Martin Beck undressed and walked around the room naked while he unpacked his suitcase. Then he went into the bathroom and took a long, cold shower.

He put on clean underclothes and a fresh shirt, and

when he had finished dressing he noticed that the time on the clock at the train station was twelve exactly. He took a cab to the main police station and walked directly up to Månsson's room.

Månsson had the windows wide open onto the court-yard, which lay in shadow at this time of day. He was in shirt sleeves, drinking beer while he leafed through a bundle of papers.

After they had greeted each other, and Martin Beck had taken off his suitcoat, settled down in the extra armchair and lit a Florida, Månsson handed him the bundle of papers.

"For a start you can take a look at this report. As you'll see, the whole thing was handled horribly from the very beginning."

Martin Beck read through the papers carefully and now and then put questions to Månsson, who filled in with details that weren't in the report. Månsson also recounted Rönn's slightly modified version of Kristiansson's and Kvant's behavior on Karolinskavägen. Gunvald Larsson had refused to have anything more to do with the case.

When Martin Beck had finished reading, he laid the transcripts on the table in front of him and said, "It's obvious that we'll have to first concentrate on questioning the witnesses properly. This really hasn't been very productive. What do they mean, anyway, by this curious phrase?"

He hunted out a piece of paper and read, " 'The deviation from the correct time of various clocks existent on the scene of the crime at the moment of the commission of the crime . . .' Does that mean anything?"

Månsson shrugged.

"That's Backlund," he said. "You've met Backlund?"

"Oh, him. I see," said Martin Beck.

He had met Backlund. Once. Several years ago. That was enough.

A car drove into the courtyard and stopped below the window. Then noises were heard, car doors being slammed shut, people running and loud voices shouting something in German.

Månsson got up slowly and looked out.

"They must have made a clean sweep on Gustav Adolf

Square," he said, "or down by the wharves. We've stepped up surveillance there, but it's mostly teenagers who have a little hash for their own use who get picked up. We seldom get at the big shipments and the really dangerous dealers."

"Same thing with us."

Månsson shut the window and sat down.

"How's Skacke doing?" Martin Beck asked.

"Fine," Månsson said. "He's an ambitious boy. Sits at home and studies every night. He does a good job, too, very careful and doesn't do anything rash. He really learned a lesson that time. He was very relieved, by the way, when he heard that you were coming, and not Kollberg."

Less than a year before, Benny Skacke had been more or less the direct cause of Kollberg's being stabbed in the stomach by a man that both of them were going to arrest at Arlanda airport.

"Good reinforcement for the soccer team too, I hear," Månsson said.

"Is that so?" said Martin Beck disinterestedly. "What's he doing right now?"

"He's trying to get hold of that man who was sitting alone several tables away from Palmgren's party. His name is Edvardsson, and he's a proofreader for *Arbetet*. He was too drunk to be questioned last Wednesday, and yesterday we couldn't get hold of him. He was probably at home with a hangover and refused to answer the door."

"If he was drunk when Palmgren was shot, maybe he's not worth much as a witness," Martin Beck said. "And when can we question Palmgren's wife?"

Månsson took a swallow of beer and wiped his mouth on the back of his hand.

"This afternoon, I hope. Or tomorrow. Do you want to deal with her?"

"Maybe it'd be better if you did it yourself. You must know more about Palmgren than I do."

"I doubt it," Månsson said. "But okay, you're the one to decide. You can talk to Edvardsson, if Skacke gets hold of him. I have a feeling that he's the most important witness so far, despite everything. Say, would you like a beer? It's warm, I'm afraid."

Martin Beck shook his head. He was extremely thirsty, but warm beer didn't appeal to him.

"Why don't we go up to the canteen and have some mineral water instead?" he said.

They each drank a bottle of mineral water standing at the bar and then returned to Månsson's room. Benny Skacke was sitting in the extra chair reading something from his note pad. He stood up quickly when they came in, and he and Martin Beck shook hands.

"Well, did you get hold of Edvardsson?" Månsson asked.

"Yes, eventually. He's at the newspaper right now, but should be home about three o'clock," Skacke said.

He looked at his notes.

"Kamrergatan 2."

"Call and say that I'll come at three," Martin Beck said.

The building on Kamrergatan seemed to be the first finished in a series of new structures; on the other side of the street were low, old houses that had been evacuated and would soon fall prey to bulldozers to make room for newer and larger apartment buildings.

Edvardsson lived on the top floor and opened the door soon after Martin Beck had rung the bell. About fifty years old, he had an intelligent face with a prominent nose and deep furrows around his mouth. He squinted at Martin Beck before he threw open the door and said, "Superintendent Beck? Come in."

Martin Beck preceded him into the room, which was frugally furnished. The walls were covered with book shelves, and on the desk by the window was a typewriter with a half-typed sheet of paper in the platen.

Edvardsson removed a stack of newspapers from the room's only armchair and said, "Please sit down and I'll get something to drink. I have cold beer in the icebox."

"Beer sounds good," Martin Beck said.

The man went out into the kitchenette and returned with glasses and two bottles of beer.

"Beck's Beer," he said. "Appropriate, eh?"

When he had poured the beer into the glasses he sat down on the sofa with one arm over the back.

Martin Beck took a big swallow of beer, which was cold and good in the oppressive heat. Then he said, "Well, you know what my visit is about."

Edvardsson nodded and lit a cigarette.

"Yes, about Palmgren. I can't exactly say I regret his passing."

"Did you know him?" Martin Beck asked.

"Personally? No, not at all. But you couldn't help but run into him in every possible connection. The impression I had was of a domineering, arrogant man—well, I've never gotten along with that type of person."

"What does that mean? 'That type'?"

"People for whom money means everything and who don't hesitate to use any means to get it."

"I'd like to hear more about Palmgren later, if you'd like to clarify what you think of him, but first I want to know something else. Did you see the gunman?"

Edvardsson ran a hand through his hair, which was a bit grizzled and lay in a wave over his forehead.

"I'm afraid I can't be of too much help. I was sitting reading and didn't really react until the fellow was already halfway out the window. At first I only noticed Palmgren, and then I saw the gunman—but kind of out of the corner of my eye. He took off very quickly, and when I got around to looking out of the window, he'd disappeared."

Martin Beck took out a crumpled pack of Floridas from his pocket and lit one.

"Have you any idea what he looked like?" he asked.

"I seem to remember that he was dressed in rather dark clothes, probably in a suit or a sport coat and pants that didn't match, and that he wasn't a young man. But it's only an impression I have—he could have been thirty, forty, or fifty, but hardly older or younger than that."

"Was Palmgren's party already seated when you got to the restaurant?"

"No," said Edvardsson. "I'd already eaten and had a whisky when they came. I live alone here, and sometimes it's nice to sit in a restaurant and read a book, and then I end up sitting there for quite a long time."

He paused and added, "Even though it gets damned expensive, of course."

"Did you recognize anyone besides Palmgren in this gathering?"

"His wife and that young man who's said to be—have been—Palmgren's right-hand man. I didn't recognize the others, but it looked as if they were employees, too. A couple of them spoke Danish."

Edvardsson took a handkerchief out of his pants pocket and wiped the perspiration off his forehead. He was dressed in a white shirt and tie, pale dacron trousers and black shoes. His shirt was soaked with sweat. Martin Beck felt his own shirt begin to grow damp and stick to his body.

"Did you happen to hear what the conversation was about?" he asked.

"To tell you the truth, I did. I'm fairly curious and think it's fun to study people, so, in fact, I was eavesdropping a little. Palmgren and the Dane talked shop—I didn't catch what it was all about, but they mentioned Rhodesia several times. He had a lot of irons in the fire, Palmgren—I even heard him say that himself on at least one occasion—and there were a number of shady deals underway, I've heard tell. The ladies talked about the kind of things that that kind of ladies usually talk about—clothes, trips, mutual acquaintances, parties ... Mrs. Palmgren and the younger of the other two talked about someone who'd had her sagging breasts operated on so that they looked like tennis balls right under her chin. Charlotte Palmgren talked about a party at "21" in New York, where Frank Sinatra had been, and someone called Mackan had bought champagne for all of them the whole night. And a million other things like that. A fantastic bra for 75 kronor at Twilfit. That it's too warm to wear a wig in the summer, so you have to put your hair up every day."

Martin Beck reflected that Edvardsson couldn't have read much of his book that night.

"And the other men? Did they talk shop, too?"

"Not very much. It seems they'd had a meeting before dinner. The fourth man—not the Dane and not the young one, that is—said something about it. No, their conversation wasn't on a very high level either. For example, they talked a long time about Palmgren's tie, which unfortunately I couldn't see since he sat with his back to me. It

must have been something special, for they all admired it,
and Palmgren said that he'd bought it for 95 francs on the
Champs-Elysées in Paris. And the fourth man told them
that he had a problem that kept him awake at night. His
daughter had actually moved in with a Negro. Palmgren
suggested he send her to Switzerland, where there are
hardly any blacks."

Edvardsson got up, carried the empty bottles out into
the kitchenette and returned with two more bottles of
beer. They were misty and looked extremely tempting.

"Yes," Edvardsson said, "that's most of what I remember from the table conversation. Not especially helpful, is
it?"

"No," Martin Beck said truthfully. "What do you really
know about Palmgren?"

"Not much. He lives in one of the largest of those old
upperclass mansions out toward Limhamn. He made a pile
of money and also spent plenty, among other things on his
wife and that old house."

Edvardsson was silent a moment. Then he asked a
question in return: "What do *you* know about Palmgren?"

"Not too much more than that."

"God save us if the police know as little as I do about
characters like Viktor Palmgren," said Edvardsson and
drank deeply from his glass of beer.

"Right when Palmgren was shot, he was giving a talk,
wasn't he?"

"Yes, I remember, he stood up and started rambling
on—the usual sort of nonsense. Welcomed them and
thanked them for good work and lectured the ladies and
had his fun. He seemed skilled at it; he sounded over-
whelmingly jovial. The whole staff withdrew so they
wouldn't disturb them, and even the music stopped. The
waiters had vanished into thin air, and I had to sit there
sucking on ice cubes. Don't you really know what Palmgren was doing, or is it a police secret?"

Martin Beck eyed the glass of beer. Took it. Took a sip
cautiously.

"I don't know very much, in fact," he said. "But there
are others who probably know. A lot of foreign business
and a real estate agency in Stockholm."

"I see," Edvardsson said and then seemed lost in thought.

After a moment he said, "The little I saw of that murderer, I already told them about the day before yesterday. Two fellows from the police were on me. One fellow who kept asking what time it was, and also a younger one who seemed a little sharper."

"You weren't quite sober at the time, were you?" Martin Beck said.

"No. Lord knows, I wasn't. And then yesterday I tied on another one, so I'm still hungover. It must be this damned heat."

Splendid, thought Martin Beck. Hungover detective questions hungover witness. Very constructive.

"Maybe you know how it feels," Edvardsson said.

"Yes, I do," said Martin Beck. Then he took the glass of beer and emptied it in one gulp. He stood up and said, "Thank you. Maybe you'll be hearing from us again."

He stopped and asked another question:

"By the way, did you happen to see the weapon the murderer used?"

Edvardsson hesitated.

"Come to think of it now, it seems to me I caught a glimpse of it, at the moment he stuck it in his pocket. I don't know much about guns, of course, but it was a long, fairly narrow thing. With a kind of roller, or whatever you call it."

"Revolving chamber," said Martin Beck. "Good-bye and thanks for the beer."

"Come again sometime," Edvardsson said. "Now I'm going to have a pick-me-up, so I can put things into a little better shape here."

Månsson was still sitting in about the same position behind his desk.

"What shall I say?" he said when Martin Beck slipped in through the door. "How did it go? Well, how did it go?"

"That's a good question. Rather badly, I think. How's it going here?"

"Not at all."

"How about the widow?"

"I'll get her tomorrow. Better be careful. She *is* in mourning."

7

Per Månsson was born and grew up in the working-class section around Möllevång Square in Malmö. He'd been a police officer for more than twenty-five years. Having lived with Malmö his whole life, he knew his city better than most—and liked it, too.

However, there was one part of the city he'd never really got to know, and this section had always made him feel uneasy. That was Västra Förstaden, with areas like Fridhem, Västervång and Bellevue, where many rich families had always lived. He could remember the famine years of the twenties and thirties, when many times as a little kid he had trudged in his clogs through the blocks of mansions on the way to Limhamn, where somehow it might be possible to find herring for dinner. He recalled the expensive cars and the uniformed chauffeurs, maids in black dresses with aprons and starched white caps, and upper-class children in tulle dresses and sailor suits. He'd felt so utterly outside of all that; the whole environment had appeared incomprehensible, like a fairy tale to him. Somehow it still felt the same way by and large, despite the fact that the chauffeurs and most of the servant girls were gone and that by now upper-class children didn't differ very much on the surface from any other children.

After all, herring and potatoes was not a bad diet. Although fatherless and poor, he'd grown up to be a big strong man, taken the "hard road" and eventually done quite well. At least he thought so himself.

Viktor Palmgren had lived in this same area; and consequently his widow probably still lived there.

So far he'd only seen pictures of the people around the fated dinner table and didn't know very much about them. About Charlotte Palmgren, however, he knew that she was considered an exceptional beauty and had once been crowned Miss Something—was it only of Sweden or of the whole universe? Then she'd made herself famous as a model and after that become Mrs. Palmgren, twenty-seven years old and at the height of her career. Now she was thirty-two and outwardly fairly unchanged, as only women can be who haven't had children, and who can afford to spend a lot of time and an unlimited amount of money on their appearance. Viktor Palmgren had been twenty-four years older than she, a fact which might give an indication of the mutual motives for the marriage. He'd probably wanted something good-looking to display to his business acquaintances and she, enough money so that she never again would need to do anything that might possibly be characterized as work. And that is the way it seemed to have worked out.

However, Charlotte Palmgren was a widow, and Månsson couldn't avoid a certain measure of conventionality. Therefore, much to his dislike, he put on his dark suit, white shirt and tie before he went down and got into the car to drive the relatively short stretch from Regementsgatan to Bellevue.

The Palmgren residence seemed to correspond to all of Månsson's childhood memories, which had perhaps become covered with a patina of slight exaggeration over the years. One could catch only a glimpse of the house from the street, a bit of the roof and a weather vane, for the hedges were not only well-clipped and richly verdant, but also very high and thick. If he wasn't mistaken, there was likely to be a wrought-iron fence behind it. The lot seemed immense, and the lawn rather resembled formal gardens. The gate to the drive was just as impenetrable as the hedge; it was of copper, green with age, high, broad, and embellished with spiraling pinnacles. On one half of the door was a row of oversized brass letters, which formed the name that was not totally unknown by now—Palmgren. On the other half was a mail slot, the button for an electric doorbell and directly over it a square opening through which potential visitors could be scrutinized before being granted admission. Clearly it wasn't a matter of just walking in any old way. As he cautiously pressed down the handle, Månsson almost expected an

alarm to start ringing somewhere inside. The door was
locked, of course, and the opening hermetically sealed.
Nothing could be seen through the mail slot—obviously it
opened into a closed metal box.

Månsson raised his hand to the doorbell, but changed
his mind, let his arm sink back and looked around.

Besides his own old Wartburg, two cars were parked by
the curb—a red Jaguar and a yellow MG. Did it seem
plausible that Charlotte Palmgren would have two sports
cars parked on the street? He stood still listening and
thought for an instant that he discerned voices from
within the park. Then the sounds died away, perhaps
stifled by the heat and the stagnant, quivering air.

What a summer, he thought. One that comes only about
once every ten years. And here you stand like a blockhead
in a tie, shirt and suit instead of lying on the beach in
Falsterbo or sitting at home in shorts with a cold drink in
your hand!

Then he thought about something else. The mansion
was old, probably from the turn of the century or so,
certainly rebuilt and modernized for a million or two.
These houses usually had a gate in the rear, where the
gardener, cooks, maids, messengers and nursemaids could
slink in without the master and mistress being irritated by
the sight of them.

Månsson walked along the hedge and turned down the
next side street. The lot seemed to extend over the whole
block, for the hedge was even, unbroken and still just as
impenetrable. He took a right again, went around to the
rear, and found what he was looking for. A pair of double
wrought-iron gates. From here the house wasn't visible,
since it was enclosed by tall trees and dense foliage.
However, he could see a big garage, rather newly built,
and an older, smaller building—a tool shed, undoubtedly.
There was no name plate on the rear entrance.

He placed his hands on both sides of the gate and
pressed. The sides swung in and open. This meant he
didn't have to find out if the gate was locked or not. In
the shade of the trees he felt how warm it really was;
drops of perspiration ran down inside his collar and ran
down his back in a tickling rivulet between his shoulder
blades. He pushed the gates shut.

On the gravel driveway to the garage, car tracks were visible; the paths that wound into the garden were covered with slate slabs.

Månsson walked across the grass under the trees in the direction of the house. This took him between rows of blooming laburnum and jasmine and, as calculated, brought him to the back of the house, which was quiet and deserted, with closed windows, kitchen and cellar stairs, and various mysterious adjoining buildings. He looked up at the house but couldn't see much of it, since he was far too close. He followed the path to the right, climbed over a flower bed, peeked around the corner and stood stock-still among the showy peonies.

The scenery was breathtaking in several respects. The lawn was very large and green, as well kept as an English golf course. In the middle was a kidney-shaped swimming pool lined with light blue tile, with clear green, shimmering water. At its farthest end there were a sauna, parallel bars and Roman rings. An exercise bicycle beside the sauna. Presumably this was where Viktor Palmgren had built up his excellent physical condition that everyone talked about. In something resembling a Bruno Mathsson chair at the edge of the pool, Charlotte Palmgren was sitting, or rather, lying, naked, her eyes closed. She had a very deep suntan, evenly apportioned over her whole body, and blond hair. If anyone had ever fostered the suspicion that she wasn't a genuine blonde, it was refuted by the fact that the sparse triangular patch of hair between her legs was so light that it appeared almost white against her suntanned skin. Her face had thin, apathetic features, a clean profile and a straight mouth. She was very thin, with almost unnaturally slender hips, a small waist and girlish breasts. Her nipples were small and pale brown and the area around them lighter than the other skin. There was nothing about her that appealed to Månsson. She could just as well have been a mannequin in a store window.

Just look at that, a naked widow!

Why not, anyway? Widows have to be naked, too, sometimes.

Månsson stood among the peonies feeling like a Peeping Tom, which of course he was.

What induced him to remain there, however, wasn't what he saw but what he heard. Somewhere in the immediate vicinity but out of sight came clinking noises from someone who was moving and doing something.

Then Månsson heard steps, and a man came forward out of the shade cast by the house. He was suntanned, too, although not nearly so deeply as Charlotte Palmgren. He was dressed in flowered Bermuda shorts and carried two tall glasses containing a pale red liquid. Straws and ice cubes. Not a bad idea at all.

Månsson recognized the man immediately from the photographs. It was Mats Linder, closest associate and protégé of Viktor Palmgren, deceased for less than forty-eight hours.

He walked across the grass toward the swimming pool. The woman in the reclining chair raised her left leg and scratched her ankle. Still without opening her eyes, she stretched out her right arm and took one of the glasses from the man's hand.

Månsson retreated behind the corner of the house. Listened. Linder said something first, "Is it too sour?"

"No, it's okay," the woman said.

He heard her put the glass down on the tiles.

"Aren't we terrible?" Charlotte Palmgren said apathetically.

"Anyway, it's damned nice."

"You can say that again."

Her voice still had the same indifferent tone.

It was quiet for a while. Then the widow said in a suggestive and affected tone, "Mats, why can't you take those stupid pants off?"

If Linder replied at all, Månsson would never find out, for he promptly left his place among the peonies.

He walked briskly and silently the same way he'd come, closed the gate behind him and continued along the hedge, went around both street corners and stopped in front of the green copper door. Without a second's hesitation he pressed the doorbell.

Chimes sounded in the distance. It didn't take more than a minute before light steps were heard approaching. The peephole was opened, and a light blue-green eye stared at him. He also saw a lock of blond hair and exaggeratedly long, technically perfect eyelashes.

Månsson had taken out his identity card and held it up in front of the opening.

"I'm sorry to bother you," he said. "My name is Månsson. Detective Inspector."

"Oh," she said childishly. "Of course. The police. Could you please wait a few minutes?"

"Of course. Am I intruding?"

"What? No, not at all. Just a couple of minutes for me to . . ."

Apparently she couldn't invent an appropriate conclusion, for the aperture banged shut and the light steps withdrew much faster than they had come.

He looked at his watch.

It took her only three and a half minutes to return and open the door. Wearing silver sandals and a severe gray dress of a light material.

She could hardly have had the time to put on anything underneath it, thought Månsson, but it wasn't necessary anyway. She had nothing special to show off or to hide.

"Please come in," Charlotte Palmgren said. "I'm so sorry you had to wait."

She locked the door and walked ahead of him to the house. Out on the street a car started. Evidently there were others besides the widow who were quick on their feet.

For the first time Månsson had the opportunity to see the mansion in its entirety and he stared at it with amazement. It wasn't a house, actually, but a kind of diminutive castle with pinnacles and towers and strange projections. Everything indicated that the original builder had suffered from a severe case of megalomania and that the architect had copied the design from a picture postcard. Recent modernizations with added porches and glass verandas hadn't improved the over-all impression. It looked atrocious, and one didn't know whether to laugh or cry or maybe send for a demolition team to blow up the whole business. The building seemed extremely substantial; dynamite was probably the only thing that could budge it. Along the drive stood a row of hideous sculptures of the type found in Germany in the Kaiser's day.

"Yes, it's a beautiful house," Charlotte Palmgren said. "But it wasn't cheap to modernize. Now everything's in tiptop shape."

Månsson managed to tear his eyes away from the house and proceeded to look at the surroundings. The lawn, as he'd already had the chance to remark, was fastidiously well kept.

The woman followed his eyes and said, "The gardener comes three days a week."

"I see," Månsson said.

"Do you want to go in or sit outside?"

"Makes no difference," Månsson said.

Every trace of Mats Linder was gone, even the glasses, but on a cart on the porch in front of the large veranda stood a seltzer bottle, a bucket of ice and some bottles.

"My father-in-law bought this house," she said, "but he died many years ago, long before Viktor and I met."

"Where did you meet?" Månsson asked irrationally.

"In Nice, six years ago," she said. "I was in a fashion show there."

She hesitated a second, then said, "Maybe we should go inside."

"Fine," Månsson replied.

"I can't offer you anything special. A drink or two, of course."

"Thank you but no."

"You understand, I'm all alone here. I've sent the servants away."

Månsson didn't say anything, and after a moment she said, "After what's happened, I thought it would be better to be alone. All alone."

"I understand. My sympathies."

She inclined her head slightly but wasn't capable of expressing anything but disgust and total apathy.

Probably she wasn't talented enough to be able to look sorrowful, Månsson thought.

"Mm-m," she said. "Let's go in then."

He followed her up a flight of stone steps beside the veranda, crossed a large gloomy hall and entered a colossal drawing room stuffed with furniture. The mixture of styles was grotesque—ultra-modern mixed with old wing chairs and semi-antique tables. She directed him to a group of four sofa units, a couch and a gigantic table with a thick plate-glass top. It looked new and expensive.

"Please sit down," she said conventionally.

Månsson sat down. The chair was the largest he'd ever seen; he sank down so deep that it felt as though he would never get back on his feet again.

"Are you sure you wouldn't like anything to drink?"

"Nothing, thanks," Månsson said. "I won't disturb you for long. But unfortunately I have to ask you several questions. As you understand, we're anxious to get hold of the person who killed Mr. Palmgren as quickly as possible."

"Yes, you *are* a policeman. Well, what should I say? It's been terribly sad, this whole thing. Tragic."

"You saw the gunman, isn't that right?"

"Yes, but it all happened so terribly fast. I sort of didn't react until afterward. Then the horrible thought struck me that he could have shot me too. All of us."

"Had you ever seen this man before?"

"No, absolutely not. I can't remember names or things like that, but I have a good memory for faces. The police in Lund asked me the same question."

"I know, but you were upset then, naturally."

"Certainly, it was horrible," she said with little conviction.

"You must have given this a lot of thought during the past few days."

"Yes, of course."

"And you did see the man clearly. You were looking in his direction. What did he actually look like?"

"Well, what can I say? He looked terribly ordinary."

"What kind of impression did he make? Was he nervous? Or desperate?"

"You know, he looked completely ordinary. Quite common."

"Common?"

"Yes, no one we'd ever associate with, I mean."

"What were your feelings when you saw him?"

"Nothing, until he pulled out the pistol. Then I was afraid."

"You saw the weapon?"

"Of course. It was some kind of pistol."

"You couldn't say what kind?"

"I don't know a thing about guns. But it was some kind of pistol. Pretty long. Like the kind they use in Westerns."

"But what could you say about the man's facial expression?"

"Nothing. He looked ordinary, as I said. I got a better look at his clothes, but I've already talked about that."

Månsson gave up on the description. Either she wouldn't or couldn't tell any more than she already had. He looked around the curious room. The woman followed his glance and said, "This sofa grouping is quite dashing, don't you think?"

Månsson nodded and considered how much it could have cost.

"I bought it myself," she said with a certain pride. "At Finncenter."

"Do you live here all the time?" Månsson asked.

"Where else would we live when we're in Malmö?" she asked sheepishly.

"But when you're not in Malmö?"

"We have a house in Estoril. We live there during the winter. Viktor often did business in Portugal. And then the company apartment in Stockholm, of course. It's on Gärdet."

She reflected and added, "But we only live there when we're in Stockholm."

"I understand. Did you usually accompany your husband on his business trips?"

"Yes, when there were social affairs, I always went along. But not to the meetings."

"I understand," Månsson repeated.

What did he understand? That for the most part she'd served as a living mannequin, something young to hang expensive creations on, things that would have been of no use to ordinary people. That for persons like Viktor Palmgren, a wife who attracted universal admiration was included in the stage properties.

"Did you love your husband?" he asked suddenly.

She didn't look surprised, but searched for an answer.

"Love sounds so silly," she said finally.

Månsson took out one of his toothpicks and began to chew on it contemplatively.

She looked at him with amazement. For the first time she displayed something resembling real interest.

"Why do you do that?" she asked.

"A bad habit I picked up when I stopped smoking."

"Oh," she said. "I see. Otherwise, there are cigarettes and cigars in the case over there."

Månsson looked at her a second. Then he tried a new tack.

"The dinner last Wednesday was almost a business gathering, wasn't it?"

"Right. They'd had a meeting in the afternoon. But I wasn't there. I was at home changing then. I was at the luncheon earlier in the day."

"Do you know what this meeting was about?"

"Business, as usual. What, I don't really know. Viktor had so many irons in the fire. He used to say that himself, too. 'I have a lot of irons in the fire.' "

"You knew all the people there, didn't you?"

"I've seen them now and then. No, as a matter of fact, not the secretary who'd come with Hampus Broberg. I'd never seen her before."

"Are you good friends with any of the others?"

"Not really."

"Not with Mr. Linder, for example? He does live here in Malmö."

"We've seen each other now and then. At company parties and things like that."

"You don't see each other privately?"

"No, only through my husband."

She was answering in a monotone and seemed completely impassive.

"Your husband was giving a speech when he was shot. What was he talking about?"

"I wasn't listening very carefully. He welcomed everyone and thanked people for their cooperation—things like that. They were all employees. Besides, we were going to leave for a while."

"Leave?"

"Yes, we were going to go sailing on the West Coast for several weeks. We have a cottage in Bohuslän—I forgot to tell you that, of course. And then we were going to leave for Portugal."

"And that meant that your husband wasn't going to see his staff for a while?"

"Right."

"And you weren't, either?"

"What? No, I was going to accompany Viktor. We were going to play golf in Portugal. Later. In the Algarve."

Månsson had lost the main battle. Her indolence made it impossible to determine when she was lying or telling the truth, and her feelings, if she had any, were well concealed. He formed a last question which he thought was idiotic and which in any case was meaningless. But it sort of belonged to the routine.

"Can you think of anyone or of any group who wanted to get rid of your husband?"

"No, I couldn't possibly."

Månsson raised himself up out of the Finnish super-armchair and said, "Thank you. I won't take up any more of your time."

"You're welcome."

She followed him to the door. He was careful not to turn his head and look at the house of mourning.

They shook hands. He thought that she held his hand strangely, but only when he was sitting in the car did he realize that she had expected him to kiss it.

She had thin hands with long, narrow fingers.

The red Jaguar was gone.

It was insufferably warm.

"Oh, hell," Månsson said to himself and turned on the ignition.

8

After a night of heavy and dreamless sleep, Martin Beck awoke late on Saturday morning, at five after nine. The evening before he'd eaten a hearty *skånsk* dinner with Månsson at the hotel, and he still felt slightly groggy, an aftereffect of what the kitchen had to offer in Scandinavia's best-known restaurant.

After opening his eyes with a sense of general well-being, he lounged for several minutes, pondering the fact that his appetite had improved, and his sensitive stomach had begun to behave quite decently since he had been separated from his wife. So, his suffering, which had gone on for so many years, had been psychosomatic, which was exactly what he had suspected all along.

The evening had been very enjoyable and rather long. Early on, Månsson had suggested that they shouldn't mull over the Palmgren case, since up to now there was so little that was concrete to say about it. This was obviously a good idea, for they were both in great need of a meal in peace and quiet, to be rounded off with a solid night's sleep. Simply to feel free for several hours and to gather their forces for continuing the investigation. The material was meager, and they both had a feeling that the case was complicated and could be painfully difficult to solve.

Martin Beck threw off the sheet and got up. He pulled up the shade and looked with pleasure out the open window. It was already hot, and the sun was beaming. Beyond Ferdinand Broberg's magnificent 1906 Post Office he saw the sparkling white hull of a boat on the Sound, blue and appealing despite the water pollution. The train ferry *Malmöhus* was making a wide swing, turning around outside of the harbor mouth in order to head the prow in the right direction. A fine boat, built at Kockum's in 1945 and constructed according to time-honored principles.

When boats still looked like boats, Martin Beck thought.

Then he took off his pajamas and went into the bathroom.

He was standing under the shower when the telephone rang.

It rang many times before he'd managed to turn off the cold water, wrap a bath towel around himself, shuffle over to the night stand and pick up the receiver.

"Yes, this is Beck."

"Malm here. How's it going?"

How's it going? The eternal question. Martin Beck frowned and said, "Hard to say at this point. The investigation has just begun."

"I tried to contact you at the police station but only found Skacke," the Chief Superintendent complained.

"I see."

"Were you sleeping?"

"No," said Martin Beck truthfully, "I wasn't asleep."

"You have to catch the murderer. On the double."

"Okay."

"A lot of pressure's been put on me. Both the Chief and the Attorney General have been on me. And now the Foreign Office is involved, too."

Malm's voice was shrill and nervous, but that was only normal.

"So it's got to be done quickly. As I said before, on the double."

"How are we supposed to do that?" said Martin Beck.

The Chief Superintendent neglected to answer his question, but that was to be expected, since he knew next to nothing about practical police work. He wasn't a very good administrator, either.

Instead he said, "This call is going through the hotel switchboard, isn't it?"

"I suppose so."

"Then you'll have to ring me from another telephone. Dial my home number. As soon as possible."

"I don't think there's any risk. You can keep talking," Martin Beck said. "In this country only the police have time to tap people's telephones."

"No, no, it's no good. What I have to say is extremely confidential and important. And this case takes precedence over anything else."

"Why?"

"That's just what I'm going to tell you. But you have to call back on a direct line. Go to the police station or somewhere. And fast. I'm in a tight spot. God knows, I wish I could get rid of the responsibility for this."

"Bull," Martin Beck said to himself.

"I can't hear. What did you say?"

"Nothing. I'll call back right away."

He hung up, dried himself and put on his clothes at a leisurely pace.

After a suitable length of time, he picked up the receiver, requested an outside line and dialed the number of Malm's home in Stockholm.

The Superintendent must have been hovering over the telephone, for he answered before the first signal had faded away.

"Yes, this is Superintendent Malm."

"Beck here."

"At last. Now listen carefully. I'm going to give you some information regarding Palmgren and his activities."

"Not a moment too soon."

"It's not my fault. I was given these details only yesterday."

He fell silent. All that could be heard was a nervous rustle.

"Well?" Martin Beck said finally.

"This is no ordinary murder," Malm said.

"There aren't any ordinary murders."

The reply seemed to confound the man. After a moment's reflection, he said, "Well, you are right, in a way. I haven't had the same practical experience as you have ..."

No, you really haven't, Martin Beck thought.

"... since mostly I've been involved with larger administrative problems."

"Now, what was Palmgren involved in?" said Martin Beck impatiently.

"He was in business. Big business. And you know, there are certain countries with which we have very sensitive relations."

"Such as?"

"Rhodesia, South Africa, Biafra, Nigeria, Angola and Mozambique, to name a few. It's difficult for our government to maintain normal contacts with these nations."

"Angola and Mozambique aren't nations," said Martin Beck.

"Now, don't get hung up on details. Anyway, Palmgren did business with these countries, among others. A large part of his operations was located in Portugal. Even though his official headquarters were in Malmö, he's thought to have made a great many of his most profitable transactions in Lisbon."

"What did Palmgren deal in?"

"Weapons, among other things."

"Other things?"

"Well, he handled practically everything. For example, he had a real estate company. Owns a lot of buildings here in Stockholm. The firm in Malmö is considered to be not much more than a façade, even if it's a very impressive one."

"Then he made piles of money?"

"Yes, to say the least. They've no idea how much."

"What does Internal Revenue have to say about that?"

"A great deal. But they don't know anything definite. Several of Palmgren's companies are registered in Liechtenstein, and they believe that most of his income went into accounts in Swiss banks. Even though his operations here were handled impeccably, they're well aware that records of the bulk of his money were inaccessible to the Internal Revenue people."

"Where does this information come from?"

"Partly from the Ministry for Foreign Affairs, and from the Revenue people. Now maybe you understand why they're so worried about this case higher up."

"No, why?"

"You really don't understand the implications?"

"Let's say that I don't quite grasp what you're getting at."

"Now listen to me," Malm said, exasperated. "In this country there's a small, but very militant, political group that violently opposes Sweden's getting involved with the countries I just mentioned. And also a much larger group of people who believe the official assurances that there aren't any Swedish interests in Rhodesia or Mozambique, for example. Palmgren's activities have been kept pretty much under cover, and still are, but from certain sources we happen to know that extremist groups here were well acquainted with them, and that he was on their black list. To use a trite expression."

"It's better to use a trite expression than one that doesn't make any sense," Martin Beck said encouragingly. "How do we happen to know all this? About the black list?"

"The Security Division of the National Police Board has done some research into the matter. Certain influential people insist that the Security Division should take over the investigation."

"Wait a second," Martin Beck said.

He put down the receiver and began hunting for cigarettes. Finally he found a crumpled pack in his right pants pocket. During this time he was thinking feverishly. The National Police Board's Security Division, known derisively as Sepo, was a special institution, despised by many but primarily renowned for its unsurpassed incompetence. On the rare occasions it had managed to break a case, or even seize a spy, without exception the culprit had been delivered by the public, trussed like a turkey on a platter and garnished with full evidence. Even the military counterespionage was more effective. Anyway, it was seldom talked about.

Martin Beck lit a cigarette and returned to the telephone.

"What in the world are you doing?" Malm asked suspiciously.

"Smoking," Martin Beck said.

The Chief Superintendent said nothing. It sounded as though he had hiccupped or possibly gasped with surprise.

"What was that about Sepo?" Martin Beck asked.

"The Security Division? It's been suggested that they should take over the investigation. And they seem to be interested in the case."

"May I ask a question? Why would Security be interested?"

"Have you thought about the murderer's *modus operandi?*" Malm said ominously.

"*Modus operandi.*" I wonder where he read that, Martin Beck thought. Aloud, he said, "Yes, I've thought about it."

"As far as I can see, it presents many similarities to a classic political killing. A fanatic who thinks about one thing only, which is to carry out the task in hand, and who doesn't worry about whether he gets caught or not."

"Yes, there's something to that," Martin Beck admitted.

"Many people think that there's a great deal to it. Among them the Security Division."

Malm paused, probably for the sake of effect. Then he said, "Now, as you know, I hold no brief for the personnel of the Security Division and have no inside knowledge of their affairs. But I've been tipped off that they're sending down one of their specialists. But then they've probably already done it. There are also secret agents stationed in Malmö."

Martin Beck put out the half-smoked cigarette from pure disgust.

"Officially, the responsibility for the investigation lies with us," said Malm. "But presumably we can count on the Security Division's making a parallel investigation, so to speak."

"I see."

"Yes, and that, of course, means avoiding conflicts."

"Certainly."

"But above all it means getting your hands on the murderer as soon as possible."

Before the secret police do, Martin Beck thought. In that case, there's no big rush for once.

"As soon as possible," Malm said with determination.

And he continued: "It'll be a feather in your cap, at the very least."

"I don't have a cap."

"This is nothing to joke about."

"I can always buy one though."

"This is nothing to joke about," Malm repeated disparagingly. "Besides, this is urgent."

Martin Beck gazed defeatedly at the sun-drenched panorama outside of the window. Hammar had been troublesome in his fashion, especially during his last few years, but at least he had been a policeman.

"What's your view on how the investigation should be set up?" Martin Beck asked blandly.

Malm did some heavy thinking. Finally he came up with the following solution: "That is a detail which I'm turning over to you and your assistants with complete confidence. You do have a great deal of experience."

It was beautifully said. The Chief Superintendent also sounded quite happy when he continued, "And now we'll give it all we've got, right?"

"Right," Martin Beck said automatically.

He was thinking about something else. Then he said,

"Then Palmgren's firm here in Malmö is more or less of a front?"

"I wouldn't go so far as to say that. On the contrary, it's probably an excellent operation."

"What kind of business is it?"

"Import and export."

"Of what?"

"Herring."

"Herring?"

"Yes," said Malm with surprise. "Didn't you know that? They buy up herring from Norway and Iceland and then export it. Where, I don't know. The whole thing is managed legitimately, as far as I can see."

"What about the company in Stockholm?"

"It's mainly a realty company, but . . ."

"But what?"

"Experts claim that Palmgren made his real fortune somewhere else, with means that we have no way of checking on or becoming involved with."

"Okay, I understand."

"Furthermore, I'd like to impress a couple of things on you."

"What things?"

"In the first place, that Palmgren was a powerful man in this country, with many influential friends, quite apart from his African and other foreign deals."

"Yeah, I get it."

"Therefore we must proceed with caution."

"I see. And secondly?"

"That you take into consideration the possibility that this could be a political killing."

"Yes," Martin Beck said and for once grew serious, "I'll take that into consideration."

With that the conversation was terminated.

Martin Beck called the police station. Månsson hadn't been heard from yet, Skacke was busy, and Backlund had gone out.

That was a good idea. Go out.

The weather was tempting, and besides, it was Saturday.

The foyer was rather crowded when he went down several minutes later. People were checking in and out in several different languages, but in the crowd in front of the reception desk was someone who couldn't help but attract attention.

He was a rather young, corpulent man, dressed in a hounds tooth checked suit of modern, youthful cut, a striped shirt, yellow shoes and socks of the same fierce color. His hair was wavy and shiny; he also had a little upturned mustache, no doubt waxed and prepared with a mustache form. The man was leaning nonchalantly on the reception desk. He had a flower in his buttonhole and was carrying a copy of *Esquire* rolled up under his arm.

He looked like a model out of a discothèque advertisement.

Martin Beck knew him. His name was Paulsson, and he was a First Assistant Detective from Stockholm.

When Martin Beck walked over to leave his room key, Paulsson gazed at him with a look that was so exquisitely empty and indolent that three other people felt it necessary to turn around and stare.

The secret police were on the scene.

Martin Beck suddenly felt an almost uncontrollable desire to laugh. Without looking at his secret colleague, he turned around abruptly and went out into the sun.

In the middle of Mälar Bridge, he turned around and studied the special style of the hotel building. It wasn't bad. The impressive façade had been preserved, and the tall *art nouveau* tower was a striking element of the cityscape. He even knew who had designed the building once upon a time—Frans Ekelund.

Paulsson was standing on the hotel steps spying. Because of his appearance, which looked almost like a disguise, there was hardly a public enemy who would not recognize him. Besides, he had an amazing gift for being seen on TV in connection with demonstrations and other public brawls.

Martin Beck smiled to himself and wandered out toward the harbor.

9

The room that Benny Skacke rented was on Kär-leksgatan, only a block from the police station. It was large and cozy, the furniture comfortable and practical, even if somewhat worn. He'd obtained the room from a police sergeant who'd been transferred to Landskrona. The landlady, a friendly, motherly old woman, was a police widow; all she required of boarders was that they be police officers.

His room was next to the hall, within convenient reach of the bathroom and kitchen, and he had unlimited access to both.

Benny Skacke was a man of habit, or rather, was in the process of making himself one. It wasn't really part of his nature to make a routine out of his existence, but he thought it would be easier for him to accomplish the tasks he'd set out for himself in order to reach his goal if he followed a definite schedule. His goal was to become Chief of Police.

Every morning he got up at six-thirty, did exercises and worked out with bar bells, took an ice-cold shower and rubbed himself dry before getting dressed. He ate a nourishing breakfast, usually consisting of sour milk and cereal, a soft-boiled egg, wholewheat bread and a glass of fruit juice. Since his working hours could be highly irregular, he had to fit his athletic training into the leisure offered during the course of the day. He swam at least three times a week, took long bicycle rides and sometimes put on his sweat suit to go jogging on Limhamn's field. He diligently took part in the Malmö policemen's soccer practice, in addition to having a position on the team and playing in all the matches on Mariedal's field. At night he studied law; he'd already completed two terms toward his law degree and hoped to be ready for the third in the fall.

At eleven o'clock every morning and at nine every evening he called his fiancée, Monica. They had become

engaged in Stockholm the week before he started working
in Malmö. A recent graduate, she had applied for a job
as a physiotherapist in Malmö, but hadn't managed to
find anything closer than Helsingborg. That was an im-
provement, at any rate, since they could now meet on the
rare occasions when their free days happened to coincide.

This warm and sunny Saturday morning, however, he
deviated from the schedule to the extent that he got up an
hour later and skipped breakfast. Instead he filled a ther-
mos with cold chocolate milk and put it in a canvas bag
along with bathing trunks and a bath towel. On his way to
the police station, he went into a bakery on Davidshall
Square and bought two cinnamon rolls and a vanilla
heart. He walked past the large copper doors of the main
entrance of the police station, turned on Verkstadsgatan
and went into the courtyard, where his bicycle was standing. It was black, a Danish make. On the oblique frame
he'd hand-painted the word POLICE in white letters. He
hoped that would scare off possible bicycle thieves.

With the bag on the carrier rack, he pedaled off
through the luxuriant foliage of Castle Park and on to the
bathhouse on Ribersborg. In spite of the early hour, it
was already blazing hot. He took a swim, sunbathed for
about an hour, and then settled down on the beach grass
and ate the lunch he'd brought along.

When Skacke entered his office at nine-thirty, his desk
was decorated with a message from Backlund:

Månsson at the widow's, Beck at the Savoy until further notice.
Answer the telephone if it rings. Back at noon.

Backlund

Skacke sat down at the desk and listened for the telephone, which didn't make a sound, while he mused over
the murder of Viktor Palmgren. What could the motive
have been? Since Palmgren had been rich, money should
be a convenient explanation. Or power. But then who
would benefit from his death? Charlotte Palmgren was the
closest and—as far as he knew—the only heir to the
money; Mats Linder should be next in line for his job.
Considering Mrs. Palmgren's much-talked-of beauty and
relative youth, the motive could also have been jealousy.

It wasn't inconceivable that she'd had a lover who'd grown tired of playing second fiddle. But in that case it was a strange way to do away with the husband. Whatever the motive was, the method seemed poorly planned. The assailant had actually escaped, but his chances of getting away must have appeared extremely small if he'd plotted the whole thing beforehand. Moreover, the victim had died after a lapse of twenty-four hours; he might have survived, if the murderer's luck had been really bad—or good. The man must have known that Palmgren would be in the dining room of the Savoy at that exact moment, unless, of course, he were a complete lunatic who'd simply barged in and shot the first guest he caught sight of.

The telephone rang. It was Chief Superintendent Malm in Stockholm, looking for Martin Beck. Skacke informed him that he was probably still at his hotel, and Malm hung up without thanking him or saying good-bye.

Benny Skacke had forgotten his train of thought and became lost in daydreams. He imagined that he came up with the solution, tracked down and caught the murderer singlehanded. He would be promoted, and after that the only direction he could go would be up. He was close to becoming Chief of Police when a new ring of the telephone interrupted his visions of the future.

It was a woman's voice. At first he didn't understand what she was saying; her *skånsk* accent was hard for a Stockholmer to comprehend. Before his transfer to Malmö, Skacke had never been in Skåne. It didn't surprise him that he found certain *skånsk* dialects difficult to understand. However, it didn't cease to amaze him that he couldn't always make himself understood. He who spoke perfectly correct Swedish.

"Uh, it's about the murder that was in the newspaper," he heard the woman say.

"Yes," he said and waited.

"This is the police I'm talking to, isn't it?" she asked suspiciously.

"Yes, this is Assistant Detective Skacke," he said.

"Assistant? Isn't your boss there?"

"No, he's away for the moment. But you can talk to me just as well. I'm working on this case, too. What did you have on your mind?"

He thought his tone inspired confidence, but the woman didn't seem at all convinced of his authority.

"Maybe it'd be better if I came over," she said solemnly. "I don't live so far away."

"Yes, please come up," said Skacke. "Just ask for Assistant De—"

"Maybe the boss will be back by then," she added and hung up.

Twelve minutes passed. Then there was a knock on the door. If the woman had sounded skeptical on the telephone, she seemed even more so when she caught sight of Skacke.

"I'd really imagined someone older," she said, as though she were choosing an article in a store.

"Very sorry," said Skacke stiffly. "But it so happens that I'm on duty at the moment. Please sit down."

He moved the armchair a little closer to the end of the desk, and the woman sat down carefully on the very edge of the chair. She was small and pudgy, dressed in a pale green summer coat and a white straw hat.

Skacke returned to his place behind the desk, and said, "Well, Mrs., uh . . ."

"Greta."

Is there such a name? Skacke thought. Apparently so.

"Well, Mrs. Gröngren. What is it you have to say about what happened last Wednesday?"

"The murder," she said. "Uh, you see, it's just that I saw the murderer. Well, I didn't know then that it was him, not until this morning when I read the newspaper. Then I understood."

Skacke leaned forward, his hands clasped on the blotter.

"Tell me about it," he said.

"Uh, I'd been over to Copenhagen shopping for groceries, you see, and then I met a ladyfriend, and we had coffee at Brønum; so I came home rather late. When I got to the corner at Mälar Bridge across from the Savoy the DON'T WALK sign was on, so I had to stand there and wait. Suddenly I saw a man jump out of one of the windows of the dining room at the Savoy—I've been there several times to eat dinner with my nephew, so I know it was the dining room. Well, my first thought was: What a rat! He's making off without paying the bill. But I couldn't do anything since the light was red, and there was no one around."

"Did you see where he went after that?" Skacke asked.

"Yes, I did. He went over to the bicycle rack to the left of the hotel, got on a bicycle and pedaled away toward Drottning Square. Then the light turned green, but I lost sight of him. I thought that the manager of the restaurant could surely afford to lose that money, so I didn't worry about it and went home."

She paused briefly.

"Well, when I crossed the street, people came out of the hotel entrance and stared, but by then he was already gone."

"Can you describe the man?" Skacke said with ill-concealed fervor and pulled over his note pad.

"Uh, he was about thirty, maybe forty. More like forty. He was quite bald—no, not bald, but almost. He had dark hair. And he had a brown suit on, a yellowish shirt and a tie—I don't know what color. Shoes black or brown, I think—must've been brown, since his suit was brown."

"What did he look like? His face, build, anything unusual about him?"

She seemed to reflect.

"He was thin," she said. "Thin body, thin face. Nothing special. Pretty tall, I thought. Shorter than you, but pretty tall. I don't know what else I can tell you."

Skacke sat quietly and looked at her for a while. Then he said, "When you lost sight of him where was he?"

"At the traffic light, I think. At the crossing on Bruks-gatan. The light must have been red there. Then the WALK sign came on, and when I walked across the street he was gone."

"Hmmm," said Skacke. "Did you see what the bicycle looked like?"

"The bicycle? Like any other bicycle, I suppose."

"Did you see what color it was?"

"No," Mrs. Gröngren said and shook her head. "Cars were going past the whole time. They got in the way."

"I see," said Skacke. "There's nothing else you can remember about this man?"

"No. Not that I can think of now. Will I get a reward for this?"

"I don't believe so," said Skacke. "The public has a moral obligation to help the police. Could I have your address and telephone number so that we can get in touch if necessary?"

The woman gave her address and telephone number. Then she stood up.

"Well, good-bye now," she said. "Do you think I'll get in the newspaper?"

"It's quite possible," Skacke said to encourage her.

He got up and followed her to the door.

"Good-bye and thanks an awful lot for the help. And for the trouble."

After he had shut the door and sat down at the desk, the door was opened again, and the woman stuck in her head.

"You know, that's right!" she said. "Before he got on the bicycle, he took something out of the inside of his jacket and put it in a box, a cardboard container, on the carrier rack. I'd completely forgotten about that."

"Oh," Skacke said, "you didn't happen to see what it was? The thing under his sport coat?"

"No, he was sort of turned away from me. The box was about this big. Almost as big as the carrier and about four inches thick. I saw it later as he was riding away."

Skacke thanked her once again, and Mrs. Gröngren left, this time apparently for good.

Then he dialed the number of the hydrofoil terminal.

When it was new, he'd written on the cover of his notebook:

Assistant Detective B. Skacke

While waiting for an answer, he wrote in front of that: *First.*

10

Just after one on Saturday afternoon, Martin Beck and Per Månsson ran into each other in the doorway to the police station canteen.

Martin Beck had strolled around in the Industrihamn docks, which were quiet and deserted on Saturdays like this during summer vacation. He'd walked all the way out to the oil wharves, where loading had been momentarily interrupted, to view the strange science-fiction landscape. Milky water stagnated in ponds surrounded by rectilinear bars of sand, on which trucks and excavators had made deep tracks. He had marveled at how much the harbor area had grown since he'd seen it for the first time about fifteen years before. He'd suddenly felt hungry—a new and pleasant phenomenon the day after a hearty meal. It doesn't take long to get used to having an appetite again, he thought contentedly. Returning to the center of the city as quickly as possible in the blazing sun, he wondered what could be on the lunch menu at the police station.

Although Månsson wasn't especially hungry, he was extremely thirsty. He had refused the drink Charlotte Palmgren offered him. But now, sitting in his stifling car, he saw the light red drinks in Mats Linder's hands, clinking with ice. They danced before his eyes. For a second he considered driving home and mixing a Gripenberger, but decided it was too early in the day and compromised. A glass of cold soda water at the canteen would have to do.

Martin Beck's hunger diminished somewhat when he entered the canteen, and since he didn't feel so sure of his stomach, he ordered a ham omelet, a tomato and a bottle of mineral water. Månsson duplicated the order.

When they were settled down with their trays, they caught sight of Benny Skacke, who was desperately looking over in their direction. Backlund was sitting across from him, with his back turned to Beck. Backlund had pushed his plate aside and was pointing his first finger threateningly at Skacke. They couldn't hear what he was saying, but to judge from the look on Skacke's face, he was giving him some kind of lecture.

Martin Beck ate his omelet quickly and then walked over to Backlund. Putting his hand on his shoulder, he said kindly, "Forgive me for borrowing Skacke awhile. There are a couple of things I have to go over with him."

Backlund seemed irritated by the interruption but could hardly protest. That cocky Stockholmer *had* been sent down by the National Police Board to head the investigation. As if they couldn't manage it themselves.

Visibly relieved, Skacke stood up and went with Martin Beck. Månsson finished his meal, and they left the canteen. Backlund gazed after them with a grieved look on his face.

They went to Månsson's room, which was moderately cool and ventilated. Månsson sat down in the swivel chair, took a toothpick from the penholder and, after peeling off the paper, stuck it in the corner of his mouth. Martin Beck lit a cigarette and Skacke went directly across the corridor to get his note pad. Then he sat down in the chair next to Martin Beck and placed the pad in his lap.

Martin Beck caught sight of the writing on the pad's cover and smiled. When Skacke saw his glance he blushed and closed the pad quickly. Then he began to give an account of what the new witness had had to say.

"Are you positive her name's Gröngren?" Månsson said skeptically.

When Skacke was through, Martin Beck said, "You'd better check that out with the crew on the hydrofoil. If it was the same man they saw standing on the afterdeck, they should've seen the box. If he still had it with him."

"I've already called," Skacke said. "The boat stewardess who saw him isn't working today. But she's making the crossing tomorrow morning, so I'll go down and talk to her then."

"Good," said Martin Beck.

"You understand Danish then," Månsson said in a doubtful tone.

"Is it really that hard?" Skacke said, wide-eyed.

Then it was time for Martin Beck to tell them about Malm's phone call and the arrival of their colleague.

"Hmm, Paulsson's his name," said Månsson. "I wonder if I haven't seen him on TV. He sound a lot like a security guy we have here, too. He's a secret agent called Persson. Always wears the same kind of suit. Dresses strangely. I thought you already knew about the herring export business, but I've never had an inkling about the weapons deals."

"That's not so strange, really," Martin Beck said. "It wasn't exactly intended that too many people should know about it."

Månsson broke the toothpick in half and put it in the ashtray.

"Well, something like that did enter my mind when the naked widow told me that Palmgren did a lot of business in Portugal."

"The *naked* widow?" Martin Beck and Skacke chorused.

Taking a new toothpick out of the penholder, Månsson said, "I was going to say the merry widow. But she wasn't—either happy or sad. She seemed indifferent to everything."

"But naked," said Martin Beck.

Månsson recounted the morning's visit to the Palmgren mansion.

"She was good-looking, huh?" Skacke said.

"No, I didn't think so," Månsson said curtly.

Then he turned to Martin Beck and said, "Do you have anything against my questioning Linder?"

"No," Martin Beck said, "but I'd really like to meet him, too. Besides, it might take the two of us to handle him."

Månsson nodded. After a while he said, "Do you believe that stuff about a political motive?"

"Sure, why not? But I'd like to know a little more about Palmgren's activities abroad. How we would work that, I don't know. Mats Linder probably isn't familiar with that part of the operations—presumably his job only includes the herring company. What was the Dane's job, by the way?"

"I don't know yet," Månsson said. "We'll have to find

that out. If nothing else works, Mogensen will surely know."

They sat quietly for a while. Then Skacke said, "If the gunman is the same guy who flew to Stockholm from Kastrup, we know he's Swedish. And if the murder had political motives, then he had to be against Palmgren's dealings with Rhodesia and Angola and Mozambique and wherever else it was. And if he was against them, then he has to be some left-wing fanatic."

"Now you're talking like Persson," said Månsson. "He sees extremists under every bush. But there's something to what you say, of course."

"To tell the truth, that same line of thought had occurred to me even before I talked to Malm. It looks amazingly like a political killing. Something very peculiar about the murderer's *modus operandi*—"

Martin Beck broke off sharply. He'd used exactly the same terminology as Malm, and that annoyed him.

"Maybe, maybe not," said Månsson. "The radical groups down here are mainly centered in Lund. I know a little about them, and they're damn peaceful for the most part. Of course Sepo doesn't think so."

"There's nothing that says he comes from around here," Skacke said.

Månsson shook his head.

"Knowledge of the local area," he said. "And if that bit about the bicycle happens to be correct."

"Just think, maybe we could get hold of it," Skacke said optimistically.

Månsson looked at him a long time. Then he shook his head again and said good-naturedly, "My dear Skacke, tracking a bicycle . . ."

Backlund knocked and stepped in without waiting for an answer; he was polishing his glasses diligently.

"Deliberations, I see," he said with irritation. "Maybe you gentlemen have also concluded where the shell went. We've hunted everywhere. Even in the food. I even made a thorough search of the mashed potatoes. There simply isn't any shell . . ."

"Sure there is," Månsson said wearily.

"But he used a revolver," Martin Beck and Benny Skacke said in the same breath.

Backlund looked as though he'd been struck by lightning.

On Sunday morning when Benny Skacke got off his bicycle at the hydrofoil's pier, *Springeren* was just entering the inner harbor. It had settled down on its keel and was gliding slowly forward to the quay.

The weather was still fantastic; not many people had chosen to cross the Sound in something that closely resembled an airplane cabin. A dozen passengers came climbing out of the boat's interior, hurried over the gangplank and through the station building to fight over the only taxi on the spot.

Skacke waited at the gangplank. After five minutes a blond girl in a hostess uniform came up on the deck. He walked up to her, introduced himself and showed her his identification.

"But I've already told the police about that man," she said. "The police in Copenhagen."

To Skacke's happy surprise, she actually spoke Swedish, but naturally with a noticeable Danish accent.

"Yes, I know," he said, "but there was something they didn't ask you about. Did you happen to notice if that man standing on the deck last Wednesday evening was carrying anything?"

The boat stewardess bit her lower lip and knit her brow.

At last she said hesitatingly, "Ye-es, now that you mention it—I recall that ... No, wait, didn't he have a box in his hand, a black cardboard box, about this big?"

She approximated the dimensions with her hands.

"Did you see if he still had the box when he came down and took a seat? Or when he went ashore?"

She pondered a moment. Then she shook her head firmly.

"No, I don't remember that. I really don't know. I only saw that he had it under his arm when he was standing up here."

"Thanks anyway," said Skacke. "That's a valuable piece of information. You haven't remembered anything else about that man since you spoke with the police in Copenhagen?"

Again she shook her head.

"No, nothing else," she said.

"Nothing else?"

She smiled at him professionally and said, "No, nothing. Now if you'll excuse me I have to get things ready for the next trip."

Skacke rode his bicycle back to Davidshall Square and went up to his room in the police station. He was actually off work, but it was close to eleven o'clock—time to call Monica.

He preferred to call from his office rather than from home. For one thing, he didn't dare talk so long at home, considering the cost; for another, his landlady was rather curious when he talked on the telephone. And he wanted to be undisturbed when he was talking to Monica.

She was off work, too, alone at home in the apartment she sublet along with a friend from work. The conversation lasted almost an hour, but what did that matter? The police department could pay. Or, better still, the taxpayer.

When Skacke hung up he had on his mind something different from the murder of Viktor Palmgren.

11

Martin Beck and Månsson met again at the police station at eight o'clock on Monday morning. Neither of them was in the best of humors; Månsson seemed indolent, slow-moving and unenterprising, and Martin Beck grim and pensive.

Without a word, they looked through their papers, but there wasn't anything encouraging. Nothing had happened on Sunday except that the town had become even warmer and emptier. When they informed the afternoon newspapers that "the state of the investigation was unchanged," there was indeed every justification for this empty and worn-out phrase. The only positive thing had been Skacke's vague information from the hydrofoil.

July is a highly unsuitable month for police investigations. If the weather is also beautiful, it's unsuitable for almost anything except for being on vacation. The Kingdom of Sweden virtually closes down; nothing functions, and it's impossible to get hold of people, simply because most of them have gone abroad or to their summer places. That includes almost every category from native professional criminals to government bodies. The relatively few policemen on duty are occupied mostly with checking up on the motley stream of foreigners or trying to keep traffic under control out on the highways.

Martin Beck would have given a lot to be able to talk to his old colleague Fredrik Melander, now Detective Inspector with the Assault and Battery Squad in Stockholm, forty-nine years of age and more than ever equipped with the police force's surest memory for names, dates, circumstances and all the other facts he'd managed to pick up during thirty years on the job. A man who never forgot anything and one of the few who might have something constructive to offer concerning this strange business with Palmgren. But Melander was definitely out of reach. He was on vacation and, as usual when off work, he had isolated himself completely in his summer cottage out on Värmdö. There was no telephone there, and none of his colleagues knew exactly where the place was. His hobby was chopping wood, but he'd chosen to devote this month of vacation to building a new, two-seater outhouse—something that only he and his tall, amazingly ugly wife were aware of, however.

Moreover, Martin Beck and Månsson should both have gone on vacation this week; the knowledge that it was sure to be put off until sometime in the nebulous future was reflected in their gloomy expressions.

On this Monday, however, there was questioning to be attended to, if at all possible. Martin Beck called Stockholm and managed after many if's and but's to persuade Kollberg to take care of Hampus Broberg and Helena Hansson, the executive secretary.

"What'll I ask them about?" Kollberg said mournfully.

"I don't really know."

"Who's the head of the investigation?"

"I am."

"And you don't know? How in the hell am I going to find out anything?"

"I'd like to get a picture of the general situation."

"The general situation? It's bad. I'm dying of heat exhaustion."

"What we need is the motive. Or, rather, we have too many to choose from. Maybe the atmosphere in the Palmgren concern can lead us to the right one."

"I see," Kollberg said skeptically. "This Hansson person, is she good-looking?"

"They say so."

"Well, there's always something to look forward to. Bye now."

Martin Beck had been close to saying, "Let me hear from you," but checked himself at the last second.

"Bye," he said and hung up.

He looked at Månsson and said, "Kollberg'll take care of the Stockholm end."

Månsson nodded and said, "Okay, he's a good man."

Kollberg was more than that, but Månsson didn't know him as well as Martin Beck did.

As a matter of fact, Kollberg was the only person Martin Beck trusted completely. He had sound judgment and was fully capable of managing on his own. Besides this he was imaginative, systematic and implacably logical. They had worked together for many years, and each understood what the other was thinking without having to exchange too many words.

Månsson and Martin Beck sat quietly and listlessly leafing through their papers.

A little after nine they got up and went down to Månsson's car, which was parked in the courtyard.

The Monday morning streets were a bit livelier, but it still didn't take Månsson more than ten minutes to drive to the tall building near the harbor where Viktor Palmgren had his main office in Sweden. By this time Mats Linder ought to be presiding in there.

Månsson parked in a highly illegal manner and put down the visor, which had a rectangular cardboard sign with the word POLICE neatly printed on the front.

They took the elevator up to the seventh story and stepped out into a large antechamber with a bright red wall-to-wall carpet and satiny wallpapered walls. There was a low table in the middle of the floor surrounded by comfortable armchairs. On the table top was a stack of magazines—they were mostly foreign, but even *Svensk Tidskrift* and *Veckans Affärer* were there. There were also two large crystal ashtrays, a teak case with cigars and cigarettes, an ebony lighter and a heavy Orrefors glass vase with red roses. Behind a long table on the left side of the room sat a blond receptionist of about twenty examining her glossy nails. In front of her was an intercom, two ordinary telephones, a steno pad in a metal stand and a gilded fountain pen on the blotter.

She had a model's figure and was dressed in a black and white dress with a very short skirt. Her stockings had an ingenious black lacework pattern, and her feet were enclosed in elegant black shoes with silver buckles. Her lipstick was almost white, and her eyelids were covered with powder-blue eyeshadow. She had long silver earrings, even, chalk-white teeth and beneath dark false eyelashes, unintelligent, clear-blue eyes. She was quite flawless, Martin Beck supposed, if you like women that way.

The girl watched them with a touch of scorn and disapproval. Then she pecked at a page of the appointment book in front of her with the long pointed nail of her first finger and said in the broadest conceivable *skånsk* accent, "You must be from the police."

She glanced at her diminutive watch and continued, "You are almost ten minutes too early. Mr. Linder is on the telephone. He's talking to Johannesburg. Please sit down for the time being. I'll notify you as soon as the conversation is completed. You're Månsson and Back, aren't you?"

"Beck."

"I see," she said indifferently.

She took the gold pen and made a nonchalant little mark in the appointment book. Then she inspected them once again, barely concealing her dislike, and made a vague gesture toward the table with the roses, crystal ashtrays and smoking articles.

"Go ahead and smoke," she said.

The way a dentist says, "Rinse."

Martin Beck felt uneasy in the setting. He glanced at

Månsson, who was dressed in a wrinkled shirt with the tail out, unpressed gray pants and sandals. He probably wasn't much more elegant himself, even though he'd put his pants under the mattress the night before. Nevertheless, Månsson seemed totally unaffected. He flung himself down in one of the armchairs, took a toothpick out of his breast pocket and leafed through a number of *Veckans Affärer* for about thirty seconds before shrugging his shoulders and throwing the magazine down on the table. Martin Beck also sat down and carefully studied the selection of expensive smoking articles in the open teak case. Then he took out one of his own Floridas, pinched the filter together and struck a match.

He looked around. The girl had returned to admiring her nails. It was absolutely quiet in the room. Something irritated him very much. After a while he realized what it was—the doors were invisible. They were there, but so well melted into the surrounding wallpaper pattern that a person actually had to make an effort to discover them.

The minutes passed. Månsson absentmindedly chewed on his toothpick. Martin Beck put out his cigarette and lit another, then stood up and walked over to where a large aquarium with shimmering green water was built into the wall. He stood studying the gaudy fish until a low buzz from the intercom interrupted this activity.

"Mr. Linder will see you now," the receptionist said.

A second later, one of the well-camouflaged doors was opened, and a dark-haired woman of about thirty-five gestured for them to come in. Her movements were rapid and precise, her look steady. A typical executive secretary, Martin Beck thought. Probably she was the one who did the work, if any real work got done within these walls. Månsson stood up and went first, with a heavy, leisurely gait, through a small room with a desk, electric typewriter, filing cabinets and many folders, arranged on shelves against the wall.

Without a word, the dark-haired secretary opened one more door and held it open for them. After they stepped in, Martin Beck had an even stronger impression that they were big, clumsy, uncouth and out of place.

During the time it took Månsson to walk straight up to the desk, behind which Mats Linder was just getting up with a grieved but kind, polite smile, Martin Beck was studying three different things in turn—the view, the furnishings and the individual they'd come to meet.

He had the ability to take stock of situations quickly and felt that it was his greatest asset in his chosen profession. While Månsson took the toothpick out of his mouth, put it in the brass ashtray and shook hands, Martin Beck had the time to grasp the essentials.

The view from the large picture windows was spectacular. Below lay the dock, or rather, the docks, bustling with activity—swarms of cargo and passenger boats, tugboats, cranes, trucks, trains and rows of containers. Beyond the harbor were the Sound and Denmark. The scene was crystal clear. He could see at least twenty boats at one time, among them several passenger boats on their way to or from Copenhagen. The panorama far surpassed the view from his own hotel window, which wasn't so bad, either. All he needed was a good pair of binoculars.

A pair of Carl Zeiss marine binoculars, made in Jena, had been included among the furnishings. They were on the right side of the large steel desk. The desk was so situated that Linder sat with his back to a windowless wall covered by a huge photographic enlargement of a fishing trawler in heavy sea, its freeboard splashed with foam, a huge cascade of water welling up from the prow. Along the starboard gunwale stood a row of men in sou'westers and oilskins, hoisting up the trawl. The contrast was striking—between struggling to catch a meager living from the sea and sitting in peace and quiet in a luxurious office where fortunes were made from these men's toil. The contrast was striking, but probably unintentional. There have to be limits to cynicism. On the wall across from the window hung three lithographs by Matisse, Chagall and Salvador Dali. In the room there were also two leather chairs for visitors and a conference table with six straight-backed rosewood chairs.

According to the detectives' information, Mats Linder was thirty years old. His appearance suited his age and position perfectly. Tall, slender and well built. Brown eyes, neatly parted hair, a thin face with a firm profile and a determined chin. Very soberly dressed.

Martin Beck looked at Månsson and felt sweatier and more wrinkled than ever.

He introduced himself and shook hands with Linder.

They sat down in the leather armchairs.

The man behind the desk leaned on his elbows and sat with his finger tips pressed together.

"Well," he said, "has the murderer been apprehended?"

Månsson and Martin Beck shook their heads simultaneously.

"Then how can I be of help to you gentlemen?"

"Did Mr. Palmgren have any enemies?" Martin Beck asked.

It was a ridiculously simple question, but a beginning had to be made somewhere. Linder, however, seemed to take the question with exaggerated gravity and to consider his answer carefully. At last he said, "When a person is involved in business of the scope that Viktor Palmgren was, he can hardly escape making enemies."

"Can you think of anyone in particular?"

"Far too many," Linder said with a wan smile. "Gentlemen, the world of business is tough today. With the credit market in its present state, there's no room for philanthropy or sentimentality. Many times it's a matter of kill or be killed. From an economic viewpoint, that is. But . . ."

"Yes?"

"But in the business world we use other methods than shooting each other. Therefore I believe that we can quite simply dismiss the theory that a slighted competitor walked into the dining room of a first-class restaurant with a pistol in his hand, in order, so to speak, to balance his books privately."

Månsson made a movement, as though something had occurred to him, but he didn't say anything. Martin Beck was forced to continue directing the conversation.

"Do you have any idea who it was who shot your boss?"

"I didn't really see him, partly because I was sitting beside Vicke—his intimate friends used to call him that—and consequently I had my back turned to the murderer, and because I didn't realize what was happening at first. I heard the shot—it wasn't loud and didn't seem very frightening—then Vicke fell forward over the table and I immediately stood up and leaned over him. It took several seconds before I realized that he was severely injured. When I turned around the gunman was gone, and the staff came rushing from all directions to help. But I told the police all this that same night."

"I know," said Martin Beck. "Maybe I didn't make myself quite clear. What I meant was, have you any idea of what kind of person might be involved?"

"A lunatic," said Mats Linder without the slightest hesitation. "Only a person who is mentally ill could act that way."

"Then Mr. Palmgren would be a victim chosen at random?"

The man reflected. Then he smiled his faint smile again and said, "That's for the police to try to figure out."

"From what I gather, Mr. Palmgren did considerable business abroad?"

"Yes, that's correct. His commercial interests were numerous and varied. What we deal with here is the original business—the import and export of fish for the canning industry. This firm was founded by old Palmgren, Vicke's father. I'm too young to have known him. As for other foreign transactions, I really know very little."

He paused and added, "But it seems highly probable that I'll have to become closer acquainted with them now."

"Who is taking over the main responsibility for ... the concern?"

"Charlotte, I suppose. She should be the sole heir. There aren't any children or any other relatives in the picture. But the corporation lawyers will have to clarify that. The firm's main lawyer had to break off his vacation very hastily. He came home on Friday night and since then has been at work going through the documents with his assistants. For the time being we are working here as usual."

Working? Martin Beck thought.

"Are you planning on being Mr. Palmgren's successor?" Månsson suddenly put in.

"No," Linder said. "I wouldn't say that, actually. Besides, I have neither the experience nor the talent required for managing a business emp—"

He broke off and Månsson didn't pursue the topic. Martin Beck didn't say anything, either. It was Linder himself who continued, "For the present I'm completely satisfied with my position here. And I can assure you that even this part of the business takes some running."

"Is herring a good business?" Martin Beck said.

The other man smiled indulgently.

"Well, we deal in more than herring. In any case, I assure you that the company's financial status is very sound."

Martin Beck felt it necessary to try a new line of attack.

"I presume that you knew all the people at the banquet fairly well."

He reflected awhile and said, "Yes. Except Mr. Broberg's secretary."

Wasn't there some animosity in his features? Martin Beck felt that there was something afoot and forged ahead.

"Isn't Mr. Broberg considerably older than you, both in terms of age and years with the Palmgren concern?"

"Yes, he's about forty-five."

"Forty-three," said Martin Beck. "And how long has he worked for Palmgren?"

"Since the middle of the fifties. About fifteen years."

It was apparent that Mats Linder disliked the subject.

"Still, you do have a more privileged position, don't you?"

"That depends on what you mean by privileged. Hampus Broberg is located in Stockholm, as vice-president of the real estate company there. He also has charge of the stock activities."

Linder's face expressed strong disapproval. Now we've got to stay with it, Martin Beck thought. Sooner or later we might get the guy to make a slip of the tongue.

"But it seems quite obvious that Mr. Palmgren had more confidence in you than in Broberg. And yet Broberg has worked for him for fifteen years and you for only ... yes, how long has it been?"

"Almost five years," Mats Linder said.

"Didn't Mr. Palmgren trust Broberg?"

"Too much," Linder said and tightened his lips as if he wanted to annul the answer and erase it from the report of the proceedings.

"Do you consider Broberg unreliable?" Martin Beck asked immediately.

"I don't want to answer that question."

"Have disagreements come up between you and him?"

Linder sat quietly awhile. It seemed as though he were trying to assess the situation.

"Yes," he said at long last.

"What were these disagreements about?"

"That's a strictly private business matter."

"Don't you consider him loyal to the firm?"

Linder said nothing. It didn't matter now, since he'd already answered the question in principle.

"Well, we'll have to talk to Mr. Broberg about that," Martin Beck said in a casual tone.

The man behind the desk took a long, thin cigarillo out of his inner pocket, peeled off the cellophane wrapper and lit it carefully.

"But I don't understand what this has to do with my boss's murder," he said.

"Maybe nothing at all," Martin Beck said. "We'll just have to see."

"Is there anything else you gentlemen would like to know?" Linder asked, puffing on the cigar.

"You had a meeting on Wednesday afternoon, didn't you?"

"Yes, that's correct."

"Where?"

"Here."

"In this room?"

"No, in the conference room."

"What was the meeting actually about?"

"Internal affairs. I'm not able to give a more detailed account of what was said, and wouldn't if I could. Let's just say that Mr. Palmgren was going to withdraw from the business for a while and wanted a report on the situation here in Scandinavia."

"Did he make any criticism during this review? Was there anything that Mr. Palmgren wasn't pleased with?"

The answer came after a short hesitation.

"No."

"Perhaps you thought that some criticism would've been in order?"

Linder didn't answer.

"You might have objections to our talking with Hampus Broberg?"

"On the contrary," Linder murmured.

"Excuse me, I didn't catch what you said?"

"It was nothing."

Silence. Martin Beck didn't think he could pursue this track much further. There had to be something rotten here, but nothing that indicated that it had anything to do with the murder.

Månsson seemed totally impassive, and Linder waited to see what would happen.

"In any case, it seems quite clear that Mr. Palmgren had more confidence in you than in Broberg," Martin Beck said, as if stating an obvious fact.

"That's possible," Linder said drily. "But anyhow, it doesn't have anything to do with his death."

"We'll just have to see," Martin Beck said.

The other man's eyes flashed. He had a hard time hiding the fact that he was furious.

"Well, we've already taken up a great deal of your precious time," Martin Beck said.

"Yes, you have, to tell the truth. The sooner this conversation is concluded, the better. For you and for me. I don't see any purpose in going over this again."

"Then we'll leave it at that," Martin Beck said, making an attempt to stand up.

"Thank you," Linder said.

His tone was sarcastic and extremely guarded.

At this point Månsson sat up and said slowly, "If you don't mind, I'd like to ask you a few questions."

"Such as?"

"What kind of relationship do you have with Charlotte Palmgren?"

"I know her."

"How well do you know her?"

"That ought to be my private affair."

"That, of course, is correct. But I'd still like you to answer the question."

"What question?"

"Are you having an affair with Mrs. Palmgren?"

Linder looked at him, coldly and deprecatingly.

After a minute of silence, he crushed his cigarillo in the ashtray and said, "Yes."

"A love affair?"

"A sexual relationship. I sleep with her sometimes, to put it simply, in language that even policemen can understand."

"How long has this relationship gone on?"

"For two years."

"Did Viktor Palmgren know about it?"

"No."

"And if he'd known about it, how would he have reacted?"

"I don't know."

"He might have objected?"

"I'm not so sure. Charlotte and I are broad-minded people. We don't care about convention. Viktor Palmgren was like that, too. Besides, their marriage was more of a practical arrangement than an emotional commitment."

"When did you see her last?"

"Charlotte? Two hours ago."

Månsson dug around in his breast pocket for another toothpick. He examined it and said, "How is she in bed?"

Mats Linder stared at him speechless. Finally he said, "Are you out of your mind?"

They stood up and said good-bye, without receiving an answer. The efficient, dark-haired secretary showed them out to the waiting room, where the blonde at the reception desk was carrying on a private conversation, cooing into one of her telephones.

When they were sitting in the car Månsson said, "Smart kid."

"Yes."

"Smart enough to tell the truth when he knows that a lie could be exposed. You can bet Palmgren had a lot of use for him."

"Mats Linder's obviously had a good teacher," Martin Beck said.

"Is he smart enough not to have people shot? That's the question," Månsson said.

Martin Beck shrugged.

12

Lennart Kollberg didn't know which way to turn.

The job he'd been assigned to seemed both repugnant and pointless. It never occurred to him, however, that it would turn out to be complicated.

He would call on a couple of people, talk to them, and that's all there would be to it.

A little before ten o'clock he left the South police station in Västberga, where all was quiet and peaceful, largely because of the shortage of personnel. There was no shortage of work, however, for all varieties of crime flourished better than ever in the fertile topsoil provided by the welfare state.

The reasons for this were cloaked in mystery—at least for those who had the responsibility of governing and for the experts who had the delicate task of trying to make the society function smoothly.

Behind its spectacular topographical façade and under its polished, semi-fashionable surface, Stockholm had become an asphalt jungle, where drug addiction and sexual perversion ran more rampant than ever. Unscrupulous profiteers could make enormous profits quite legally on pornography of the smuttiest kind. Professional criminals became not only more numerous but also better organized. An impoverished proletariat was also being created, especially among the elderly. Inflation had given rise to one of the highest costs of living in the world, and the latest surveys showed that many pensioners had to live on dog and cat food in order to make ends meet.

The fact that juvenile delinquency and alcoholism (which had always been a problem) continued to increase surprised no one but those with responsible positions in the Civil Service and at the Cabinet level.

Stockholm.

Not much was left of the city where Kollberg was born and grew up. With the sanction of the city planners, the steam shovels of real estate speculators and the bulldozers of the traffic "experts" had devastated most of the respectable old settlement. By now the few sanctuaries of culture that remained were pitiful in appearance. The city's character, atmosphere and style of life had disappeared, or rather, changed, and it wasn't easy to do anything about it.

Meanwhile more squeaks were appearing in the police machinery, which was overworked, partly because of the shortage of men. But there were other, more important reasons.

It was less important to recruit more policemen than to get better ones—no one seemed to have thought of that.

Thought Lennart Kollberg.

It took a while to get out to the housing project managed by Hampus Broberg. It was located far to the south, in an area that had been countryside in Kollberg's youth, a place where he used to go on school excursions when he was a child. It resembled far too many of the rent traps built during recent years—an isolated group of high-rise apartments, slapped together quickly and carelessly, whose sole purpose was to make as large a profit as possible for the owner while at the same time guaranteeing unpleasantness and discomfort for the unfortunate people who had to live there. Since the housing shortage had been kept alive artificially for many years, even these apartments were in great demand, and the rents were close to astronomical.

Presumably the realty office occupied the best rooms—those built with the greatest care. However, even in these, moisture had seeped through, and the doorposts had warped so much that they'd already come loose from the masonry.

The greatest drawback from Kollberg's point of view, however, was that Hampus Broberg wasn't to be found there.

In addition to Broberg's private office, which was spacious and rather stylishly furnished, there was a conference room and two small rooms, which were inhabited by a caretaker and two female employees—the first a woman of fifty and the second a girl who had barely turned nineteen.

The older woman looked like a real monster. Kollberg guessed that her main duty was to threaten eviction and to refuse repairs. The girl was clumsy and ugly, had acne and looked bullied. The caretaker seemed resigned. He must have had the thankless job of seeing to it that the drains and toilets worked just well enough to get by.

Kollberg proceeded on the assumption that he should talk to the monster.

No, Mr. Broberg wasn't here. He hadn't shown up since Friday afternoon. Then he'd been in his office for about ten minutes and then left again, carrying a briefcase.

No, Mr. Broberg hadn't said anything about when he was coming back.

No, neither of the ladies' names was Helena Hansson, nor had they ever heard of anyone by that name.

However, Mr. Broberg did have another office, in the city. On Kungsgatan, to be exact. Both he and Miss Hansson would certainly be there.

No, Mr. Palmgren didn't concern himself with the upkeep of the properties. Since the area had been built up four years ago, he'd only been there on two occasions, both times in the company of Mr. Broberg.

What did they do at the office? Collect rents and keep the tenants in order, of course.

"And that's not the easiest thing in the world," said the monster caustically.

"Okay, I get the picture," Kollberg said. And left.

He got into his car and drove north toward Stockholm.

On the way he passed temptingly close to his own home in the borough of Skärmarbrink. His family was there— his daughter Bodil, who would soon be two years old, and above all Gun, who seemed to grow prettier and more irresistible every day. Kollberg was a sensualist, and had been careful to choose a wife who would comply with his exacting demands.

He steeled himself, however, sighed deeply, wiped the sweat off his forehead with his shirt sleeve and drove on toward the center of Stockholm. He parked on Kungsgatan and stepped out. Then he went into the entrance to check that he'd gone to the right address.

According to the directory, the house contained mostly film companies and law offices, but it also had what he was looking for.

On the fourth floor, there was listed not only HAMPUS BROBERG INC., but also VIKTOR PALMGREN LOAN & FINANCE.

Kollberg rode up on a creaking, aged elevator and found that both company plaques decorated the same snuff-colored door. He grasped the doorknob and found the door locked. There was a doorbell, but he ignored it and, true to habit, hammered on the door with his fist.

A woman opened, looked at him with big brown eyes and said, "What in the world is the matter?"

"I'm looking for Mr. Broberg."

"He isn't here."

"Is your name Helena Hansson?"

"No, it isn't. Who are you?"

Kollberg pulled himself together and took his identification card out of his back pocket.

"Excuse me," he said. "It must be the fault of this heat."

"I see," she said. "The police."

"Right. The name's Kollberg. May I come in for a minute?"

"Of course," the woman said and stepped aside.

The room he entered looked like a run-of-the-mill office with tables, folders, typewriter, filing cabinets and all the usual accessories. Through a half-open door he could see into another room, which was apparently Hampus Broberg's private office. Smaller than the secretary's, but more comfortable, it seemed almost entirely taken up by a desk and a large safe.

While Kollberg was looking around, the woman had turned the lock on the door. Then she stared at him inquiringly and said, "Why did you ask me if my name was Hansson?"

She was about thirty-five years old, slender and dark, with thick eyebrows and short hair.

"I thought you were Mr. Broberg's secretary," Kollberg said absentmindedly.

"Actually I am Mr. Broberg's secretary."

"Well, in that case . . ."

"My name isn't Hansson," she continued, "and it never has been."

Looking at her obliquely, he saw that she wore two broad gold bands on the ring finger of her left hand.

"What is your name, then?"

"Sara Moberg."

"You weren't in Malmö last Wednesday when Mr. Palmgren was shot?"

"Certainly not."

"We were told that Mr. Broberg was in Malmö at the time and that his secretary was with him."

"In that case it wasn't me. I never go along on his trips."

"And the secretary's name was Hansson," Kollberg said stubbornly, taking a dog-eared piece of paper out of his pants pocket.

He glared at it and said, "Miss Helena Hansson. That's what it says here."

"I don't know anyone by that name. Besides, I'm married and have two children. As I said before, I never go along on trips."

"Then who could this Miss Hansson have been?"

"No idea."

"Maybe an employee in some other branch of the company?"

"I've never heard of her, at any rate."

The woman looked at him sharply and said, "Until now."

Then she added vaguely, "Of course, there are traveling secretaries, as they're called."

Kollberg dropped the subject.

"When did you last see Mr. Broberg?"

"This morning. He came in a little after ten and stayed in his office for about twenty minutes. Then he left. For the bank, I think."

"Where do you think he is now?"

Glancing at the clock, she said, "Probably at home."

Kollberg consulted his piece of paper.

"He lives out on Lidingö, doesn't he?"

"Yes, on Tjädervägen."

"Is he married?"

"Yes. They have a daughter who's seventeen. But she and his wife aren't home. They're in Switzerland on vacation."

"Do you know that for a fact?"

"Yes. I ordered their plane tickets myself. Last Friday. It must have come up quickly, for they left the same day."

"Has Mr. Broberg been working as usual after what happened in Malmö last Wednesday?"

"Well, no," she said. "No, you could hardly say that. It was very tense around here on Thursday. You see, we didn't know anything definite then. On Friday we found out that Mr. Palmgren had died. Mr. Broberg was in on Friday for maybe an hour altogether. And today, as I said, he was here for about twenty minutes."

"Did he say when he planned to get back?"

The woman shook her head.

"Is he usually in the office longer than that?"

"Oh yes, he's here most of the time. Sits in his office."

Kollberg walked over to the inner door and let his eyes wander over Hampus Broberg's room. He took note of three black telephones on the desk and an elegant suitcase standing next to the safe. The suitcase wasn't big, but it was made of pigskin and had two straps buckled over the top. It looked brand-new.

"Do you know if Mr. Broberg was here on Saturday or Sunday?" he asked.

"Well, somebody was here. We aren't open on Saturday, so I was off work as usual over the weekend. But when I came in this morning I noticed right away that someone had moved things around."

"Can this someone have been anyone else but Broberg?"

"Hardly. We're the only two who have keys to this place."

"Do you think he'll come back today?"

"Don't know. Maybe he went to the bank and then home. That seems quite likely."

"Lidingö," murmured Kollberg. "Tjädervägen."

He was getting even farther away from home.

"Good-bye," he said abruptly and left.

It was sweltering hot in the car by now, and he perspired profusely on the way to Lidingö.

As he crossed the bridge over Värtan and saw the big ships in Frihamnen and the hundreds of pleasure boats full of half-naked vacationers with tans, he reflected that it was idiotic to rush around like this. Of course he should have stayed in his office, used the telephone and asked these people to come to Västberga. But then none of them would have come, and he would've been burned up about that. Besides, Martin Beck had said that it was urgent.

The houses built along Tjädervägen on Lidingö didn't belong to the super-deluxe class, but they were still light-years away from the decrepit housing project he'd visited earlier. Nobody who lived here was so unfortunate as to have to be milked by characters like Palmgren and Broberg. Large, expensive bungalows with meticulous lawns lined both sides of the street.

Hampus Broberg's house seemed closed and completely dead. Car tracks led up to the garage doors, but when Kollberg peeked in one of the small side windows, he found the garage empty. Everything indicated that, until quite recently, two cars had been parked there. No one responded to his ringing and pounding, and the blinds behind the large windows were drawn, so that it was impossible to catch a glimpse of what the house looked like inside.

Kollberg panted as he walked over to the house next door. It was larger and more fashionable than Broberg's; the name on the door was that of a noble family. At least it sounded noble.

He rang the bell and the door was opened by a tall blond woman. She looked cool, and her manner was aristocratic.

When he had identified himself, she peered at him disdainfully and made no move to ask him to come in.

When he stated his business she said coldly, "We are not in the habit of spying on our neighbors. I don't know Mr. Broberg and am unable to help you."

"That's too bad."

"Perhaps for you, but not for me."

"Then please excuse me," Kollberg said.

She looked at him appraisingly and asked a very startling question, "Tell me, who sent you here anyway?"

Both her voice and her clear blue eyes expressed suspicion. She might have been between thirty-five and forty. Extremely well preserved. She reminded him vaguely of someone, but he couldn't recall who.

"Well, good-bye," he said dejectedly and shrugged his shoulders.

"Good-bye," she said emphatically.

Kollberg got into his car and consulted his slip of paper.

Helena Hansson had given an address on Västeråsgatan in Vasastaden and a telephone number. He drove to the police station on Lejonvägen on Lidingö, where several plainclothesmen were brooding over the week's pools coupon while they drank soft drinks out of paper cups.

"Do you know what Go Ahead Deventer could be?" one of them said.

"No idea," Kollberg said.

"What about Young Boys?"

"What were those names again?"

"Go Ahead Deventer and Young Boys. They're soccer teams. Playing in the pools cup matches. But we don't know where they're from. You know, the pools cup."

Kollberg shrugged his fat shoulders. Soccer was one of the things that weren't of the least interest to him.

"Go Ahead Deventer must be from Deventer," he said. "That's a city in Holland."

"Damn. The National Homicide Squad *would* know about things like that. Do you think they're any good?"

"As a matter of fact, I only came here to borrow the telephone," Kollberg said wearily.

"Go ahead. Use any one you want."

Kollberg dialed Helena Hansson's number and got the out-of-order signal. Then he called the telephone company and was consoled with the information that the telephone in question was no longer in use.

"Do you know anything about a Mr. Hampus Broberg?" he asked the two betting policemen.

"Sure, he lives on Tjädervägen. And to live like him, you've got to have plenty of money."

"We only have the better sort of people out here," said one of the policemen.

"Have you ever had reason to have anything to do with him?"

"Nope," the other policeman said and poured out more Loranga orange. "We maintain law and order here."

"This isn't Stockholm," said the first one virulently.

"And if we have any crimes, they're high-class stuff. People don't go around bashing each other's heads in with axes. There aren't any old bums or doped-up kids under every bush. I think we'll put our money on Go Ahead Deventer, anyway."

They had completely lost interest in Kollberg.

"Bye," he said gloomily and left them.

During the long drive to Vasastaden in Stockholm, he considered the fact that even Lidingö had a generous portion of crime behind its polished façade. The only difference was that people were richer and could hide their dirty linen more easily.

There was no elevator in the apartment building on Västeråsgatan, and he had to trudge up five flights of stairs in five different stairwells. The house was dilapidated—neglected by the landlord as usual—and big fat rats ran among the garbage cans on the asphalt courtyard.

He rang doorbells here and there. Several times doors were opened, and various people stared at him in alarm.

People here were afraid of the police—perhaps with good reason.

He didn't find Helena Hansson.

No one could say if a person by that name lived or had lived there. Giving information to the police obviously wasn't a popular pastime, and besides, people in apartment buildings like this one generally knew very little about each other.

Kollberg stood out on the street and wiped his face with a handkerchief that was already soaked with hours of perspiration.

He reflected for several minutes.

Then he gave up and drove home.

An hour later his wife said, "Lennart, why do you look so miserable?"

He had showered, eaten, made love to her and then showered again, and was now sitting wrapped in a bath towel, downing a can of cold beer.

"Because I feel miserable," he said. "That damn job
..."

"You should quit."

"It's not that easy."

Kollberg was a policeman, and he still couldn't help
trying to be as good a policeman as possible. Somehow
that drive had been built into his psyche; it was like a
burden that, for some reason, he had to carry.

The order he'd received from Martin Beck was simple,
a routine matter, and now, because of it, he was at his
wit's end. He scowled and said, "Gun, what's a traveling
secretary?"

"Usually some kind of call girl, who goes around with
her nightgown, toothbrush and birth control pills in a
briefcase."

"Then she's nothing but a whore."

"Right. Available for people like businessmen who are
too lazy to pick up some girl in the place they're staying."

On reflection, he realized that he needed help. He
couldn't get it out in Västberga, where they were hard-
pressed for people during vacation.

A moment later he sighed, went over to the telephone
and called the Stockholm police on Kungsholmsgatan.

The person who answered was the last person he
wanted to talk to.

Gunvald Larsson.

"How's it going?" he said sullenly. "What do you think?
I'm up to my neck in stabbings, fights, robberies and
insane foreigners who are sky-high on LSD. And almost
nobody here. Melander is on Värmdö, and Rönn went
to Arjeplog last Friday night. Strömgren is on Majorca.
And people seem to get more aggressive in this heat. Lose
their judgment entirely. What the hell do you want?"

Kollberg detested Gunvald Larsson, who was, in his
opinion, only a big, dumb thug with snobbish ways. As far
as his judgment went, what was there to say? Gunvald
Larsson had lost his in the cradle.

Thought Kollberg. But he said aloud, "Well, it's about
the Palmgren affair."

"I don't want to have a thing to do with it," Gunvald
Larsson said immediately. He'd already had enough trouble
with it.

Kollberg recounted the tale of his sorrows anyway.

Gunvald Larsson interspersed it with bad-tempered grunts. Once he interrupted and said, "Sitting there jabbering about it won't get you anywhere. It's not my job."

But something must have attracted his attention, for when Kollberg finished, he said, "Did you say Tjädervägen on Lidingö? What was the number?"

Kollberg repeated the number.

"Hmm," Gunvald Larsson said. "Maybe I can do something for you."

"That's decent of you," Kollberg forced himself to say.

"To tell the truth, I'm not doing it for your sake," Gunvald Larsson said, as though he really meant it.

He did, too.

Kollberg wondered why he'd become interested. Generosity wasn't one of Gunvald Larsson's characteristics.

"About this Hansson whore," Gunvald Larsson said dismally. "You'd better talk to the Vice Squad."

"Yes, I'd thought of that."

"Well, of course. It all fits together—she had to show identification down there in Malmö at the first questioning. But she could have made up any damn address she pleased. So probably her name really is Helena Hansson."

Even Kollberg had thought of that, but refrained from making further comment.

He hung up and immediately dialed again.

This time he asked to be connected with Åsa Torell of the Vice Squad.

13

As soon as the conversation was over, Gunvald Larsson went down, got into his car and drove straight to Lidingö.

His face was taut, set in a strangely grim smile.

He looked at his big hairy hands resting on the steering wheel and chuckled to himself with satisfaction.

Out on Tjädervägen he gave only a passing glance to

Broberg's house, which looked just as deserted as before. Then he went over to the house next door and rang the bell. The door was opened by the same cool, blond woman who had dismissed Kollberg so ignominiously a couple of hours earlier.

When she caught sight of the gigantic man on the step her attitude changed.

"Gunvald," she said with consternation. "How in the . . . how can you have the gall to show your face here?"

"Oh," he said banteringly, "true love never dies."

"I haven't seen you for more than ten years, and that I'm grateful for."

"What a nice thing to say!"

"Your picture was in the newspapers last winter. I burned them all up in the fireplace."

"You really are sweet."

She knit her blond eyebrows suspiciously and said, "Did you send that fat guy out here earlier today?"

"As a matter of fact, no. But I'm here for the same reason."

"You must be crazy."

"You think so?"

"After all, I can only tell you the same thing I told him. I don't spy on my neighbors."

"You don't? Well, are you going to let me in? Or should I kick your whole goddamned rosewood door in, alabaster paneling and all?"

"You should just die of shame. But you're probably too thick for that."

"This is getting better all the time."

"Well, I'd rather you came in than stand on the steps and disgrace me."

She opened the door. Gunvald Larsson stepped in.

"Where is that henpecked husband of yours?" he asked.

"Hugold is at the Chief of Staff's office. He has a great deal of responsibility and is very busy now. The General is on vacation."

"Kiss my ass," said Gunvald Larsson. "And he hasn't even managed to knock you up in thirteen years, or however long it's been?"

"Eleven," she said. "And watch yourself. I'm not alone, either."

"Is that so? Do you have a lover, too? Little cadets, maybe?"

"You can spare me the vulgar remarks. An old friend dropped by for tea. Sonja. Maybe you remember her."

"No, I don't, thank goodness."

"She hasn't had an easy time of it," the woman said, touching her blond hair lightly. "But she has a respectable profession anyway. She's a dentist."

Gunvald Larsson didn't say anything. He followed her into a very large, elegant living room. On a low table was a silver tea service, and a tall, slim woman with brown hair sat on the couch nibbling on an English biscuit.

"This is my eldest brother," said the blonde. "Unfortunately. Gunvald's his name. He's a . . . policeman. Before he was just a thug. The last time I saw him was more than ten years ago and before that the times were few and far between."

"C'mon now, you behave now," Gunvald Larsson said.

"You would say that. Where were you, for instance, the last six years Father was alive?"

"At sea. I was working. And that's more than can be said of any other member of the family."

"You made us take all the responsibility," she said bitterly.

"And who laid their mitts on all the money? And everything else?"

"You'd already squandered your part of the inheritance before you received your dishonorable discharge from the Navy," she said icily.

Gunvald Larsson looked around.

"Oh, fuck," he said.

"What do you mean by that?"

"Exactly what I said. Oh, fuck. Like, where did you get that two-foot silver rooster?"

"Portugal. We bought it in Lisbon during a world cruise."

"How much did it cost?"

"Several thousand kronor," she said indifferently. "I don't remember exactly. What are you called now? Patrolman?"

"First Assistant Detective."

"Father would turn over in his grave. You mean to say

you haven't even managed to become a superintendent or whatever it's called? How much do you make?"

"That's none of your business."

"What are you doing here? Maybe you want to borrow money? I wouldn't be surprised."

She looked at her girlfriend, who had been following the discussion in silence, and added matter-of-factly, "He's renowned for his insolence."

"Right," Gunvald Larsson said and sat down. "Now bring another cup."

She left the room. Gunvald Larsson looked at the childhood friend with a gleam of interest. She didn't return the look, and neither of them said anything.

His sister came back with a tea glass in a silver holder, placed on a small engraved silver tray.

"What are you doing here?" she said.

"You know that already. You're going to tell me every single thing you know about this Broberg and his boss. His name was Palmgren and he died last Wednesday."

"Died?"

"Yes. Don't you read the newspapers?"

"Maybe I do. But that's none of your business."

"He was murdered, moreover. Shot."

"Murdered? Shot? What kind of horrible doings *are* you involved in?"

Gunvald Larsson impassively poured tea into his glass.

"Look, I've already told you. I don't spy on the neighbors. And I said so to that other clown you sent along to me this morning."

Gunvald Larsson took a swallow of tea. Then he put the glass down with a bang.

"Quit making a spectacle of yourself, Kid Sister. You're as curious as a cat and have been ever since you started walking. I know you know a helluva lot about Broberg. About Palmgren, too, for that matter. I'm convinced that you and that lousy husband of yours know both of them. I have a fairly good idea of how things work in those distinguished circles of yours."

"Being vulgar isn't going to get you anywhere. I'm not going to say anything anyway. Least of all to you."

"Sure you are. Otherwise . . ."

She looked at him derisively and said, "Otherwise, what?"

"Otherwise I'll get a local patrolman in uniform to go around with me to every house in a mile's radius. I'll introduce myself and say that my sister is such a goddamn idiot that I have to ask other people for help."

She stared at him speechless. At last she said tonelessly, "Do you mean you'd have the nerve to . . ."

"You're damn right, that's what I mean. So you'd better cough something up right now."

Her friend was now following the dialogue with discreet but obvious interest.

After a long, strained silence, his sister said resignedly, "Yes, I suppose you really are capable of doing something like that."

And immediately afterward, "What do you want to know?"

"Do you know Broberg?"

"Yes."

"And Palmgren?"

"Casually. We've been at a party or two together. But . . ."

"But what?"

"It's nothing."

"Well, what has Broberg been up to these last few days?"

"It's none of my business."

"Quite right. But I've got a damn good idea that you've been peeking every time anyone has made a move in that house. Well?"

"His family went away last Friday."

"I know that already. What else?"

"He sold his wife's car that same day. A white Ferrari."

"How do you know that?"

"A buyer was here. They stood outside of the house bargaining."

"Well, how about that! What else?"

"I don't think Mr. Broberg's slept at home the last few nights."

"How do you know that? Have you been in his house to check?"

With a despairing look, she said, "You're worse than ever."

"Now answer, goddammit."

"It's hard to keep from noticing what goes on in the house next door."

"Yeah, especially if you're nosy. So he hasn't been there?"

"In fact, he's been there several times. From what I've seen, he's moved some things out."

"Has anybody besides that car dealer been there?"

"We-e-ell . . ."

"Who and when?"

"On Friday he came with a blond girl. They stayed for a couple of hours. Then they carried some things out to the car. Suitcases and some other things."

"I see. Keep going."

"There were some people there yesterday. A very distinguished couple and a guy who looked like an attorney. They walked around looking at everything, and the guy who I think was an attorney took notes the whole time."

"What do you think it was all about?"

"I think he was trying to sell the house. I think he was successful, too."

"Did you hear what they said?"

"I couldn't help hearing bits and pieces."

"Of course," Gunvald Larsson said drily. "It sounds like he sold the house?"

"Yes."

"With the furniture and the rest of the crap?"

"What a filthy mouth you have!"

"You don't have to worry about that. Just answer. Why do you think he really managed to sell the house?"

"Because I heard snatches of the conversation. For example, they said that quick deals are always the best and that the transaction favored both parties, under the circumstances."

"Tell me more."

"They parted like old friends. Shook hands and slapped each other on the back. Broberg handed over some things. Keys, among other things, I think."

"What happened then?"

"They drove away. In a black Bentley."

"What about Broberg?"

"He stayed behind for a couple of hours."

"And did what?"

"Burned something in the fireplaces. Both chimneys smoked for a long time. I thought . . ."

She broke off.

"What did you think?"

"That it was peculiar, considering the weather. There's a heat wave."

"And then?"

"He went around drawing all the blinds. Then he drove away. I haven't seen him since."

"Kid Sister," said Gunvald Larsson kindly.

"Yes, what is it?"

"You would've made a good cop."

She made an indescribable grimace and said, "Are you going to go on torturing me?"

"Sure. How well do you know Broberg?"

"We've seen each other now and then. That's hard to avoid when you're neighbors."

"What about Palmgren?"

"Casually, as I said. We were at several parties together at Broberg's house. Once we had a party in the garden here, and he came. You know, in situations like that one always invites the neighbors, on principle. Palmgren just happened to be at Broberg's then, so he came over, too."

"Was he alone?"

"No. His wife was with him. Young and terribly charming."

"I see."

She didn't say anything.

"Well," Gunvald Larsson said, "what's your opinion of these people?"

"They're very well-to-do," she said neutrally.

"You are, too. You and your phony baron."

"Yes," she said, "that's correct."

"Birds of a feather flock together," Gunvald Larsson said philosophically.

She looked at him for a long time and then said sharply, "I want you to understand something, Gunvald."

"What?"

"That these people, Broberg and Palmgren, weren't like us. I mean, they do have a lot of money, especially Palmgren. Did, rather. But they lack style and finesse. They're ruthless businessmen who step on everyone and everything in their way. I've heard that Broberg is some kind of profiteer and that Palmgren did very questionable business abroad. For people like that, their money does give them admission to all the most select circles, but they still lack something. They'll never be completely accepted."

"Um-hmm, well, there's something to that, let me tell you. Then, in other words, you don't accept Broberg?"

"No, I do, but solely because of his money. It was the same thing with Palmgren. His fortune gave him influence pretty much everywhere. You must realize that this society has grown dependent on people like Palmgren and Broberg. In many cases, they have more leverage in the way the country's run than either the Government or Parliament and such. So even people like us have to accept them."

Gunvald Larsson looked at her with disgust.

"Well, if you say so," he said. "But I think that in the not-too-distant future, things are going to happen that will make you and that whole damn upper-class riffraff of yours extremely surprised."

"What would that be?"

"Are you so damn stupid that you don't notice what's happening around us? In the whole world?"

"Don't shout at me," she said coldly. "We aren't children any more. And now, I think it's time for you to get lost."

"I already was. You forget I've been a sailor."

"Hugold is coming any minute. And I don't want you here then."

"He has short working hours, I gather."

"Yes, he does. People with highly qualified jobs often do. Good-bye, Gunvald."

He stood up.

"Well, you've been helpful, at any rate," he said.

"I wouldn't have said a word if you hadn't blackmailed me."

"Yeah, I realize."

"As far as I'm concerned, it could easily be another ten years before I see you again."

"For me too. Bye-bye."

She didn't answer.

Her girlfriend stood up and said, "I'd better be off now, too."

Gunvald Larsson looked at her. She was tall and slim—tall enough to come up to his shoulder at least. Gracefully and elegantly dressed. Just enough make-up. Just right, generally speaking. He hadn't seen a car outside and said, "Can I give you a lift into town?"

"Yes, please."

They left.

Gunvald Larsson glanced over at the house that evidently wasn't Broberg's any longer and shrugged.

When they were sitting in the car he checked to see if she was wearing a wedding ring. She wasn't.

"Excuse me, I didn't catch your name," he said.

"Lindberg. Sonja Lindberg. I remember you from when I was little."

"Oh, really?"

"You were much taller than I was, of course. Then as now."

He found her attractive. Maybe he should ask her out. Well, it could wait. No hurry. He could call her up one of these days.

"Where should I drop you off?" he asked.

"On Stureplan, please. My practice is on Birger Jarlsgatan. I live there too."

Good, he thought. That makes asking unnecessary.

Neither of them said anything before he'd stopped on Stureplan.

"Good-bye and thank you," she said and extended her hand.

He took it. It was slender, dry and cool.

"Bye, Sonja," he said.

He closed the door and drove on.

In his office on Kungsholmsgatan there were about fifteen messages, including one from Kollberg, who was in Västberga and wanted him to call back.

Gunvald Larsson got the most urgent work out of the way before he dialed the number of the South police station.

"Hello," said Kollberg.

Gunvald Larsson related what he'd heard but avoided naming the source.

"Good job, Larsson," said Kollberg. "Then it looks like he's planning to skip the country."

"He's probably left already."

"I don't think so," said Kollberg. "That suitcase I told you about before is still there in his room on Kungsgatan. I just called his secretary, and she said that Broberg had called her half an hour ago and said he wouldn't make it back to the office before five."

"He must be living at some hotel," said Gunvald Larsson pensively.

"Probably. I'll try to check it out. But it isn't conceivable that he's registered in his correct name."

"Hardly," said Gunvald Larsson. "By the way, did you get hold of that broad?"

"Not yet. I'm sitting here now waiting for the Vice Squad to call back."

Silence.

After a while he complained, "I'm really pushed for time. If I can't make it back to Kungsgatan before five, could you see to it that you or somebody else keeps an eye on his damn usury office?"

Gunvald Larsson's natural impulse was to say no. He took the letter-opener out of the penholder and picked between his big front teeth in a preoccupied manner.

"Yes," he said at last. "I'll arrange it."

"Thanks."

Thank my dear sister, Gunvald Larsson thought. Then he said, "One more thing."

"What?"

"Broberg was eating at the same table when Palmgren was shot."

"So what?"

"How in hell can he have anything to do with the murder?"

"Don't ask me," Kollberg said. "Everything seems very hush-hush. Maybe Martin knows."

"Beck," said Gunvald Larsson with distaste.

That was the end of the conversation.

14

Lennart Kollberg had to wait slightly more than an hour for the information from the Vice Squad. Meanwhile he sat, heavy, inert and sweaty, at his desk out in Väst-berga. What had looked like a simple matter to dispose of that morning—talking to two witnesses—had somehow developed into hot pursuit.

Hampus Broberg and the mystifying Helena Hansson suddenly emerged as two people wanted by the police, while Kollberg sat clinging to the threads of the dragnet like some kind of spider. The remarkable thing was that he still didn't know why he was out to get these two people. No charge had been filed against either of them; they had already been questioned by the police in Mal-mö, and common sense seemed to indicate that neither could reasonably have had anything to do with the murder of Viktor Palmgren.

However, he couldn't shake off the feeling that it was important to get hold of them as quickly as possible.

Why?

It's only the policeman's occupational disease creeping up on you, he thought gloomily. A total wreck after twenty-three years of service. Can't think like a normal human being any more.

Twenty-three years of daily contact with police officers had made him incapable of maintaining sensible relations with the rest of the world. In fact, he never felt truly free, not even with his own family. There was always something gnawing at his mind. He'd waited a long time to build this family, because police work wasn't a normal job, but something you committed yourself to. And it was obvious you could never get away from it. A profession involving daily confrontations with people in abnormal situations could only lead in the end to becoming abnormal yourself.

Unlike the overwhelming majority of his colleagues, Kollberg was capable of penetrating and analyzing his own situation clearly. Which he did, surprisingly and unfortunately, with unclouded vision. His problem lay in being both a sensualist and a man of duty, in a profession where sentimentality and personal involvement were luxuries which in nine cases out of ten you couldn't allow yourself.

Why do policemen associate almost exclusively with other policemen? he wondered.

Naturally because it was easier that way. Easier to keep the necessary distance. But also easier to overlook the morbid camaraderie in the force, which had flourished, unchecked, for many years. Essentially that meant that policemen isolated themselves from the society they were supposed to protect and, above all, be integrated with.

For example, policemen didn't criticize other policemen, with rare exceptions.

A rather recent sociological study had shown that vacationing policemen, who were more or less forced to mix with other people, were very often ashamed to admit that they were officers of the law. This was a result of the definition of their role and of the many myths that surrounded their profession.

Constantly encountering fear, distrust or open contempt could make anyone paranoid.

Kollberg shuddered.

He didn't want to be a fear-monger and he didn't want to be distrusted or despised. He didn't want to be paranoid.

However, he did want to get hold of two people whose names were Hampus Broberg and Helena Hansson. And he still didn't know why.

He went out to the lavatory for a drink of water. Although the faucet had been running for several minutes, the water was still lukewarm and flat.

He groaned and sank down at his desk again. Distractedly he drew a small five-pointed star on the blotter. One more. And another after that.

When he had drawn seventy-five five-pointed stars, the telephone rang.

"Yes, Kollberg."

"Hi, this is Åsa."

"Have you found out anything?"

"Yeah, I think so."

"What?"

"We've located this Hansson person."

Åsa Torell paused. Then she said, "At least I'm pretty sure it's the right person."

"So?"

"She's on our books."

"As a hooker?"

"Yes, but upper class. She comes closest to what we'd call a call girl."

"Where does she live?"

"On Banérgatan. This other address is wrong. As far as we know, she's never lived on Västeråsgatan. However, the telephone number didn't just come out of the clear blue. It looks like she had that contact number earlier."

"What about the name? Is Helena Hansson her real name?"

"We're fairly sure of that. She had to show identification down in Malmö last Wednesday, so I don't think she could've cheated on that point."

"Does she have a record?"

"Oh, yes. She's been a prostitute since she was a teenager. Our division's had a great deal to do with her, although not so often during recent years."

Åsa Torell was quiet a moment. He could imagine vividly how she looked at that very instant. She was probably hunched over a desk, just like him, biting her thumbnail contemplatively.

"She appears to have begun like most of the others, usually without being paid. Then she began walking the street, and apparently she's had enough class to work herself up into a more profitable bracket. Belonging to a call-girl ring is considered almost respectable by those kind of people."

"Yeah, I can imagine."

"As a matter of fact, call girls are the pick of the crop among prostitutes. They don't take just any job—only the ones that are guaranteed to be lucrative. Just calling herself a traveling secretary, or even an executive secretary, as she seems to have done in Malmö, shows that she has style and can move in quite high society. There's a big difference between selling the goods on Regeringsgatan and being able to sit at home in an apartment in Östermalm waiting for telephone calls. She probably has a group of regulars and at most takes one assignment or whatever you'd call it a week. Or something like that."

"Does your division have any direct interest in her? At the moment?"

"Yes. That's what I wanted to convey to you. If she's involved in some other kind of crime and is afraid of getting caught, we may have a chance of uncovering a whole call-girl ring."

"We could always try to scare her. Send someone over there to pick her up."

Kollberg thought again. He continued, "Of course, I'd be quite willing to meet her myself, at her home. There's something strange about this whole affair. What it is, I don't know yet."

"What do you mean?"

"I have the feeling that she's more involved in this affair with Broberg and Palmgren than we suspect. Do you know her?"

"I only know what she looks like—from pictures we have here," Åsa Torell said. "Judging from them, she looks very proper and businesslike. But of course that's one of the keys to success in that particular line of business."

"Certainly, they have to be able to keep up a good front. It's important for them not to make any false moves at social events."

"Right. From what I've heard, some of these girls can even take shorthand. At least they can do enough to fool most people."

"Do you have her phone number?"

"No."

"Too bad."

"Maybe, maybe not," said Åsa Torell. "The girls in this business change numbers pretty often. They have unlisted phones as a matter of course, and even then their subscriptions are usually registered under different names. And ..."

"And ..."

"And that shows that they're real pros. Big time."

She was quiet awhile. Then she asked, "Why is it so darned urgent for you to get hold of her?"

"To be honest with you, I don't really know."

"You don't know?"

"No. Martin wants her questioned, mostly as a routine measure, about what she saw or didn't see that night in Malmö."

"Well, that's not a bad place to start," said Åsa Torell. "Then maybe the first will lead to the second."

"Just what I was hoping," said Kollberg. "According to Larsson, she was at Hampus Broberg's home on Lidingö last Saturday, and I'm as good as convinced that Broberg is working on something really shady."

"I have a hard time imagining she'd be directly involved in Palmgren's murder. But then most of what I know comes from the newspapers these last few days."

"No. I can't see a direct connection with this shooting, either. However, there are a number of ramifications to this case, and I have a feeling they have to be followed up, even if they don't fall directly in my division."

"What do you think Broberg is up to?"

"Some kind of large-scale financial swindle. He appears to be converting all his assets here into cash incredibly fast. I suspect he's preparing to leave the country today."

"Why don't you call in the fraud boys?"

"Because there's not much time. Before those guys have the time to get onto this, Broberg'll probably be far out of reach. Maybe the Hansson girl, too. But Palmgren's murder does give us a lever. Both of them were witnesses, which means I can move in on them."

"I admit I'm only a novice," said Åsa Torell. "And hardly a murder investigator, besides. But does Martin feel that one of the people who were at the dinner would have gone all out to get Palmgren out of the way, for his own benefit?"

"Yes, that seems to be one of the theories."

"Then this person would've hired a murderer?"

"Yes. Something like that."

"It seems farfetched, if you ask me."

"I think so, too. But it's happened before."

"I know. What other possibilities are they considering?"

"For one thing, a purely political killing. Even Sepo's got into the act. From what I've heard, a man of theirs has been sent down to Malmö."

"That must be terribly pleasant for Martin and the rest of them."

"Yeah, it really is. Of course, Sepo is doing its own investigation as usual. It'll be ready in a year or two, and then they'll go into action."

"And Martin who just loves politics," said Åsa Torell.

What she meant was that Martin Beck detested everything even remotely related to politics and that he promptly retreated into a shell every time there was any mention of demonstrations, assassinations or political involvement.

"Hmm," said Kollberg. "Anyway, now it appears that Palmgren earned most of his millions from something that was the exact opposite of foreign aid. Like making indecent profits on international armaments sales. So neither Martin nor any of the others rules out the possibility that he was actually got out of the way for political reasons. As a kind of warning to others in the same line of business."

"Poor Martin," said Åsa Torell.

There was a certain warmth in her voice now.

Kollberg smiled to himself. He'd become well acquainted with Åsa Torell after Åke Stenström's death, and he thought a lot of her, both for her quick intelligence and for her qualities as a woman.

"Oh, well," he said. "I suggest that you and I go over to see this lovely lady as soon as possible and see if we can weasel something interesting out of her. I'll take the car and pick you up on the way. We'll have to chance it that she's home."

"Okay," Åsa Torell said. "But . . ."

"But what?"

"Well, I'm warning you, she's going to be a pretty hard nut to crack, and we'd be smart to take it easy—at least in the beginning. I know I'm only a beginner, and maybe it sounds crazy to be giving you advice, but I've had some experience with this clientele. Somebody like Helena Hansson knows all about how to act with the police. From long, hard practice, you understand. I don't think the strong-arm treatment would be worth much."

"You're probably right."

"By the way, who's keeping an eye on Broberg?"

"If we're lucky, we may find him in the lady's arms," Kollberg said. "Otherwise, Gunvald Larsson has offered his services, strangely enough."

"Then there'll be strong-arm tactics anyway," Åsa Torell said caustically.

"I suppose so. Let's say I'll come by to pick you up in about twenty minutes."

"Sure, that's fine. See you soon."

"Bye."

Kollberg sat for a while with his hand on the receiver. Then he called Gunvald Larsson.

"Yeah," the latter said antagonistically. "What in hell is it now?"

"We've located the girl."

"Okay," Gunvald Larsson said indifferently.

"I'm going to see her now with Åsa Torell."

"Okay."

"You sound even crosser than usual."

"For good reason," Gunvald Larsson said. "Twenty minutes ago a Turk got his guts ripped open with a stiletto on Hötorget. The devil only knows if he'll pull through. When I saw him it seemed like he had a hard time keeping his insides together."

"Did you catch the person who did it?"

"No. But we know who it was."

"Another Turk?"

"No, not at all. A first-rate, pure-bred Stockholm kid. Seventeen years old and stoned out of his mind. We're hunting for him now."

"Why did he do it?"

"Why? That's a helluva question. He probably got the idea that he could solve the foreigner problem all by himself. It gets worse and worse for every passing day."

"That's true," said Kollberg. "Gunvald, I don't think I'll have enough time to make it to Broberg's office."

"Don't worry about it," Gunvald Larsson said. "It'll all

work out. I'm beginning to get interested in this guy myself."

They hung up simultaneously, without another word.

Kollberg was left wondering what had made Gunvald Larsson so unusually helpful.

He called the finance company on Kungsgatan.

"No, I haven't heard from Mr. Broberg," said Sara Moberg.

"The suitcase is still in his room?"

"Yes. I told you that the first time you called."

"Excuse me, I just wanted to check."

He also called the realty office that he'd visited in the morning.

They hadn't seen Hampus Broberg there either, or even heard from him, for that matter.

He went out to wash his hands, put a note on his desk and proceeded down to the car.

Åsa Torell was waiting for him on the steps outside of the main police station on Kungsholmsgatan.

Kollberg pulled up by the sidewalk and watched approvingly as she walked down the wide steps and crossed the walk.

In his eyes she was an exceptionally attractive woman, with her short dark hair and big brown eyes. She was small, but had a very promising figure, with fine broad hips. Both slender and firm.

Her manner was highly sensual, but as far as he knew, she'd given up sex after Stenström's death.

He wondered how long that could last.

If I hadn't already had the good sense to find a first-rate wife . . .

Thought Lennart Kollberg.

Then he stretched out his arm and opened the right front door.

"Climb in, Åsa," he said.

She sat down beside him, put her shoulder bag on her lap and advised him, "Now we'll take it easy, like we said."

Kollberg nodded and started the car.

Five minutes later they stopped in front of an old apartment building on Benérgatan.

They got out on either side of the car.

"You should be careful when you walk right into the street like that," said Åsa Torell.

Kollberg nodded again.

"You're so right," he said.

He yearned for a clean shirt.

15

The apartment was on the third floor, and the name Helena Hansson was actually on the door plate.

Kollberg raised his right fist to pound on the door, but Åsa Torell restrained him by putting her hand on his arm and rang the doorbell instead.

Nothing happened, and after half a minute she rang again.

This time the door was opened, and a young blond woman peered at them with questioning blue eyes.

She was wearing plush slippers and a white bathrobe. It looked as if she'd just taken a shower or washed her hair, for she had a bath towel wound around her head like a turban.

"Police," Kollberg said, hauling out his identification card.

Åsa Torell did the same, but didn't say anything.

"You are Helena Hansson, right?"

"Yes, of course."

"We're here about what happened in Malmö last week. We'd like to talk to you a moment."

"I already told the police down there what little I know. The same evening."

"That conversation clearly wasn't very exhaustive," Kollberg said. "You were naturally rather upset at the time, and testimony given under such conditions tends to be rather sketchy. So we always question witnesses again, when they've had several days to think things over. May we please come in for a moment?"

The woman hesitated. It was obvious she was about to say no.

"It won't take too much of your time," Kollberg said. "This is a purely routine procedure for us."

"Yes," said Helena Hansson. "I don't have much time, but ..."

She stopped, and they let her think through the conclusion of her sentence in peace.

"Can you please wait out here for a second, while I put something on?"

Kollberg nodded.

"I've just washed my hair," she added. "It'll only take a minute or two."

Cutting off further discussion, she closed the door in their faces.

Kollberg put a warning finger to his lips.

Åsa Torell promptly knelt down and opened the lid of the mail slot, soundlessly and cautiously.

There were sounds from inside the apartment.

First the clicks from a telephone dial.

Helena Hansson was trying to call someone. She obviously got an answer, asked for someone in a low voice and was connected. Then nothing, but Åsa Torell had unusually good hearing and thought she heard the phone ringing for a long time on the other end. At last the woman inside said, "Oh, he's not. Thank you."

The receiver was replaced.

"She tried to call someone she didn't get hold of," Åsa Torell whispered. "Through a switchboard, I think."

Kollberg formed a name on his lips.

"Broberg."

"She didn't say Broberg. I would've caught that."

Kollberg made a warning face again and pointed dumbly to the mail slot.

Åsa Torell put her right ear against the opening. It was her best one.

Various sounds came from inside, and she knit her thick black eyebrows.

After a couple of minutes she straightened up and whispered, "She was doing something in a hurry, obviously. Packing a suitcase, I think, because I thought I heard her lock it. Then she carried or dragged something across the floor and opened and closed a door. Now she's getting dressed."

Kollberg nodded thoughtfully.

A little later Helena Hansson opened the door again. She had a dress on, and her hairdo was suspiciously neat. Both Kollberg and Åsa Torell noticed immediately that she'd put on a wig over her damp hair.

They were innocently standing as far away in the stàir well as possible. Åsa Torell had lit a cigarette and was smoking nonchalantly.

"Please come in," Helena Hansson said.

Her voice was pleasant and surprisingly cultivated.

They went in and looked around.

The apartment included a hall, one room and kitchen. It was fairly spacious and attractive, but impersonally furnished. Most of the furnishings seemed new; many of them indicated that the person who lived there at least wasn't short of money. Everything was neat and tidy.

The bed was big and wide. Kollberg looked at the thick bedspread and could clearly see a rectangular impression, as though something like a suitcase had lain there recently.

There were a sofa and comfortable armchairs in the room. Helena Hansson made a vague gesture toward them and said, "Sit down, please."

They sat down. The woman was still standing.

"Would you like something to drink?"

"No, thank you," Kollberg said.

Åsa Torell shook her head.

Helena Hansson sat down, took a cigarette from a pewter mug on the table and lit it. Then she said calmly, "Well, what can I do to help you?"

"You already know why we're here," said Kollberg.

"Yes. That horrible night in Malmö. But there isn't much more I can tell you than that—that it was horrible."

"Where were you seated at the table?"

"At the corner on one side. My dinner partner was a Danish businessman. His name was Jensen, I believe."

"Yes. Mr. Hoff-Jensen," said Kollberg.

"Oh, yes, that was his name."

"What about Mr. Palmgren?"

"He was sitting on the other side. Diagonally across from me. Directly opposite me was the Dane's wife."

"That means you were sitting facing the man who shot Mr. Palmgren?"

"Yes, that's right. But everything happened so fast. I barely had the time to grasp what was going on. Besides, I doubt if anyone understood anything until afterward."

"But you saw the murderer?"

"Yes. But I didn't think of him as a murderer."

"What did he look like?"

"I've already said what I know. Do you want me to repeat it?"

"Yes, please."

"I only have a very general impression of his appearance. As I said, everything happened so fast, and I wasn't concentrating very much on the people around me. I was mostly lost in my own thoughts."

She spoke calmly and seemed thoroughly sincere.

"Why weren't you concentrating, as you worded it?"

"Mr. Palmgren was making a speech. What he was saying didn't apply to me, and I was listening with half an ear anyway. I didn't understand most of what he was talking about; I was smoking and thinking about other things."

"Let's get back to the gunman. Did you recognize him?"

"No, not at all. He was a complete stranger to me."

"Would you be able to pick him out if you saw him again?"

"Maybe. But I couldn't be sure."

"What was your impression of him?"

"That he was a man of thirty-five, or maybe forty. He had a thin face and dark hair—not much of it."

"How tall was he?"

"About average height, I suppose."

"How was he dressed?"

"Fairly neatly. I think his jacket was brown. At any rate, he had a pale-colored shirt and a tie on."

"Can you say anything else about him?"

"Not much. He looked pretty ordinary."

"How would you place him socially?"

"Socially?"

"Well, for example, did he look like someone with a good job, plenty of money?"

"No, I don't think so. More like a clerk or a worker of some kind. I got the impression he was quite poor."

She shrugged and added, "But you shouldn't take what I say too seriously. The fact is I only caught a glimpse of him. Since then I've tried to sort out my impressions, but I'm not positive. Part of what I think I saw could be pure ... maybe not fantasy, but ..."

She searched for the right words.

"Construction after the fact," Kollberg suggested.

"Exactly. Construction after the fact. You catch a glimpse of someone or something, and then afterward, when you try to recall the details, it comes out wrong."

"Did you see the weapon he used?"

"In a flash, so to speak. It was some kind of pistol, rather long."

"Do you know much about guns?"

She shook her head.

"No, nothing at all."

Kollberg tried a new approach.

"Had you met Mr. Palmgren before?"

"No."

"And the rest of the party? Were you acquainted with them?"

"Only Mr. Broberg. I'd never met the other people before."

"But you'd known Broberg for some time?"

"He had hired me on several occasions."

"In what capacity were you in Malmö?"

She looked at him with surprise.

"As a secretary, of course. Mr. Broberg does have his own regular secretary, but she never accompanies him on trips."

She spoke openly and confidently. It all appeared very well rehearsed.

"Did you take any shorthand notes or minutes during this trip?"

"Certainly. There was a meeting earlier in the day. I took notes on what was discussed then."

"What was discussed?"

"Various kinds of business matters. To tell the truth, I didn't understand very much of it. I just wrote it down."

"Do you still have the shorthand notes?"

"No. I transcribed all of them when I returned home on

Thursday and left the minutes with Mr. Broberg. I threw the shorthand away."

"I see," Kollberg said. "How much did you get for this work?"

"A fee of two hundred kronor—plus traveling and living expenses, of course."

"Oh. Was it a difficult job?"

She shrugged again.

"Not particularly."

Kollberg exchanged a glance with Åsa Torell, who as yet hadn't opened her mouth.

"That should be all for me," Kollberg said.

Helena Hansson lowered her eyes.

"Just one more thing. When the police in Malmö questioned you immediately after the murder, you gave an address on Västeråsgatan here in the city."

"Did I?"

"That was wrong, wasn't it?"

"I really hadn't given it a thought. Don't even remember it. But I was in a daze at the time. In fact, I used to live on Västeråsgatan. I must've simply made a mistake in the general commotion."

"Hmm," said Kollberg. "Yeah, that can happen to anyone."

He stood up and said, "Thank you for the help. I'm through now. Good-bye."

He walked toward the door and left the apartment.

Helena Hansson looked enquiringly at Åsa Torell, who was still sitting in her chair, silent and immobile.

"Was there anything else?" Helena Hansson said uncertainly.

Åsa Torell gazed at her for a long time. They were sitting across from each other. Both women were about the same age, but the similarities ended there.

Åsa Torell let the silence deepen and take effect, then she crushed her cigarette in the ashtray and said slowly, "You're no more a secretary than I'm the Queen of Sheba."

"How dare you say a thing like that?" Helena Hansson said with agitation.

"My colleague, who just left, works for the Homicide Squad."

Helena Hansson looked at her in bewilderment.

"However, I don't," said Åsa Torell. "I'm with the Vice Squad here in town."

"Oh," the other woman said.

Her shoulders collapsed.

"We have a whole dossier on you," said Åsa Torell in an unsparing monotone. "It covers ten years. You've already been picked up fifteen times. That's quite a few."

"All right, but you can't send me up for this, you old slut," Helena Hansson said defiantly.

"Careless of you not to have a typewriter at home. Or even a steno pad. Unless it's in the briefcase over there."

"Don't start poking around in my things without a warrant, you bitch. I know my rights."

"I'm not planning to touch anything here without a warrant," Åsa Torell said.

"What in hell are you doing here then? I can't ever be pulled in for this."

Åsa Torell didn't say anything.

"Besides, dammit, I have the right to go where I want with who I want."

"And go to bed with who you want? Yes, that's perfectly correct. But you don't have the right to be paid for it. How big was that 'fee,' anyway?"

"Do you think I'm so damned stupid I'd answer that question?"

"It isn't necessary. I know the going rate. You got a thousand kronor tax-free and all expenses paid."

"You know a helluva lot," Helena Hansson said impertinently.

"We know most everything about these things."

"Only don't get the idea you can send me up, you goddamned, fucking . . ."

"I probably can. Don't worry. It'll all work out."

Suddenly Helena Hansson sprang up and flung herself across the table, her fingers tensed like claws.

Agile as a cat, Åsa Torell got to her feet and parried the attack with a simple blow that threw the other woman backwards, down into the chair.

A vase of carnations had toppled onto the floor; neither of them bothered to pick it up.

"No scratching," said Åsa Torell. "Just take it easy."

The woman stared at her. It actually looked as though she had tears in her watery blue eyes. The wig had slipped to one side.

"So you're a fighter, too, you fucking whore?" she whined.

She sat still for a while with a desperate look on her face. Then she worked herself up to a new counteroffensive and said hysterically, "Go away, dammit. Leave me alone. Come back when you really have something."

Åsa Torell dug around in her shoulder bag and took out a pencil and note pad.

"What I'm really interested in is something else," she said. "You've never worked free-lance and surely aren't now, either. Who's running the show?"

"Are you so goddamned stupid you think I'll tell you?"

Åsa Torell walked over to the telephone, which was on the dressing table. It was a pale gray Dialogue model. She bent over and jotted down the number, which the telephone company had issued as a sort of small service. Then she picked up the receiver and dialed the number. She got a busy signal.

"Wasn't too clever of you to leave the slip on with the correct number," she said. "You'll get sent up for this telephone, no matter whose name the line's registered under."

The woman slumped even lower in her chair and looked bitter but resigned.

After a moment she looked at the clock and complained, "Can't you get the hell out of here now? You've already shown how smart the cops can be."

"Not yet," said Åsa Torell calmly. "Just hang on."

Helena Hansson now seemed totally confused. She clearly hadn't counted on anything like this. It lay beyond the scope of her instructions and didn't fit with the directions she'd followed earlier. Moreover, the fact that this policewoman had complete knowledge of her past was sufficient to make her drop all pretense.

Still she seemed curiously nervous and kept looking at the clock.

She realized that the other woman was waiting for something, but couldn't figure out what it was.

"Are you going to stand there staring at me for much longer?" she said resentfully.

"No. This won't take long."

Said Åsa Torell and looked at the woman in the chair. She didn't feel anything at all for her. Not even dislike and definitely not compassion.

The telephone rang.

Helena Hansson made no attempt to get up to answer, and Åsa Torell didn't move from the spot.

Six rings echoed in the room.

Then everything returned to the status quo.

Åsa Torell was standing beside the dressing table, her arms hanging loosely and her feet slightly apart.

Helena Hansson was huddled up in the armchair, staring ahead with expressionless eyes.

Once she mumbled, "Well, you can give me a break, can't you?"

And immediately after, "How in the hell can a chick be a cop. . . ?"

Åsa Torell could have asked a question in return but refrained.

The deadlock was broken ten minutes later by heavy pounding on the outer door.

Åsa Torell answered, and Kollberg came in with a piece of paper in his hand. He was flushed and sweaty. It was evident that he'd been hurrying.

He stopped in the middle of the floor, breathed in the sinister atmosphere, glanced at the overturned vase of flowers and said, "Have you ladies been scuffling?"

Helena Hansson looked up at him. There was neither hope nor surprise now; all her professional polish had vanished.

"What the hell do you want now?" she said.

Kollberg held out the piece of paper and said, "This is a warrant to search this apartment. Complete with stamp and signature. I requested it myself, and the prosecuting attorney has given his approval."

"Go to hell," Helena Hansson said thickly.

"No thanks," Kollberg said amiably. "We're going to look around a little."

Åsa Torell nodded toward the closet door.

"I think it's in there," she said.

She took Helena Hansson's purse from the dressing table and opened it.

The woman in the chair didn't react.

Kollberg opened the closet door and pulled out a suitcase.

"Not so big, but incredibly heavy," he mumbled.

He put it on the bed and unbuckled the straps.

"Found anything interesting?" he asked Åsa Torell.

"A round-trip ticket to Zurich and a hotel voucher. She's booked on a flight at a quarter to ten tomorrow morning from Arlanda. Return flight from Zurich at seven-forty the day after tomorrow. The hotel room is reserved for one night."

Kollberg pushed aside a top layer of clothing and various other rubbish and began to rummage around in the bundles of paper lining the bottom of the suitcase.

"Stocks," he said. "A helluva lot of them!"

"They aren't mine," Helena Hansson said tonelessly.

"I didn't think so," Kollberg said.

He walked over and opened the black briefcase.

It contained exactly what his wife had said.

A nightgown, several pairs of panties, cosmetics, a toothbrush and bottles of pills.

It was almost laughable.

He looked at the clock. It was already five-thirty, and he hoped that Gunvald Larsson had kept his promise and was on his toes.

"That's all for now," he said. "You can come with us now."

"Why?" Helena Hansson said.

"Off the cuff I can inform you that you're suspected of intent to engage in illegal traffic in currency," Kollberg said. "You can count on being taken into custody, but that's not my business."

Kollberg looked around, shrugged his shoulders and said, "Åsa, will you see that she gets what they usually take along at a time like this."

Åsa Torell nodded.

"Pigs," said Miss Hansson.

16

Everything happened on that Monday.

Gunvald Larsson stood by the window in his office, looking out over his city. On the surface it didn't look so bad, but he was too aware of the hotbed of crime that smoldered all around him. True, he came into contact only with assault and battery cases, but they were more than enough. Moreover, they were usually the most unpleasant to deal with. Six new robberies, each one more brutal than the other, and no clues for the time being. Four cases of wife-beating, all rather severe. And one case of the reverse: A woman had attacked her husband with an iron. Larsson had had to go there himself, to an address on Bastugatan on the South Side. The shabby apartment looked like a slaughterhouse. Everything was covered with blood, and he even got bloodstains on his new pants.

In Gamla Stan an unwed mother had thrown her one-year-old child out of a window on the third floor. The child was seriously injured, though the doctors said it would survive. The mother was seventeen years old and hysterical. Her only reason had been that the baby was screaming and wouldn't listen to her.

At least twenty fairly bloody fights in the city center alone. He didn't even want to think what the reports from the modern slum areas in the suburbs would look like.

The telephone rang.

He let it ring for a while before answering.

"Larsson."

Grunting fiercely.

The Turk who'd had his stomach ripped open had died at South Hospital.

"Uh-hmm," he said indifferently.

He wondered if the man's death had really been necessary. The hospitals were filled to overflowing; whole sections were closed because of vacations and a general personnel shortage. There was also a shortage of blood donors.

The assailant had already been caught. A patrol car had picked him up in a junkie hangout in a condemned house in Birkastaden. He was completely dazed and couldn't answer at all when he was addressed. He'd had the bloody stiletto on him, in any case. Gunvald Larsson had looked at him for half a minute and sent for the police doctor.

Apart from the robberies, which seemed well planned, these were all what are called unpremeditated crimes, almost comparable to accidents. Unhappy people, nervous wrecks, were driven into desperate situations against their wills. In almost all the cases, alchohol or drugs were of decisive importance. It may have been partly due to the heat, but more basic was the system itself, the relentless logic of the big city, which wore down the weak-willed and the maladjusted and drove them to senseless actions.

And the lonely. He wondered how many suicides had been committed during the last twenty-four hours and felt almost relieved that it would still be a while before he found out. Those reports were still out in the various police stations where the material was processed and the reports compiled.

It was now twenty minutes to five, time for him to be relieved.

He should've been able to drive home to his bachelor den in Bollmora, shower, put on slippers and a clean bathrobe, drink a cold bottle of ginger ale (Gunvald Larsson came near to being a teetotaler), take the telephone off the hook and spend the evening with a piece of escapist literature.

But now he'd assumed responsibility for something that had nothing to do with him at all. This thing with Broberg, an undertaking he alternately regretted and looked forward to with a certain vindictive delight. If Broberg was a criminal—and Gunvald Larsson was convinced he was—then he was exactly the type of criminal Gunvald Larsson took pure pleasure in sending to jail. A slumlord. A loan shark. Unfortunately, they were usually untouchable, although everyone knew they existed and lived in the best of health, within the formal limits of the inflexible law.

He'd decided not to do this alone. On the one hand, because he'd operated on his own and in his own way many times during his years on the force and had been criticized many times for it. For that matter, so often that his prospects of ever being promoted, as things stood now, seemed negligible. On the other, because he didn't want to take any risks and because this ought to look neat.

For once he was following the rule book, and precisely for that reason he should, of course, be prepared for everything to go haywire.

But where would he find a partner?

There was no one available in his own section, and Kollberg had said that the situation was identical out in Västberga.

In desperation he called the fourth precinct and managed after many if's and but's to get a positive answer.

"If it's all *that* important," the Superintendent said, "maybe I can let you have a man."

"That's generous of you."

"Do you think it's easy, keeping *you* supplied with people too? When it should be the other way around?"

"No, no," Gunvald Larsson said. "I know."

A large part of the uniform force stood glowering outside of various embassies and tourist agencies. Doing no good at all, furthermore, since they couldn't accomplish anything constructive if sabotage or demonstrations were in the offing. Now the National Chief of Police had even forbidden the men to play with their batons, which had been the only bit of entertainment this senseless, deadly dull work had to offer.

"Well," Gunvald Larsson said, "who is this guy?"

"His name's Zachrisson. Comes originally from Maria. Usually works as a plainclothesman."

Gunvald Larsson furrowed his blond eyebrows sternly.

"I know him," he said, without a trace of enthusiasm.

"I see. Well, that ought to be an advan—"

"Just make damned sure he doesn't have a uniform on," said Gunvald Larsson. "And that he's outside the building at five minutes to five."

He thought for a moment and added, "And when I say outside, I don't mean for him to stand right outside the door with his arms crossed like some old bouncer."

"I understand."

"Fine," said Gunvald Larsson and hung up.

He arrived at the building on Kungsgatan at exactly five to five and immediately discovered Zachrisson standing with a sheepish look on his face, staring at a store window with a display of women's underwear.

Gunvald Larsson inspected him grimly. His plainclothes attire was limited to a sport coat. Otherwise he was dressed in regulation pants and shirt with the matching police tie. Any idiot could see he was an officer of the law at a hundred yards. Moreover, he was standing with his feet apart, hands behind his back, rocking back and forth on the balls of his feet. The only thing needed to complete the picture was a paper bag containing his cap and baton.

When he caught sight of Gunvald Larsson he straightened up, and it almost looked as though he was going to stand at attention. Zachrisson had unpleasant memories of their previous work together.

"Just take it nice and easy," said Gunvald Larsson. "What's that in your right coat pocket?"

"My pistol."

"Couldn't you have had the sense to wear a shoulder holster?"

"I couldn't find one," Zachrisson said lamely.

"Christ, then put the hardware inside your waistband."

The man promptly stuck his hand into his pocket.

"Not here, for chrissake," Gunvald Larsson said. "Go and do it in the doorway. Discreetly."

Zachrisson obeyed.

When he returned his appearance was somewhat improved. But not much.

"Now listen here," Gunvald Larsson said. "We can expect a guy to show up here and walk into the building sometime after five. He looks something like this."

He showed him a picture, which was dwarfed by his enormous right hand. It was poor, but the only one he'd been able to get hold of.

Zachrisson nodded.

"He's going to walk into the building and, if I'm not mistaken, he'll be coming out again in a matter of minutes. He'll probably then be carrying a black pigskin suitcase with two straps around it."

"Is he a robber?"

"Yeah, something like that. I want you to stay outside of the building near the door."

Zachrisson nodded once more.

"I'm going up the stairs. I may grab him there, but I may prefer not to. It's very likely that he'll come in a car and park right in front of the door. He'll be in a hurry, and he may leave the engine running while he's inside. The car ought to be a black Mercedes, but that's not definite. If by any chance he comes out on the sidewalk with the suitcase in his hand without me, then you must stop him, at any cost, from driving away until I can make it out here."

The policeman put on a determined look.

"And for chrissake, try to look like an ordinary human being. Not like you were on guard outside of the U.S. Trade Center."

Zachrisson blushed slightly and looked puzzled.

"Okay," he mumbled.

And shortly after, "Is he dangerous?"

"Could be," Gunvald Larsson said nonchalantly.

His own opinion was that Broberg was about as dangerous as a flea.

"Now try to remember everything," he said.

Zachrisson recovered his dignity with some difficulty and nodded.

Gunvald Larsson walked in the door. The hall was large and deserted, and it looked as if most of the offices had already closed.

He walked up the stairs. Just as he passed the door with the two plaques, HAMPUS BROBERG INC. and VIKTOR PALM-GREN LOAN & FINANCE, a dark-haired woman of about thirty-five locked it from the outside. Obviously the secretary.

A glance at his Ultratron showed that it was exactly five o'clock. Punctuality is a virtue.

The woman pressed the button for the elevator without glancing at him. He walked halfway up the next flight of stairs, stood absolutely still and waited.

The wait was fairly long and extremely uneventful. During the next fifty minutes, the elevator was used three times, and on two occasions individuals of no interest to him walked down the stairs—apparently people who had worked overtime for one reason or another. When this happened Gunvald Larsson walked up and met them on the floor above. Then he returned to his post. At three minutes to six he heard the elevator come creaking up and heavy steps approaching. This time they were coming from down below. The elevator stopped, and a man stepped out. He had a bunch of keys in his hand, and, for all Gunvald Larsson knew, it could very well be Hampus Broberg. If so, dressed in a hat and overcoat despite the heat. He unlocked the office, went in and closed the door.

At that moment the person who was tromping up the staircase walked past the door to Broberg's office and came on up. He was heavy-set and wearing work clothes and a flannel shirt. When he caught sight of Gunvald Larsson he stopped short and said loudly, "What are you doing, hanging around here, huh?"

"It's none of your business," Gunvald Larsson whispered.

The man smelled of beer or akvavit, or both.

"It is too my goddamn business," the man said obstinately. "I'm the janitor here."

He set himself in the middle of the staircase, with one hand on the wall and the other on the handrail, as if to block the way.

"I'm a policeman," Gunvald Larsson whispered.

At that very second the office door was opened, and Broberg, or whoever it was, came out with the famous suitcase in his hand.

"Policeman!" said the janitor in a rough, booming voice. "You'd better prove that one before I . . ."

The man carrying the suitcase didn't hesitate a fraction of a second, decided against the sluggish elevator and scooted down the stairs at top speed.

Gunvald Larsson was in an awkward situation. There was no time for bickering. If he hit the guy in the work clothes he'd probably fall down the stairs and break his neck. After a short hesitation he decided to brush him aside with his right hand. This should have been quite easy, but the janitor resisted and grabbed hold of Gunvald Larsson's jacket. When he tried to break loose he heard the material give way and rip. Furious about this new damage to his wardrobe, he turned halfway around and struck the man on the wrist. The janitor let go with a groan, but Broberg now had a considerable head start.

Gunvald Larsson plunged down the stairs. Behind him he heard savage curses and uncertain, shuffling steps.

The state of affairs in the hall on the ground floor was perfectly ludicrous.

Zachrisson had come inside the street door, of course, and was standing with his legs apart. He'd opened his jacket and was fumbling for his pistol.

"Stop! Police!" he howled.

Broberg had stopped abruptly without letting go of the suitcase, which he was carrying in his right hand. He stuck his left hand into the pocket of his overcoat and pulled out a gun, aimed at the ceiling and fired. Gunvald Larsson didn't hear a ricochet and was almost certain that it was a starting gun, a stage revolver or some kind of toy.

Zachrisson flung himself down on the marble floor and shot, but missed. Gunvald Larsson flattened himself against the wall. Broberg ran toward the back of the large hall, away from the policeman by the outer door. There was probably a back door. Zachrisson shot again and missed. The man carrying the suitcase was only ten feet from Gunvald Larsson and was still moving toward the inside of the building.

Zachrisson fired three shots. All of them hit wide.

What in hell do they learn at the Police Academy? Gunvald Larsson wondered.

Bullets ricocheted back and forth between the stone walls.

One of them entered the heel of Gunvald Larsson's right shoe, putting paid to a peerless example of Italian craftsmanship.

"Cease fire!" he roared.

Zachrisson fired again, but there was just a click. He'd probably forgotten to fill the magazine.

Gunvald Larsson took three strides forward and, without a second's hesitation, struck Hampus Broberg on the jaw, as hard as he could. He heard a crunch under his fist, and the man slumped down in a sitting position.

The custodian came down the stairs, swearing and panting heavily.

"What the hell. . . ?" he gasped.

Gun smoke lay like a light blue fog over the hall. The smell of cordite was penetrating.

Zachrisson stood up, looking perplexed.

"What were you aiming for?" Gunvald Larsson said angrily.

"The legs . . ."

"Mine?"

Gunvald Larsson picked up the weapon that had fallen out of Broberg's hand. As he'd suspected, it was a starting gun.

Outside on the street a vociferous crowd was gathering.

"Are you nuts?" the custodian said. "That's Mr. Broberg."

"Shut up," said Gunvald Larsson and dragged the man on the floor to his feet.

"Take the suitcase," he said to Zachrisson. "If you can manage it."

He led the captive out through the door, gripping his right arm tightly. Broberg held his chin in his left hand. Blood trickled out between his fingers.

Without looking around, Gunvald Larsson forced his way through the jabbering crowd and walked over to his car. Zachrisson plodded after him with the suitcase.

Gunvald Larsson shoved the prisoner into the back seat and got in himself.

"Think you can get us to Headquarters?" he asked Zachrisson.

The latter nodded dejectedly and squeezed in behind the steering wheel.

"What's going on?" asked a dignified citizen in a gray suit and beret.

"We're making a film," Gunvald Larsson said and slammed the door.

"Get this goddamn thing moving," he said to Zachrisson, who was fumbling with the ignition.

Finally he got the car started.

On the way to Kungsholmen Zachrisson asked a question that had obviously been on his mind.

"Aren't you armed?"

"Idiot," said Gunvald Larsson wearily.

As usual he was carrying his police pistol on a waist-band clip.

Hampus Broberg said nothing.

17

Hampus Broberg said nothing, because he was both unwilling and unable. Two of his teeth had been knocked out, and his jawbone was fractured.

At nine-thirty that night Gunvald Larsson and Kollberg were still leaning over him, shouting senseless questions.

"Who shot Viktor Palmgren?"

"Why did you try to escape?"

"You hired a killer, didn't you?"

"It's no good denying!"

"You'd better come clean."

"Well, who's the gunman?"

"Why don't you answer?"

"The game's up, anyway, so start talking."

Now and then Broberg shook his head, and when Palmgren's murder was mentioned he contorted his already contorted features into an expression that was probably intended to be a sardonic smile.

Kollberg could imagine what this grimace meant, but not much more.

During the introductory formalities and later, in passing, they'd asked him if he wanted to call his lawyer, but the prisoner still shook his head.

"You wanted Palmgren out of the way so you could sneak off with the money, didn't you?"

"Where is the gunman?"

"Who else was in on the plot?"

"Spill it!"

"You're being held in custody."

"You're in a bad fix."

"Why are you trying to protect other people?"

"Nobody's bothering to protect you."

"Well, come out with it."

"If you tell us who committed the murder it may count in your favor later on."

"You'd be wise to cooperate with us."

Now and then Kollberg tried a gentler approach.

"When were you born? And where?"

Gunvald Larsson ran true to form, the whole time trying to adhere to the doctrine that you have to begin from the beginning.

"Okay, let's take it from the beginning again. When did you decide that Viktor Palmgren had to be got out of the way?"

Grimace. Shake of the head.

Kollberg thought he could read the word "idiots" on the man's lips.

For an instant it struck him that that was quite an adequate description.

"If you won't talk, write on the pad there."

"Here's a pencil."

"We're only interested in the murder. Others will have to take care of the other stuff."

"Do you realize you're suspected of conspiracy?"

"As accessory to first-degree murder?"

"Are you going to confess or not?"

"It'd be best for everyone if you did it now. Right away."

"Let's take it from the beginning. When did you decide that Palmgren had to be killed?"

"Out with it!"

"You know we have enough evidence to have you booked. You're already in custody."

That was true. No doubt about it. In the suitcase were stocks and other securities worth something like half a million kronor, according to a quick calculation. They were homicide detectives, not financial experts, but they knew a little about illegal traffic in currency and securities.

They'd found a one-way ticket to Geneva via Copenhagen and Frankfurt in a folder in the inside pocket of Broberg's suit coat. The ticket was in the name of a Mr. Roger Frank.

In the other inside pocket there was a forged passport,

bearing Broberg's picture, but also with the name Roger Frank, engineer.

"Well, how about it?"

"The best thing you can do is clear your conscience."

At last Broberg took the ballpoint pen and wrote some words on the steno pad.

They leaned over the table and read:

Get me a doctor.

Kollberg drew Gunvald Larsson aside and said in a low voice, "Maybe that's what we should do. We can't keep on like this for hours."

Gunvald Larsson frowned and said, "Guess you're right. Is there anything to show he set up that damned murder? Seems to me that's highly unlikely."

"Right," Kollberg said reflectively. "Right."

They were both tired and felt like going home.

But they rounded things off by repeating several questions:

"Who shot Palmgren?"

"We know you didn't shoot him, but we also know you know who did it. What's his name?"

"And where is he?"

"When were you born," said Gunvald Larsson, who was not really concentrating. "And where?"

Then they gave up, sent for the police doctor on call and turned Broberg over to the guards in the detention ward.

They got into their cars and went home, Kollberg to his wife, who was already asleep, Gunvald Larsson to grieve over his ruined clothes.

Before Kollberg fell into bed he tried to call Martin Beck but couldn't reach him.

Gunvald Larsson didn't consider calling Beck or anyone else. He took a long shower and thought about the bloodstains on his pants, his ripped jacket and ruined shoes. Before going to sleep he read two pages of a book by Stein Riverton.

Kollberg had witnessed a more instructive interrogation earlier in the evening.

As soon as he and Åsa Torell had brought Helena Hansson into a bare, inhospitable room at the Vice Squad headquarters, the girl broke down completely and reeled off a confession that had run as freely as her tears. They had to turn on a tape recorder to catch everything she had to say.

Yes, she was a call girl.

Yes, Hampus Broberg was a regular customer of hers.

He'd given her the suitcase, the plane ticket and the hotel voucher. She was going to fly to Zurich and leave the suitcase in the hotel's safe deposit box. He was going to come from Geneva the next day and pick it up.

She was going to get ten thousand kronor for her trouble, if everything went well. She didn't know what was in the suitcase.

Hampus Broberg had said they couldn't risk taking the same plane.

When the police arrived she'd tried to contact Broberg at the Carlton Hotel, where he was staying under the name of Frank, but couldn't reach him.

The fee for the job in Malmö had been fifteen hundred kronor, not a thousand.

She also blurted out the various contact numbers of the call girl ring she belonged to.

She said she was completely innocent, really, and didn't know what it was all about.

She was a prostitute, but then she wasn't the only one, and she'd never done anything else.

She knew absolutely nothing about the murder.

At any rate, no more than she'd already told them.

Kollberg was inclined to believe her on that point, as well as on the others.

18

In Malmö Paulsson was on the lookout.

The first days—Saturday and Sunday—he'd concentrated on the hotel personnel; he wanted, so to speak, to close in on his prey. He knew from experience that it was easier to carry out an assignment if you knew who it was you were looking for.

He took his meals in the hotel dining room and between times remained in the lobby. He soon found out that hiding behind a newspaper in the restaurant with his ears pricked up gave meager results. Most of the guests spoke foreign languages that were incomprehensible to him, and if the staff discussed Wednesday's event among themselves, they didn't do it in the proximity of his table.

Paulsson decided to play the curious guest who'd read about the drama in the newspaper. He called over the waiter, an apathetic young man with sideburns and a dazzling white jacket several sizes too large.

Paulsson tried to start up a conversation about the shooting, but the waiter wasn't interested and answered in monosyllables. Every now and then his eyes wandered toward the open window.

Had he seen the murderer?

Ye-e-es.

Wasn't he one of those long-haired types?

No-o-o.

Did he really not have long hair, or was he sloppily dressed at least?

Maybe his hair was a little long. Didn't see too well. He had a jacket on, anyway.

The waiter pretended he had something to do in the kitchen and left.

Paulsson reflected.

If someone usually had long hair and a beard and wore jeans and baggy jackets, it was, of course, the easiest thing in the world to disguise himself. All he had to do was cut his hair, shave and put on a suit, and then no one would recognize him. The problem with such a disguise was that it would take quite a while for that person to regain his former appearance. Therefore he ought to be easy to find.

Paulsson felt happy about this conclusion.

However, many of these left-wingers looked like ordinary people. He'd noticed that many times when he'd been on duty during demonstrations in Stockholm. It had often annoyed him. People who wore work clothes and had big red Mao buttons on their shirts were easy to identify, even when they weren't in groups. But the job was complicated by people who were treacherous enough to go around in business suits, smooth-shaven and clean-cut, with their leaflets and subversive literature in neat briefcases. This meant that he didn't have to go to unhygienic extremes in his own disguise, but it was annoying all the same.

The headwaiter came over to his table.

"Was the meal good?" he asked.

He was short, had close-cropped hair and a humorous twinkle in his eye. He must surely be more alert and talkative than the waiter.

"It was very good, thank you," Paulsson said.

Then he switched to *the* topic.

"I was just thinking about what happened last Wednesday. Were you here at the time?"

"Yes, I was working that night. Horrible. And they haven't caught the murderer, either."

"Did you see him?"

"Uhn—you see, it all happened so fast. When he first came in I wasn't in the dining room. I didn't come in until after he'd fired. So you could say I just caught a glimpse of him."

Paulsson had a brilliant idea.

"He didn't happen to be colored?"

"Excuse me?"

"I mean a Negro, to be blunt. He wasn't a Negro?"

"No, why would he be a Negro?" said the headwaiter with genuine surprise.

"There are rather light-colored Negroes, as you may know. Who don't even look like Negroes, really, if you don't look too closely."

"No, I've never heard of that. Other people saw him much better than I did, so you'd think some of them would've noticed if he was a Negro. And said it. No, he couldn't have been."

"Well, okay," Paulsson said. "It was just an idea that struck me . . ."

Paulsson spent Saturday night in the bar, where he consumed a great number of various nonalcoholic drinks.

When he ordered his sixth, a Pussyfoot, even the bartender, who wasn't easily surprised, looked somewhat astonished.

On Sunday night the bar was closed, and Paulsson

stayed in the lobby. He prowled around the reception
desk, but the clerk seemed very busy, talked on the
telephone, studied the ledger, helped guests and now and
then hurried off on an urgent errand with elbows raised
and long coat tails flapping after him. Finally Paulsson
was able to exchange a few words with him, but didn't
receive support for any of his theories. The clerk was
particularly emphatic about the fact that the man was not
a Negro.

Paulsson finished off the day with a pusztaschnitzel in
the grill. There the clientele was significantly more numerous and youthful than in the dining room, and he over-
heard several interesting conversations from the tables
nearby. At the table next to Paulsson's, two men and a
girl were talking about things that, to his great displea-
sure, he couldn't fathom, but at one point they even
mentioned the murder of Viktor Palmgren.

The younger man, with long red hair and a bushy
beard, expressed his contempt for the deceased and his
admiration for the assailant. Paulsson studied his appearance carefully and made a mental note of it.

The next day was Monday, and Paulsson decided to
extend the search to Lund. There were students in Lund,
and where there were students there had to be radical
elements. Up in his room he had long lists of names of
people in Lund who could be suspected of holding deviant
opinions.

So in the afternoon he took the train to the university
town, which he had never visited before, and set off
through the town to search out the students.

It was hotter than ever, and Paulsson perspired in his
checkered suit.

He found his way to the university, which was dead and
abandoned in the blazing sun. No revolutionary activities
seemed to be going on. Paulsson recalled the picture he'd
seen of Mao swimming in the Yangtze Kiang. Maybe the
Lund Maoists were in the Höje River, following the
Chairman's example.

Paulsson took off his jacket and went to have a look at
the cathedral. He was surprised that the notorious Giant
Finn statue was so small and bought a picture postcard of
him to send to his wife.

On his way from the cathedral he caught sight of a
notice announcing a dance that the Student Union was
going to have that night. Paulsson decided to go to it, but
since it was still early in the evening, he had to find some
way to pass the time.

He wandered around the town, which was deserted for
the summer, strolled under the tall trees in the city park,
sauntered along the gravel paths of the Botanical Gardens
for a long time and suddenly felt very hungry. He ate a
simple dinner at Storkällaren and then sat over a cup of
coffee, watching what little activity there was on the
square outside.

He didn't have the vaguest idea of how to organize the
search for Viktor Palmgren's killer. Assassinations hardly
ever occurred in Sweden—he couldn't remember any political murder occurring in modern times. He wished that
the information he had to go on wasn't so vague and that
he knew a little better where to start looking.

When it was dark, and the street lamps had been turned
on, he paid the check and went to find the discothèque.

That venture was also unproductive. About twenty
teenagers were drinking beer and dancing to deafening
rock music. Paulsson talked to several of them, but it
turned out that they weren't even students. He drank a
small mug of beer and then took the train back to
Malmö.

He ran into Martin Beck in the hotel elevator. Even
though they were alone in the elevator, the latter stared
fixedly at a point above Paulsson's head, whistling silently
to himself. When the elevator stopped he winked at Paulsson, put a finger to his lips and walked out into the
corridor.

19

On Monday afternoon Månsson called his Danish
colleague.

"What do you think you're doing?" Mogensen said.

"Calling during working hours. Do you think I sit here sleeping at the Bureau of Investigation, too?"

"Beg your pardon," Månsson said.

"Oh, I understand, it's so urgent you can't hold off until tonight. Well, let's hear it, I'm just sitting here twiddling my thumbs."

"Ole Hoff-Jensen," said Månsson. "He's a director of some company that's a part of an international concern owned by Viktor Palmgren. You know, the guy who was shot dead here last week. I'd like to know what kind of company and where its office is. As soon as possible."

"Okay, I get it," Mogensen said. "I'll call back."

Half an hour passed.

"That wasn't so hard," said Mogensen. "Are you listening?"

"Sure. Go ahead," Månsson said and grasped his pencil.

"Mr. Ole Hoff-Jensen is forty-eight years old, married, and has two daughters. His wife's name is Birthe; she's forty-three. They live on Richelieus Allé in Hellerup. The firm is an air freight company called Aero-fragt, which has its main office on Kultorvet in Copenhagen and space out at Kastrup airport. The company has five planes of the DC-6 type. Anything else you want to know?"

"No thanks. That's enough for the moment. How are you, by the way?"

"Horrible. And hot. I think this heat drives people insane. The city's packed with nut cases. Swedes galore. Farewell."

The instant Månsson hung up it occurred to him that he'd forgotten to ask for the telephone number of the airline.

He asked the switchboard to get it, which took a while. When he finally reached Aero-fragt he was informed that Hoff-Jensen couldn't be reached until the following day, and that he could meet with him after eleven o'clock.

It's just as well, Månsson thought. I couldn't have taken another director today.

He spent the remainder of Monday afternoon working on some routine business, which did, after all, have to be taken care of.

On Tuesday morning he picked up Martin Beck outside

of the hotel. He'd planned for them to take the hydrofoil to Copenhagen, but Martin Beck explained that he wanted to ride on a real boat, and that they might as well combine work with pleasure and eat lunch during the crossing. He'd found out that the train ferry Malmöhus was due to leave in twenty minutes.

There weren't many passengers on board. Only two tables in the dining room were occupied. They made a round of the smorgasbord to sample the herring, had wienerschnitzel and then went forward to the lounge to drink coffee.

The Sound was as smooth as glass, but the view wasn't entirely clear. The silhouette of Ven shimmered in the haze, but it wasn't possible to distinguish either Backafallen or the small white church. Martin Beck studied the lively traffic with interest and was delighted when he caught sight of a steam-driven freighter with a graceful hull and a beautiful, straight chimney.

Over coffee Martin Beck outlined what Kollberg and Gunvald Larsson had found out from Broberg and Helena Hansson. It was bad enough, but didn't really seem to contribute to the murder investigation.

They took a train from the boat to Central Station and then went on foot across Rådhus Place and through the narrow streets to Kultorvet. Aero-fragt's office was on the top floor of an old building, and since there wasn't an elevator, they had to climb up the steep, cramped flights of stairs.

Although the building was old, the interior decoration of the office was ultramodern. They entered a long, narrow corridor with many doors covered with padded green imitation leather. The wall space between the doors was filled with large photostat copies of old types of airplanes, and under each picture there was a small leather armchair and a brass ashtray on a pedestal. The corridor led into a large room with two lofty windows onto the square.

The receptionist, who was sitting with her back to the window at a white steel-frame desk, was neither young nor very pretty. She had a pleasant voice, however; Månsson recognized it from his telephone call the previous day. She also had gorgeous, strawberry blond hair.

She was talking on the telephone and gestured politely

to them to wait in chairs on one side of the room.
Månsson dropped into one of the armchairs and took out
a toothpick. He'd replenished his supply from the condi-
ments rack in the train ferry's dining room. Martin Beck
remained standing and looked at the old tile stove in one
corner of the room.

The telephone conversation was being carried on in
Spanish, a language in which neither Martin Beck nor
Månsson was proficient, and they soon grew tired of
listening.

At last the strawberry blonde finished talking and stood
up with a smile.

"You gentlemen are from the Swedish police, I gather,"
she said. "Just a moment, and I'll notify Mr. Hoff-Jensen."

She disappeared through a pair of double doors covered
in the same imitation leather, although here they were
coffee brown, with large, shiny brass studs. The doors
closed noiselessly behind her, and even though Martin
Beck strained his ears, he couldn't distinguish voices from
within. Barely a minute passed before the doors were
opened again, and Hoff-Jensen came toward them with
outstretched hand.

He was athletic and suntanned. His broad smile revealed a row of dazzling white, flawless teeth under a
well-tended mustache. He was dressed in a style of studied
unconventionality, in an olive green shirt of thin raw silk,
a darker jacket of soft Irish tweed, chestnut brown trousers and beige moccasins. The thick curly hair that showed
at the neck of his shirt was silvery against his bronzed
skin. He had a broad chest and a large head with powerful facial features. His closely-cropped hair was platinum
blond, as was his mustache. His hips seemed unnaturally
narrow in relation to the heavy upper half of his body.

After he'd shaken hands with Martin Beck and Månsson, he held the door open for them. Before closing it, he
said to the secretary, "I don't want to be disturbed for
anything."

Hoff-Jensen waited until the policemen had each taken
a seat, then he settled down behind the desk. He leaned
against the back of his chair and picked up the cigar that
was smoldering on an ashtray within easy reach.

"Well, gentlemen, you're here about poor Viktor, I assume. You haven't found the guilty man?"

"No, not yet," Martin Beck said.

"I really don't have much more to say than what I said when we were questioned that terrible night in Malmö. Everything happened in a matter of seconds."

"But you had the time to see the gunman, didn't you?" Månsson said. "You were sitting facing in that direction."

"Certainly," Hoff-Jensen said and puffed on his cigar.

He reflected a moment before continuing.

"But before the shot was fired I hadn't noticed the man, and afterward it took me a minute to grasp what had happened. I saw Viktor fall onto the table, but didn't understand right away that he'd been shot, even though I did hear the shot. Then I saw the man with the revolver— I think it was a revolver—rush to the window and disappear. I was taken by surprise and didn't have time to take note of what he looked like. So, gentlemen, you see that I can't be of much help to you."

He lifted his arms and let them fall on the padded arms of the chair in a gesture of apology.

"But you did see him," Martin Beck said. "You must have some impression."

"If I had to describe the man I'd say that he looked middle-aged, a little shabby, perhaps. I don't think I ever saw his face; by the time I looked up he already had his back to me. He must have been in good shape to have got through that window so fast."

He leaned forward and put the cigar out in the ashtray.

"What about your wife?" Månsson asked. "Did she see anything in particular?"

"Not a thing," Hoff-Jensen answered. "My wife is a very sensitive, impressionable woman. It was a terrible shock for her, and it took her several days to get over it. Besides, she was sitting beside Viktor and so had her back to the criminal. You won't insist on questioning her?"

"No. It may not be necessary," Martin Beck said.

"That's kind of you," Hoff-Jensen said and smiled. "Well, in that case . . ."

The man gripped the arm rests as if to stand up, but

Månsson hastened to say, "We have a couple more questions, if you don't mind, Mr. Hoff-Jensen."

"Ye-es?"

"How long have you been head of this company?"

"Since it was formed eleven years ago. As a young man I was a pilot, then I studied advertising in the United States and was publicity director for an airline before Viktor made me head of Aero-fragt here in Copenhagen."

"What about now? Are you carrying on as usual, despite his death?"

Hoff-Jensen extended his arms and displayed his beautiful set of false teeth.

"The show must go on," he said.

It was quiet in the room. Martin Beck looked sideways at Månsson, who'd sunk deeper into the chair and was staring disgustedly at the golf bag full of clubs propped up against the tile stove.

"Who will be head of the concern now?" said Martin Beck.

"Well, that's a good question," said Hoff-Jensen. "Young Linder is still too green, probably. And Broberg, uh, like me, I imagine, has his hands full."

"How did you get along with Mr. Palmgren?"

"Very well, I'd say. He had complete confidence in me and in the way I ran the company."

"Exactly what does Aero-fragt do?" Martin Beck asked and realized immediately what the answer would be.

"It flies freight, as the name implies," Hoff-Jensen said.

He held out a cigar case to Månsson and Martin Beck, and when both shook their heads he took a cigar himself and lit it. Martin Beck lit a Florida, exhaled the smoke and said, "Yes, I understand that, but what kind of freight? You have five planes, isn't that right?"

Hoff-Jensen nodded and studied the coal on his cigar. Then he said, "The freight consists mainly of the company's own products, primarily canned fish. One of the planes is also equipped with freezer storage. At times we run charter flights. Some firms in Copenhagen call on us for various carrrying jobs—and other interested parties, for that matter."

"What countries do you fly to?" Martin Beck asked.

"Mostly European, if you don't include the Eastern European countries. Africa sometimes."

"Africa?"

"Mostly charter. That's seasonal," Hoff-Jensen said and looked pointedly at his watch.

Månsson sat up straight, took the toothpick out of his mouth and pointed it at Hoff-Jensen.

"How well do you know Hampus Broberg?"

The Dane shrugged.

"Not very well. We see each other sometimes at board meetings, like last Wednesday. We talk on the telephone now and then. That's all."

"Do you know where he is now?" asked Månsson.

"In Stockholm, I suppose. His home is there. And his office."

Hoff-Jensen seemed surprised by the question.

"What kind of a relationship did Palmgren and Broberg have?" Martin Beck asked.

"Good, as far as I knew. They may not have been exactly close friends, the way Viktor and I were. We played golf together a lot and saw each other outside business hours. I'd say that Viktor and Hampus Broberg were more like boss and employee."

Something in his tone betrayed a feeling of contempt for Hampus Broberg.

"Had you ever met Mr. Broberg's secretary before?" Månsson asked.

"The blond girl? No, that was the first time. A sweet kid."

"How many employees do you have?" Martin Beck asked.

Hoff-Jensen stopped to think.

"Twenty-two at present," he said. "It varies a little, depending on . . ."

He broke off and shrugged.

"Well, on the season, the nature of the business and so on," he said nebulously.

"Where are your planes now?" Martin Beck asked.

"Two are at Kastrup. One is in Rome and one on Sao Tomé for engine repairs. The fifth is in Portugal."

Martin Beck stood up abruptly and said, "Thank you.

Can you let us know if you think of something else? Will
you be staying here in Copenhagen in the near future?"

"Yes, I will," Hoff-Jensen said.

He put down the cigar but remained sitting quietly in
the chair.

In the doorway Månsson turned around and said,
"You don't by any chance know who could've wanted
Viktor Palmgren dead?"

Hoff-Jensen picked up his cigar, gazed steadily at
Månsson and said, "No, I don't know. Obviously the
person who shot him. Good-bye, gentlemen."

They walked down Købmagergade to Amager Square.
Månsson glanced toward Læderstræde. He knew a
girl who lived there. She was a sculptor from Skåne, who
preferred to live in Copenhagen. He'd met her in connection with an investigation a year earlier. Her name was
Nadja, and he liked her very much. They met now and
then, usually at her place, slept with each other and had a
good time together. Neither of them wanted to make a
commitment, and they were careful not to encroach too
much on each other's lives. During the past year, their
relationship had been practically flawless. Månsson's only
problem was that he no longer enjoyed his weekend get-
togethers with his wife in the same way; he would rather
have been with Nadja.

Strøget teemed with people, most of whom seemed to
be tourists. Martin Beck, who detested crowds, dragged
Månsson through the throng outside of the entrance to
Magasin du Nord and in on Lille Kongensgade. They each
drank a bottle of Tuborg at cellar temperature in Skind-
buksen, which was also crowded, although the people were
more congenial than on the street.

Månsson persuaded Martin Beck to take the hydrofoil
home. The boat's name was *Svalan,* and Martin Beck felt
sick during the crossing. Forty minutes after they left
Danish soil they walked in the door to Månsson's office.

On the desk was a message from the Technical Squad:

> *Ballistic study finished.*
> *Wall*

20

Martin Beck and Månsson looked at the bullet that had killed Viktor Palmgren. It was lying in front of them on a sheet of white paper, and their shared opinion was that it looked small and innocent.

It had been somewhat knocked out of shape by the impact, but not very much, and even then it hadn't taken the experts many seconds to establish the caliber of the weapon. As a matter of fact, you didn't even have to be an expert to know that.

"A .22," Månsson said thoughtfully. "That seems strange."

Martin Beck nodded.

"Who the hell tries to kill somebody with a .22?" Månsson said.

He inspected the small nickel-cased projectile and shook his heavy head.

Then he answered his own question: "Nobody. Especially if it's not premeditated."

Martin Beck cleared his throat. As usual, he was coming down with a cold, although it was the middle of the hottest summer he'd seen in many years.

How would it be in the fall? When moisture and raw fogs closed in on the country, saturated with every species of virus from the whole wide world.

"In America it's almost considered proof that the gunman is a real craftsman," he said. "A kind of snobbishness. It shows the murderer is a real pro and doesn't bother to use more than what's absolutely necessary."

"Malmö isn't Chicago," Månsson said laconically.

"Sirhan Sirhan killed Robert Kennedy with an Iver Johnson .22," said Skacke, who was hanging around in the background.

"That's right," Martin Beck said, "but he was desperate and emptied the whole magazine. Fired like crazy all over the place."

"He was an amateur, anyway," Skacke said.

"Yes. And the shot that killed Kennedy was a chance hit. The rest of the bullets hit other people in the crowd."

"This guy took careful aim and fired a single shot," Månsson said. "From what we know, he cocked the gun with his thumb before pulling the trigger."

"And he was right-handed," said Martin Beck. "But then almost everyone is."

"Hmm," said Månsson. "There's something screwy about this."

"Yeah, there really is," Martin Beck said. "Are you thinking about anything in particular?"

Månsson grumbled under his breath for a minute. Then he said, "What I'm thinking about is that the fellow acted so professional. Especially with the gun. And he knew exactly who he was going to shoot."

"Yes . . ."

"And yet he only fired one shot. If he'd been unlucky the bullet could've struck the skull and ricocheted. As it turned out, it struck obliquely, and that was enough to take away some of the momentum."

Martin Beck had wondered about that, too, but couldn't arrive at any logical conclusion from the reasoning.

In silence they began to study the report of the technicians who'd examined the bullet.

Ballistic science had made great progress since 1927, when it made its international breakthrough during the lengthy, famous trial of Sacco and Vanzetti in Dedham, Massachusetts, but the principles were still the same. Then Calvin Goddard had brought out the helixometer, the micrometer microscope and the comparative microscope, and since then great numbers of criminal cases throughout the world had been decided on the basis of ballistic evidence.

If the bullet, the shell and the weapon were available it was the simplest thing in the world for any specialized criminologist to establish whether a particular projectile had been fired from a particular gun or not. If two of the components were available—usually the bullet and the cartridge—it was fairly easy to deduce the type of weapon.

Different makes of gun leave different characteristics on

the shell as well as on the bullet in the second that the firing pin hits the detonator cap and the bullet goes its way out through the bore. After Harry Söderman, who'd been an apprentice of Locard in Lyons, constructed the first Swedish comparison microscope in the early thirties, they had slowly but surely built up an exhaustive collection of tables, from which one could read off the effect of different types of gun on the cartridge used.

But, in this case, the science, despite its generally acknowledged precision, let them down because they only had the bullet to go on and because, moreover, it was misshapen.

Nonetheless, the ballistics man had compiled a list of possible weapons.

Martin Beck and Månsson could contribute several that weren't possible. Only a little common sense was required for that.

First and foremost, all automatics were eliminated—they reject the shell when the barrel recoils, and no shell had been found in this instance. It's true that shells can end up in the most unlikely places—in a dish of mashed potatoes, for example, as Backlund had suspected, in clothes or just about anywhere. There had been examples of spent cartridges finding their way into pockets and pants cuffs and not being discovered until much later.

But the testimony seemed to be conclusive. Even if no one involved seemed to be a weapons expert, everything pointed to one thing—that the murderer had used a revolver. Which, as everyone knows, doesn't reject shells; they stay in the cartridge cylinder, waiting patiently until someone takes them out.

The statement from the ballistics expert was very long, and even when Martin Beck and Månsson had spent an hour of their precious time cutting it down, it was still pretty lengthy.

"My, my," Månsson said, scratching his head. "This document doesn't give us much to go on, unless we can locate either the gun or something else that points in some definite direction."

"Like what?" Martin Beck asked.

"Don't know," said Månsson.

Martin Beck wiped the perspiration off his forehead

with a folded handkerchief. Then he unfolded it and blew his nose.

He looked at the list of revolvers and babbled dismally, "Colt Cobra, Smith & Wesson 34, Firearms International, Harrington & Richardson 900, Harrington & Richardson 622, Harrington & Richardson 926, Harrington & Richardson SideKick, Harrington & Richardson Forty-Niner, Harrington & Richardson Sportsman . . ."

"Sportsman," Månsson said to himself.

"I'd like to have a word with these Harrington and Richardson guys," Martin Beck said. "Why can't they be satisfied with one model?"

"Or none at all," Månsson said.

Martin Beck turned the page and continued to mumble.

"Iver Johnson Sidewinder, Iver Johnson Cadet, Iver Johnson Viking, Iver Johnson Viking Snub . . . We should be able to cross that one out. Everybody says the barrel was long."

Månsson walked over to the window and looked thoughtfully out over the station courtyard. He wasn't listening any more. He heard Martin Beck's voice only as background noise.

"Herter's .22, Llama, Astra Cadix, Arminius, Rossi, Hawes Texas Marshal, Hawes Montana Marshal, Pic Big Seven—God, is there no end to this."

Månsson didn't answer. He was thinking of something else.

"I wonder how many revolvers there are in this city alone," Martin Beck said.

The question could hardly be answered. They must have been legion—inherited, stolen and smuggled. Hidden away in closets and drawers and old trunks. Illegal, of course, but people didn't worry about that.

And then, naturally, there were people who actually had licenses, but not many.

The only ones who definitely didn't have revolvers, or at least didn't wear them, were policemen. The Swedish police were equipped with 7.65 mm Walther pistols, stupidly enough. Although it's easier to change the magazine on automatics, they have the unpleasant habit of getting caught in clothing and other things, just when it's important to draw fast. "To snag," as it is called in the jargon.

They were interrupted in their reflections when Skacke knocked on the door and came in.

"Somebody has to talk to Kollberg," he said. "He doesn't know what he's going to do with these people in Stockholm."

21

What to do with Hampus Broberg and Helena Hansson was a problem, to put it mildly.

In addition, Martin Beck and Kollberg had to resolve the matter on the telephone, which took quite a while.

"Where are they now?" Martin Beck said.

"On Kungsholmsgatan."

"In custody?"

"Yes."

"Can we get them booked?"

"The prosecuting attorney thinks so."

"*Thinks?*"

Kollberg sighed deeply.

"What are you trying to say?" Martin Beck asked.

"They're being held for planning to violate the currency laws. But for the moment there isn't any formal charge against them."

Kollberg paused significantly. Then he said, "This is what I'm trying to say. The only conclusive evidence against Broberg is that he had a forged passport in his pocket and fired a blank from a starting gun when Larsson and that trigger-happy patrolman were about to pick him up."

"Yes?"

"And the broad's confessed that she peddles her ass. She also had a suitcase full of securities. She says Broberg gave her the suitcase and the securities and the ticket and the whole works and offered her ten grand to smuggle everything into Switzerland."

"Which is probably true."

"Sure. The problem is that they never had time to get

under way. If Larsson and I'd had our heads on straight, we would've let them keep going for a while. We could've tipped off customs and the passport check-point so they would've got caught out at Arlanda."

"Then you mean there won't be enough evidence?"

"Right. The prosecuting attorney claims there's a possibility the judge will refuse the arrest warrant and will think it's enough to issue an injunction against their leaving his jurisdiction."

"And let them go?"

"Exactly. Unless you . . ."

"What?"

"Unless you can convince the prosecuting attorney down there in Malmö that they're being held because they have vital information about Palmgren's murder. If you can do that we can book them and send them down to you. That's what the lawyers suggest."

"What do you think?"

"Not too much. It seems really obvious that Broberg was planning to make off with an ungodly amount of money. But if we take that approach, the matter has to be handed over to the Fraud boys."

"But does Broberg have anything to do with the murder?"

"Let's just say that since last Friday his conduct has been dictated by the fact that Palmgren died on Thursday night. It looks clear as day, doesn't it?"

"Yes. Seems like the only logical explanation."

"However, Broberg has the world's best alibi for the murder itself. Just like Helena Hansson and the other people sitting at the table."

"What does Broberg say?"

"He's reported to have said 'Ow!' when the doctor bandaged his jaw. Otherwise he hasn't said a word—literally."

"Wait a second," Martin Beck said.

He wiped off the sweaty telephone receiver with his handkerchief.

"What are you doing?" Kollberg asked suspiciously.

"Sweating."

"Then you should see me. To get back to this goddamn

Broberg, he's not very cooperative. For all I know, this money and all these stocks could actually be his."

"Hmm," Martin Beck said. "If that were true, where would he have got them?"

"Don't ask me. The only thing I know about money is that I don't have any."

Kollberg seemed to be thinking over this sorrowful remark. Then he said, "Anyway, I have to have something to tell the prosecuting attorney."

"How is it with the girl?"

"A lot easier, as far as I can see. She's talking her head off. The Vice Squad is reeling in the whole call-girl outfit, which is apparently spread out over the whole country. I just talked to Sylvia Granberg, and she claims they can hold Helena Hansson without any trouble, at least as long as their investigation lasts."

Sylvia Granberg was a sub-inspector with the Vice Squad and, among other things, Åsa Torell's boss.

"And besides they have some interests to tend to in Malmö," Kollberg went on. "So if you want to meet Helena Hansson you shouldn't run into any trouble."

Martin Beck said nothing.

"Well?" Kollberg said finally. "What should I do?"

"It would undoubtedly be interesting if certain confrontations took place," Martin Beck mumbled.

"I can't hear what you're saying," complained Kollberg.

"I've got to do some thinking about this. I'll call you in about half an hour."

"Absolutely no later. Any time now everybody's going to jump on me and start yelling. Malm, the Chief of Police and the whole bunch."

"Half an hour. I promise."

"Good. Bye now."

"Bye," Martin Beck said and hung up.

He sat for a long time with his elbows on the desk, his head buried in his hands.

After a while the picture grew clearer.

Hampus Broberg had converted all his assets into cash in Sweden and tried to escape from the country. He'd first got his family to safety. Everything suggested that his situation had become untenable the moment Palmgren died.

Why?

In all likelihood, because he'd embezzled large sums of money during the course of many years from the Palmgren enterprises he controlled, primarily the real estate agency, the stock transactions and the finance company.

Viktor Palmgren had trusted Broberg, who could consequently feel relatively secure as long as the head of the company was alive.

But with Palmgren gone, he didn't dare remain longer than was absolutely necessary. Thus he'd felt in danger, if not of his life, at least of financial ruin and perhaps a long prison term.

In danger from whom?

Hardly the authorities, for it didn't seem likely that the police or Internal Revenue could ever straighten out Palmgren's tangled affairs. Even if it were possible, it would in any case take a very long time, probably years.

The one who had best access was Mats Linder naturally.

Or possibly Hoff-Jensen.

But Linder's aversion to Broberg was so strong that he'd been unable to conceal it during the police enquiry.

Hadn't he strongly hinted that Broberg was a swindler? That Palmgren had trusted his man in Stockholm too much?

In any case, Linder had the best chances in an eventual struggle for power over the Palmgren millions.

If Broberg had embezzled large amounts, Linder was in the position of being able to demand an immediate audit of the various companies' accounts and bring a charge against him.

However, Linder had as yet taken no action, even though he must know or at least suspect that he didn't have much time.

The police had stopped Broberg instead, but it had happened almost by accident.

Which could indicate that Linder was in a precarious position himself and didn't dare take the risk of possible recriminations.

Anyhow, Broberg didn't seem to have had anything to

gain from Palmgren's death, and above all he hadn't expected it.

Everything he had done since Friday had been relative to Palmgren's sudden death, as Kollberg had quite correctly pointed out, but everything indicated that he had acted quickly, almost in panic, and so must have been virtually unprepared.

Then didn't this clear Broberg of any suspicion concerning the murder proper?

Martin Beck felt convinced of one thing—if there really had been a conspiracy behind the act of violence, that conspiracy was economic, not political.

Then who had something to gain from doing away with Palmgren?

There could be only one answer.

Mats Linder.

The man who'd already managed to win Palmgren's wife and who held the best cards in the financial power game.

Charlotte Palmgren was much too content with her existence to get involved in plots at such a high level. Besides, she was simply too stupid.

Hoff-Jensen certainly didn't have sufficient control of the Palmgren business empire.

But would Linder really take such an obvious risk?

Why not?

When you play for high stakes you have to take big risks.

It would be interesting to confront Hampus Broberg with Mats Linder and hear what the two gentlemen had to say to each other.

What about the girl?

Had Helena Hansson only been a paid pawn? Clearly a functional one, useful as secretary, smuggling courier and bedmate.

Her own statements indicated that, and there wasn't actually any reason to doubt them.

But lengthy experience showed that a great deal was revealed in bed. And Broberg was one of her regular clients.

Martin Beck's thoughts matured into a decision.

He got up and left the room. Took the elevator down

to the ground floor, where the public prosecution authorities had their offices.

Ten minutes later he was sitting behind the desk in his borrowed room again, dialing the number to Västberga.

"Fabulous!" Kollberg said. "You're right on the dot."

"Yeah."

"And?"

"Have them booked."

"Both of them?"

"Yes. We need them as witnesses down here. They're essential to the investigation of the murder."

"Really?"

Kollberg sounded skeptical.

"They should be sent here as soon as possible," Martin Beck said with conviction.

"Okay," Kollberg said. "Just one more thing."

"What?"

"Can I be dropped from this damn case from now on?"

"I think so."

After the telephone conversation, Martin Beck remained seated for a while, still deep in thought. But now he was more preoccupied with Kollberg and the hint of doubt in his voice.

Were these people really essential to the investigation of the murder?

Maybe not, but he had another, more personal, reason for his request. He'd never seen even a picture of either Broberg or Helena Hansson, and he was merely curious. He wanted to see what they looked like, talk to them, establish some kind of human contact and then see what his own reactions were.

Hampus Broberg and Helena Hansson were formally placed under arrest before Stockholm's Civic Court at five minutes after ten the following morning, Wednesday, July 9. They left Stockholm on the noon plane the same day, Broberg accompanied by a warden and Helena Hansson by a female prison guard and Åsa Torell, who was going to discuss joint investigation work with her colleagues in Malmö.

They landed at Bulltofta at a quarter to two.

22

On the tip of Amager, immediately south of Kastrup airport, is Dragør. It's one of the smaller towns in Denmark, with about four to five thousand inhabitants, and now probably best known for its large new ferry harbor. In the summertime ferries shuttle between Dragør and Limhamn on the Swedish side, carrying all the Swedish cars traveling to and from the Continent. The ferries do a steady business even during the winter, mostly with heavier vehicles, trucks, buses and trailers. All year round housewives travel from Malmö to Dragør to buy tax-free merchandise on board and groceries, which are cheaper in Denmark.

Not so very long ago the little port had a reputation as a resort, and there was constant activity in the harbor, where fishing boats lay rail by rail.

As a health resort, Dragør had the advantage of being within commuting distance of Copenhagen. Now the proximity to the capital city is merely a disadvantage; the water off Dragør's piers and beaches is so polluted that it isn't suitable for either swimming or fishing.

The town and its buildings, however, haven't changed appreciably since the days when ladies lazily twirled their parasols on the beach promenade, carefully shielding their alabaster complexions against the ruinous rays of the sun, and along the shore gentlemen dressed in jersey bathing suits hardly flattering to their beerbellies, cautiously sampled the waters for their medicinal effects.

The houses are squat and picturesque, painted or plastered in a variety of gay colors, the gardens are verdant, smelling of berries, flowers and lush vegetation, and the winding streets narrow and often paved with cobblestones. The stinking automobile traffic that roars to and from the ferries sweeps past the outskirts of the town, and relative peace reigns in the old quarter between the harbor and the highway.

Summer vacationers still come to Dragør, despite the poor swimming. All the rooms in the Strand Hotel were taken on this Tuesday early in July.

It was three o'clock in the afternoon, and on the veranda outside of the hotel, a family of three was just finishing their late lunch. The parents lingered over a cup of coffee and a coffee ring, but the boy, who was six and whose name was Jens, couldn't sit still any longer.

He ran excitedly back and forth between the tables, constantly nagging his parents.

"Can't we go now? I want to look at the boats. Finish your coffee. Hurry up. Let's go now. Can't we go down to the boats now?"

And so on until his mother and father gave in and stood up.

Hand in hand, they strolled down toward the old harbor pavilion, which is now a museum. There were only two fishing boats tied up in the harbor—there were usually more—meaning that several had to be out in the Sound, catching mercury-contaminated plaice.

The boy stopped at the edge of the pier and began to throw stones and sticks into the muddy water. He saw several interesting objects bobbing against the side of the wharf, but they were too far away for him to reach them.

The ferry harbor was down the beach. Several cars were lined up on the large asphalt approach waiting for the ferry, which could be seen drawing closer out on the sparkling water.

The three vacationers turned and wandered slowly back along the pier and in among buildings and houses. They stopped on Nordre Strandvej and chatted with an acquaintance who was out walking his dog.

Then they continued along the road to where the houses ended and Kastrup airport began. There they turned off to the right and went down to the beach.

Jens found the wreck of a green plastic boat at the edge of the beach and played with it, while his parents sat in the beach grass and watched. At last he tired of this and went exploring for things that had been washed up. He found an empty milk carton, a beer can and a condom and then bitterly regretted showing his finds to his parents, who made him throw everything away again.

At the moment his father stood up and shouted at him, he caught sight of something intriguing at the water's edge. A box, it looked like. Maybe a treasure chest. He ran to pick it up.

His father took the box from him, of course. He screamed a little in protest but soon gave up. He knew it didn't do any good.

Jens' parents examined the box. It was waterlogged, and the black grainy paper, which had been glued to the thick cardboard, had come loose in some places.

But it wasn't dented, and the lid, which wasn't quite closed, seemed undamaged.

When they looked closer they could make out printing on the top:

ARMINIUS .22

And right underneath, in smaller letters:

Made in West Germany.

The box aroused their curiosity somewhat.

They opened it cautiously, so as not to damage the soaked lid.

The inside of the box was lined with polystyrene, compressed from the kind of plastic particles that get washed up in countless millions on the Swedish and Danish beaches on the Sound, the Baltic and the North Sea.

Two one-inch-deep profiles had been cut out of the white polystyrene block. One of them was in the shape of a revolver with a very long barrel; the other was less well defined, and they couldn't tell immediately what it was.

"A box for a toy gun," said the woman and shrugged her shoulders.

"Don't be silly," the man said. "There was a real revolver in this box."

"How do you know that?"

"It even says the make on the lid. An Arminius .22. And look here. This space is for an extra butt, so you can exchange it for one with a larger gripping surface."

"Uh," the woman said. "I think guns are horrible."

The man laughed.

He didn't throw the box away, but kept carrying it as they walked up toward the road.

"It's only a box," he said. "Nothing to be scared of."

"But still," the woman said. "What if the revolver or

the pistol had still been in there, loaded, and Jens found it and . . . ?"

The man laughed again and stroked his wife's cheek.

"You and your imagination," he said. "If the revolver had been in there the box would never have floated ashore. It's a pretty heavy number, a .22 like this. Besides, there couldn't have been a gun in this box when it was thrown in the sea. Nobody throws away an expensive thing like a revolver . . ."

" . . . unless he's a gangster who wants to get rid of a murder weapon," his wife interrupted. "What if . . ."

She stopped short and yanked at her husband's sleeve.

" . . . What if that's it? I think we should take this box to the police station."

"Are you crazy? And be laughed at?"

They started walking again. Jens ran in front of them; he'd forgotten his treasure box.

"Well, but even so," she said. "You never know. It can't do any harm. We'll go to the police."

The wife was stubborn, and the man, who'd had ten years' experience of it, knew it was usually easier to give in than to disagree.

And so it happened that a quarter of an hour later Police Sergeant Larsen in Dragør had his blotter ruined by a wet revolver box from West Germany.

23

Whereas everything happened on Monday and something on Tuesday, nothing at all happened on Wednesday. Nothing that furthered the investigation, anyway.

Martin Beck had the feeling as soon as he awoke. That it would be a peculiar day.

He felt ill at ease and dissatisfied. He'd gone to sleep late and awakened early, with a leaden taste in his mouth and his head throbbing with unfinished trains of thought.

The same subdued mood prevailed at the police station. Månsson was silent and pensive, thumbing through his papers time and again and systematically crushing his never-ending toothpicks between his teeth. Skacke seemed discouraged, and Backlund polished his glasses with an injured look on his face.

Martin Beck knew from experience that lulls of this sort occurred during every difficult investigation. They could last for days and weeks and all too often could never be broken. The material they had to work on led nowhere, all their resources appeared exhausted, and all the clues reduced to empty nothingness.

If he'd followed his instinct, he would simply have dropped everything, taken the train to Falsterbo, lain down on the beach and let the rare Swedish warmth wash over him. The morning newspapers had reported water temperatures of 70°, which really was unusually warm for the Baltic.

But, of course, a Chief Inspector doesn't do that, especially in the midst of looking for a murderer.

It was all extremely annoying. He needed both physical and mental activity, but didn't know what to do. So he was even less capable of telling anyone else what to do. After a few hours of blatant inactivity, Skacke asked frankly, "What should I do?"

"Go ask Månsson."

"I already did."

Martin Beck shook his head and walked into his room. He looked at the clock. Still only eleven.

Almost three hours till the plane bringing Broberg and Helena Hansson was due in Malmö.

For want of anything better to do, he called Palmgren's office and asked to speak to Mats Linder.

"Mr. Linder isn't available," the blond receptionist said lazily. "But . . ."

"But what?"

"I can connect you with his secretary."

Mats Linder was indeed unavailable. He had left for Johannesburg on the Tuesday afternoon flight from Kastrup.

On urgent business.

For the moment he wasn't even available in Johannesburg, in case anyone should have the absurd idea of trying to call him there.

Since the plane was still in the air.

It was uncertain when Mr. Linder would return.

Had the trip been planned?

Mr. Linder always planned his trips very carefully.

Said the efficient secretary authoritatively.

Martin Beck hung up and looked reproachfully at the telephone.

Hmm. The confrontation between Broberg and Linder just went down the drain.

Struck by a thought, he lifted the receiver again and dailed Aero-fragt's number on Kultorvet in Copenhagen.

Certainly.

Mr. Hoff-Jensen had suddenly been obliged to leave for Lisbon that morning.

It would be possible to reach him later at the Hotel Tivoli on Avenida da Liberdade.

But for the moment the plane was still in the air.

It was uncertain when he would return to Denmark.

Martin Beck conveyed the news to Månsson, who shrugged apathetically.

At two-thirty Broberg and Helena Hansson finally arrived.

In addition to the prison warden and an enormous bandage, Broberg arrived with his lawyer.

He didn't say anything, but the lawyer was not at a loss for words.

Mr. Broberg *couldn't* talk, since he'd been subjected to the most vicious kind of police brutality. And even if he'd been able to say anything, he had nothing to add to what he'd already stated in his testimony exactly one week ago.

The lawyer continued his prepared speech, now and then throwing murderous glances at Skacke, who was operating the tape recorder. Skacke blushed.

Martin Beck didn't, however. He sat with his chin cupped in his left hand and gazed intently at the man with the bandage.

Broberg was a completely different type from Linder and Hoff-Jensen. He was heavy-set, had red hair and coarse, brutal features. Squinty, pale blue eyes, a pot belly and the kind of head that would have sent him posthaste to the gas chamber if the late Lombrosi's criminological theories had been correct.

The man was simply loathsome to look at and was also ostentatiously and tastelessly dressed. You almost felt sorry for him, Martin Beck thought.

The lawyer felt professionally sorry for Broberg. He talked and talked, and Martin Beck let him, even though the man must have been repeating largely what he'd said to no avail at the court proceedings.

But the guy had to do what he had to do for the fat fee he would get when he eventually managed to have Broberg acquitted—or almost—and Gunvald Larsson and Zachrisson penalized for breach of authority.

And he wouldn't mind if that did happen. Martin Beck had long been depressed about Gunvald Larsson's methods, but had refrained from intervening, in the sacred name of loyalty.

When the lawyer reached the end of the saga of Brobergian suffering, Martin Beck said, still without taking his eyes off the prisoner, "Mr. Broberg, you can't talk then?"

A shake of the head.

"What is your opinion of Mats Linder?"

A shrug of the shoulders.

"Do you think he's capable of assuming responsibility for the company?"

Another shrug.

He examined Broberg for almost a minute longer and tried to catch the expression in his dull, unsteady eyes.

The man was obviously scared, but he also looked ready for a fight.

At last Martin Beck said to the lawyer, "Well, I gather that your client has been upset by the events of the past week. For the time being, maybe we should call it a day."

Everyone looked equally surprised—Broberg, the lawyer, Skacke and even the warden.

Martin Beck got up and went to hear how Månsson and Backlund were getting along with Helena Hansson.

He met Åsa Torell in the corridor.

"What's she saying?"

"A whole lot of stuff. But hardly anything you can use."

"What hotel are you staying at?"

"Same as you. The Savoy."

"Then maybe we could eat dinner together tonight?"

If they could, perhaps there'd be a pleasant end to this otherwise dismal day.

"It might be difficult," Åsa Torell said evasively. "I may have a lot to do here today."

She avoided meeting his eyes. Which was easy, since she didn't even come up to his shoulder.

Helena Hansson talked and talked. Månsson sat stock-still at the table. The tape recorder hummed. Backlund paced up and down the room with a shocked expression on his face. A death blow must have been dealt to his belief in the purity of life.

Martin Beck stood just inside the door, his elbows propped on a metal cabinet, and observed the woman while she repeated word for word what she'd said previously to Kollberg.

But now nothing was left of the semi-respectable façade or the thinly applied veneer.

In fact, she looked thoroughly unnerved and worn out. Just a whore, who'd got out of her depth and was scared to death. Tears trickled down her cheeks, and she soon started giving details of everyone and everything in her line of business, obviously in the hope that she would get off lightly.

It was all very depressing, and Martin Beck left as quietly and considerately as he'd come.

He returned to his room, now empty and even warmer than before.

He observed that the chair Hampus Broberg had sat in was moist from perspiration, both on the seat and the back.

The telephone rang.

Malm, of course.

Who else?

"What the he—what in the world are you up to?"

"The investigation."

"Just a minute," Malm said irritatedly. "Was it not understood, even quite clearly stated, that this investigation would be conducted as discreetly and efficiently as possible?"

"Yes."

"Do you consider a wild shooting match and a fight in the middle of Stockholm to be discreet?"

"No."

"Have you seen the newspapers?"

"Yes. I've seen the newspapers."

"How do you think they'll look tomorrow?"

"Don't know."

"Isn't it going a little too far for the police to pressure for the arrest of two people who are probably completely innocent?"

The Chief Superintendent had a point there, obviously, and Martin Beck didn't answer right away.

"Well," he said at last, "maybe it will look a little peculiar."

"Peculiar? Do you realize down there that I'm on the firing line for this?"

"That's too bad."

"I can tell you that the Chief of Police is just as upset as I am. We've been conferring for hours up in his room ..."

Mules may ease each other's itch, thought Martin Beck. That had to be a quotation from Latin.

"How did you get in to see him?" he asked innocently.

"How I got in to see him?" Malm echoed. "What are you talking about? Is that your idea of a joke?"

It was well known that the Chief of Police was reluctant to talk to people. Rumor had it that some high official had even threatened to haul a fork truck up to the National Police Board and force the doors of the holy of holies in order to have a face-to-face conversation. However, the dignitary in question had a great weakness for giving speeches, both to the nation and to defenseless groups of his private army.

"Well," Malm said, "can you at least say that an arrest is imminent?"

"No."

"Do you know who the murderer is, but need more evidence?"

"No."

"Do you know what circles he moves in?"

"Not the slightest idea."

"That's absurd."

"You think so?"

"What in the world do you want me to say to the parties concerned?"

"The truth."

"What truth?"

"No progress."

"No progress? After a week of investigation? With our best men on the case?"

Martin Beck took a deep breath.

"I don't know how many cases I've worked on, but it's quite a number by now. And I can assure you that we're doing our best."

"I'm convinced of that," Malm said in a conciliatory manner.

"But that's not what I really wanted to say," Martin Beck continued. "Just that a week can be a very short time. It hasn't even been a week now, as you may know. I got here on Friday, and today's Wednesday. Some time ago we arrested a man who committed a murder sixteen years before. That was two years ago and therefore before your time."

"Okay, I know all that. But this isn't an ordinary murder."

"You said that before."

"There could be international complications," Malm said with a touch of desperation in his voice. "In fact, there already are."

"In what way?"

"Repeated pressure has been put on us by several foreign embassies. And I'm fairly certain that there are Security men from abroad already here. They're sure to turn up soon in Malmö or Copenhagen."

He paused. Then he said in a wavering voice, "Or here in my office."

"Oh, well," Martin Beck said consolingly, "they can't mess things up much more than Sepo, at any rate."

"The Security people? A man of theirs is in Malmö. Are you working together?"

"I wouldn't say that exactly."

"Haven't you met?"

"I've seen him."

"Is that all?"

"Yes. And only because I couldn't avoid it."

"We haven't received any positive information from them, either," Malm said despondently.

"Did you expect any?"

"I can't help feeling that you're taking this much too lightly."

"If that's true, you're wrong. I never take a murder lightly."

"But this is not an ordinary murder."

Martin Beck had a feeling he'd heard that before.

"You can't go at it any old way," Malm said, putting heavy stress on the words. "Viktor Palmgren was a celebrity, both here and abroad."

"Yeah. I gather he appeared in the weeklies every week or so."

"Hampus Broberg and Mats Linder are also prominent citizens."

"I see."

"You can't treat them any old way."

"Of course not."

"At the same time you must be very careful what you leak to the press."

"I don't leak a thing myself."

"As I told you last time, it could cause irreparable damage if certain of Palmgren's activities became public knowledge."

"Who would be irreparably damaged?"

"Who do you think," Malm said agitatedly. "The nation, naturally. This nation of ours. If it became known that members of the Government had been aware of certain transactions, then ..."

"Then?"

"Then the political consequences could be devastating."

Martin Beck detested politics. If he had political views he kept them strictly to himself. He'd always tried to dodge assignments that might have political consequences. Generally, he offered no opinion when political crimes came up in a conversation.

But this time he couldn't help saying, "For whom?"

Malm let out a sound as though he'd been stabbed in the back.

"Do everything you can," he pleaded.

"Okay," Martin Beck said mildly. "I'll do everything I can ..."

After a second he added, "Stig."

That was the first time he'd called the Chief Superintendent by his first name. And hopefully the last.

The remainder of the afternoon passed in a melancholy mood.

The Palmgren investigation had bogged down.

However, it was unusually lively at the police station. The Malmö police force raided two brothels downtown, much to the indignation of the employees and to the even greater shame of the customers who'd been hauled in.

Åsa Torell had obviously been right when she said she'd have a lot to do.

He left the police station about eight, still feeling dissatisfied and vaguely worried.

His appetite deserted him, so there was no question of having a hearty *skånsk* dinner. He forced down a sandwich and a glass of milk, anyway, at the Mitt-i-City cafeteria on Gustav Adolf Square.

He chewed his food carefully and slowly. Through the window he studied the teenage vagrants, who were smoking hash and trading it for stolen records around the rectangular stone basin on the square.

No policemen were in sight, and the staff of the Bureau of Child Welfare must have had other things to do.

Eventually he strolled along Södergatan, diagonally across Stortorget and down toward the harbor. When he got back to the hotel it was ten-thirty.

In the lobby his eyes immediately fell on two men sitting in the easy chairs to the right of the entrance to the dining room. One of them was tall and bald and had a thick black mustache. He was also incredibly suntanned. The second man was a hunchback, almost a dwarf, with a pale face, sharp features and intelligent black eyes. Both were impeccably dressed, the mustachioed one in dark blue shantung and the hunchback in a well-cut pale gray suit with a vest. Both men had shiny black shoes, and both were motionless, staring vacantly straight ahead. A bottle of Chivas Regal and two glasses were on the table between them.

Foreigners, thought Martin Beck. The hotel swarmed

with foreign guests, and on the flagpoles outside he'd seen at least two national flags he didn't recognize.

As he picked up the room key, he saw Paulsson come out of the elevator and walk over to the two men's table.

24

Up in his room the maid had prepared everything for the night, turned down the bed, put out the bedside rug, closed the window and drawn the curtains.

Martin Beck turned on the bedside lamp and glanced at the TV set. He had no desire to turn it on and, besides, the programs were probably all over by now.

He took off his shoes, socks and shirt. Then he pulled open the drapes and opened out the double windows.

A faint breath of cool air, just barely noticeable, floated in from outside.

He propped his hands on the window sill and gazed out over the canal, the train station and the harbor.

He stood there for a long time in pants and fishnet undershirt and thought about nothing, on the whole.

The air was warm and unmoving, the sky filled with stars.

Illuminated passenger boats came and went; the train ferry bellowed in the harbor entrance. The traffic on the streets was almost nonexistent, and there was a long row of taxis outside of the train station with their vacant signs on and their front doors open. The drivers stood in clusters and passed the time of day, and the cars were painted in a variety of quite bright colors, not black as in Stockholm.

He didn't want to go to bed. He'd already read the evening newspapers and he'd forgotten to pick up a book. He could go down and buy one, but then he'd have to get dressed again. Yet he didn't want to read either, and if he did, the Bible and the telephone directory were always close by. Or the autopsy report, but he knew it almost by heart.

So he stood there by the window and looked, feeling
curiously alone and shut off. Totally of his own choosing,
since he could have been sitting in the bar or at Månsson's home or in a thousand different places.

Something was missing, but he didn't really know what.

After he'd stood there for quite a while he heard
someone tapping on the door. Very lightly. If he'd been
sleeping or in the shower, he wouldn't have heard it.

"Come in," he said, without turning his head.

He heard the door open.

Maybe it was the murderer, striding in with his revolver
raised, ready for action. If he aimed for the back of the
head this time, too, Martin Beck would fall forward out of
the window and, if he were unlucky, he would be dead
before he was smashed on the sidewalk far below.

He smiled and turned around.

It was Paulsson in his houndstooth suit and his canary
yellow shoes.

He looked unhappy. Even his mustache didn't seem
quite as elegant as usual.

"Hi," he said.

"Hi."

"May I come in?"

"Sure," Martin Beck said. "Sit right down."

He went over and sat down on the edge of his bed.

Paulsson squirmed in his chair. His forehead and cheeks
glistened with perspiration.

"Take off your jacket," Martin Beck said. "We're not
too particular about formalities here."

Paulsson hesitated for a long time, but finally he began
to undo the buttons on the double-breasted jacket and
struggled out of it. He folded it very carefully and laid it
over the arm of the chair.

Under the jacket he was wearing a shirt with broad
pale green and orange stripes. Plus a pistol in a shoulder
holster.

Martin Beck wondered how long it would take him to
get at the gun, if he first had to go through all that
complicated unbuttoning process.

"What's on your mind?" he asked calmly.

"Uh . . . I wanted to ask you something."

"Go ahead. What?"

"You don't have to answer, of course."

"Don't be silly. What is it?"

"Well . . ."

And then finally it came, visibly after the exercise of a great deal of self-control, "Have you gotten anywhere?"

"No," Martin Beck said.

From pure courtesy he returned the question, "Have you?"

Paulsson shook his head wistfully. Lovingly stroked his mustache, as if it gave him renewed strength.

"This seems pretty complicated," he said.

"Or else it may be very simple," Martin Beck said.

"Simple?" Paulsson said.

Questioningly and incredulously.

Martin Beck shrugged.

"No," Paulsson said, "I don't think so . . . And the worst thing is . . ."

He broke off. With a hopeful glint in his eye, he said, "Have they been raking you over the coals, too?"

"Who?"

"Oh, the bosses. In Stockholm."

"They seem a little nervous," Martin Beck said. "What's the worst thing, you were going to say?"

"This is going to be a large-scale international investigation, politically complicated. With ramifications in all directions. Tonight two foreign security agents arrived. At the hotel."

"Those two characters sitting in the lobby a while ago?"

Paulsson nodded.

"Where are they from?"

"The little man is from Lisbon and the other one from Africa. Loranga Marcuse, or whatever it's called."

"Lourenço Marques," Martin Beck said. "It's in Mozambique. Do they have an official assignment here?"

"I don't know."

"Are they even policemen?"

"Security agents, I think. They introduce themselves as businessmen. But . . ."

"What?"

"But they identified me right away. Knew who I was. Strange."

Extremely strange, Martin Beck thought. Aloud he said, "Have you talked to them?"

"Yes. They speak very good English."

Martin Beck happened to know that Paulsson's English had serious shortcomings. Maybe he was good at Chinese or Ukrainian or something else that was valuable to the security of the realm.

"What did they want?"

"They asked things I really didn't get. That's why I bothered you like this. First they wanted to see a list of the suspects."

"So?"

"To tell you the truth, I don't have a list like that. Maybe you do?"

Martin Beck shook his head.

"Of course, I didn't say that," Paulsson said cunningly. "But then they asked me something I didn't get at all."

"What was that?"

"Well, as I understood it, but it has to be wrong, they wanted to know which people from the overseas provinces were suspected. The overseas provinces ... But they said it several times in different languages."

"You understood correctly," Martin Beck said kindly. "The Portuguese claim that their colonies in Africa and other places have an equal status with the provinces in Portugal itself. Apparently they meant people—above all political refugees—from places like Angola, Mozambique, Macao, Cape Verde Islands, Guinea and so on."

Paulsson's face suddenly lit up.

"Well I'll be—!" he said. "Then I did hear right after all."

"What did you tell them?"

"Nothing definite. They seemed pretty disappointed."

Well, that was easy to imagine.

"Are they planning to stay here?"

"No," Paulsson said. "They're going on up to Stockholm. To talk to their embassy. By the way, I'm flying up there tomorrow, too. Have to report. And study the archives."

He yawned and said, "Better go to bed. It's been a tough week. Thanks for the help."

"With what?"

"These . . . overseas things."

Paulsson got up, put on his jacket and buttoned all the buttons with great care.

"Bye," he said.

"Good night."

In the doorway he turned around and said ominously, "I think this is going to take years."

Martin Beck sat still for two minutes. Then he grinned to himself, took off the rest of his clothes and went into the bathroom.

He stood under a cold shower for a long time, wrapped the bath towel around himself and returned to his place by the window.

It was quiet and dark outside. All activity seemed to have ceased, both in the harbor and at the railroad station.

A police car rolled slowly past. Most of the cab drivers had given up and driven home.

Martin Beck stood gazing out into the silent summer night. It was still warm, but he felt cool and fresh after the shower.

After a while he felt it was time to go to bed. Sooner or later it had to happen, after all, even if sleep still seemed far away.

He frowned at his pyjamas, which were lying on his pillow. They looked pleasant now, but would inevitably be sweaty and cling to his body when he awoke.

He put them in the closet. Folded the blanket neatly and put it away under the bed. Hung out the big towel on the drying rack in the bathroom.

Then he lay on his back in the bed, folded the sheet almost down to his waist and clasped his hands behind his head. He lay watching the ceiling, where the reflection from the reading lamp threw indistinct shadows.

He was thinking, but with neither precision nor concentration.

After he'd lain like that for fifteen or maybe twenty minutes there were more taps on the door. Very light this time, too.

Good God! he thought. Could he really stand more dribble about espionage and secret agents? Naturally it would be easiest to pretend to be asleep. Or was that neglect of duty?

"Okay, come in," he said with a sense of doom.

The door was opened cautiously, and Åsa Torell came into the room, dressed in slippers and a short white nylon robe, tied with a sash around her waist.

"You weren't sleeping, were you?"

"No," Martin Beck said.

After a moment he added foolishly, "You weren't, either?"

She smiled and shook her head. Her short dark hair shone.

"No," she said. "I just got in. I've scarcely had time to take a shower."

"I heard you had your hands full today."

She nodded.

"Yeah. Darn it. We've hardly eaten today. Just a couple of sandwiches."

"Sit down."

"Thanks. You're not too tired?"

"You don't get tired from doing nothing."

She still hesitated, with one hand on the doorknob.

"I'll just get my cigarettes," she said. "My room isn't more than two doors away."

She left the door ajar. He still lay with his hands behind his head and waited.

After twenty seconds she was back, closed the door soundlessly and padded over to the chair where Paulsson had been in agony about an hour before. She kicked off her slippers and drew her legs under her. She lit a cigarette and inhaled deeply several times.

"Oh, wow!" she said. "It's really been a helluva day."

"Are you beginning to have second thoughts about being a policewoman?"

"Yes and no. You see so much misery that you only heard about before."

She looked thoughtfully at her cigarette and continued, "But sometimes you do have the feeling you're doing a little good, too."

"Yes," he said, "once in a while."

"Did you have a bad day?"

"Yes, very. Nothing new or constructive. But it's like that a lot."

She nodded.

"Do you have any ideas?" he said.

"Huh-uh. How could I have, really? Except to say Palmgren was a bastard. A lot of people must have had good reason to hate him. What I mean is that maybe it doesn't have to be so complicated as some people seem to think. Revenge. Pure and simple."

"Yes, I've thought about that, too."

She fell silent.

When the cigarette was finished she lit another. She smoked Danish cigarettes—Cecil, in a green, white and red pack.

Martin Beck turned his head and looked at her feet, which were thin and gracefully arched, with long, straight toes.

Then he raised his eyes to her face. She looked preoccupied, and her eyes had a faraway look.

He continued to watch her. After a while she relaxed, lifted her head slightly and looked straight into his eyes.

Hers were big and brown and serious.

A moment ago she'd been preoccupied; now, suddenly, she was intensely present.

They went on looking at each other.

She put out her cigarette, and this time she didn't light another.

She moistened her lips and bit the end of her tongue. Her teeth were white, but slightly uneven. Her eyebrows thick and dark.

"Well?" he said.

She nodded slowly and said very quietly, "Well, sooner or later. Why not now?"

She got up and sat down on the edge of the bed.

She didn't move for a while. They still looked into each other's eyes.

Martin Beck freed his left arm. His hand brushed against her slim fingers. He tugged lightly at her sash.

"There's no hurry," he said.

She looked deep into his eyes and said, "Yours are gray. Actually."

"And yours are brown."

Åsa Torell smiled without parting her lips. Then she raised her right hand, slowly undid the knot, half stood up and let the robe fall to the floor.

He pushed the sheet away, and she sat down again, her right leg raised so that her foot rested against the left side of his chest.

"Have you thought about this before?" she said.

"Yes. Have you?"

"Sometimes. Once in a while during the past year."

They exchanged a few more words.

"Has it been a long time?"

"Terribly long. Not since—"

She broke off and said, "What about you?"

"Same here."

"You're good," she said.

"You are, too."

It was true. Åsa Torell was good, and he'd known it for a long time.

She was small but firm. Her breasts were small but the nipples were large, erect and dark brown. The skin over her midriff and abdomen was smooth and supple and the copious hair between her legs curly and almost coal black.

Her hand was lying spread out on his left leg and slid slowly upward. Her fingers were thin but long, strong and purposeful.

She was very open.

After a moment he moved his hands to her shoulders. She changed position and lay on top of him—soft, deep and wide open and soon filled with him.

She panted in short, quick breaths against his shoulder and soon afterward against his mouth.

When she was lying on her back she felt very solid and secure, and her legs were strong around his back and hips.

When she left it had been light for a couple of hours.

She put on her robe and slippers and said, "Bye and thanks."

"Same to you."

Thus it had happened, and would never happen again. Or maybe it would.

He didn't know.

He did know, however, that he was old enough to be

her father, even if that place hadn't been occupied for exactly twenty-seven years.

Martin Beck reflected that Wednesday hadn't ended so badly, despite everything. Or could it be that Thursday had begun well?

Then he fell asleep.

They saw each other again several hours later, at the police station. In passing, Martin Beck said, "Who booked you the room at the Savoy?"

"I did. But Lennart told me to do it."

Martin Beck smiled to himself.

Kollberg, of course. The schemer. Well, this time, anyway, he would never know for certain whether he'd been successful or not.

25

At nine o'clock on Thursday morning the situation in the tracking center was at a standstill. Martin Beck and Månsson were sitting across from each other at the large desk. Neither of them said anything. Martin Beck was smoking, and Månsson wasn't doing anything. He'd used up his toothpicks.

At twelve minutes after nine, Benny Skacke made the first active contribution of the day by coming into the room with an enormously long strip of teletype in his hand. He stopped inside the door and started skimming through it.

"What's that?" Martin Beck asked.

"The list from Copenhagen," Månsson said dully. "They send out one like that every day. Missing persons, cars that've disappeared, things they've found, anything like that."

"A whole lot of girls who've run away," Skacke said. "Nine of them, no, ten."

"Well, it's that time of year," Månsson said.

"Lisbeth Møller, twelve years old," Skacke mumbled.

"Missing from her home since Monday, drug addict. And she's twelve years old?"

"Sometimes they turn up here," Månsson explained. "Most of the time they don't, of course."

"Stolen cars," Skacke said. "A Swedish passport, issued to Sven Olof Gustafsson, Svedala, fifty-six years old. Confiscated at a prostitute's place in Nyhavn. His billfold, too."

"Drunken pig," said Månsson laconically.

"A steam shovel from a tunnel construction site. How can anybody swipe a steam shovel?"

"It's been done," Martin Beck said.

"Drunken pig," said Månsson. "Is there anything under guns? They usually come toward the end."

Skacke scanned down the listing.

"Sure," he said. "Several of them. A Swedish army pistol, 9mm, Husqvarna, has to be old. A Beretta Jaguar ... Box for an Arminius .22, five boxes of 7.65 mm ammunition ..."

"Stop there," Månsson said.

"Yes, what was that about a box?" Martin Beck said.

Skacke went back up the list.

"A box originally for an Arminius .22," he said.

"Found where?"

"Floated ashore on the beach between Dragør and Kastrup. Found by a private individual and left with the police in Dragør. Last Tuesday."

"Isn't Arminius .22 on our list?" Martin Beck said.

"It sure is."

Said Månsson, suddenly alert, his hand already on the telephone receiver.

"Yeah, sure," Skacke said. "The box. The box on the bicycle ..."

Månsson energetically harassed the Copenhagen police switchboard. It took a moment before he was connected with Mogensen.

Mogensen had never heard of the box.

"No, I appreciate that you can't keep track of all that junk," Månsson said patiently. "But it *is* on your own damn list. Wait a second ..."

He looked at Skacke and said, "What number is it on the list?"

"Thirty-eight."

"Thirty-eight. Three, eight," Månsson said into the receiver. "Yes, it could be important for us . . ."

He listened a minute. Then he said, "By the way, do you know anything more about Aero-fragt and Ole Hoff-Jensen?"

Pause.

"Yes, that'd be fine," Månsson said and hung up.

He looked at the other two.

"They're going to check it out and then call us back."

"When?" Martin Beck asked.

"Mogensen is usually pretty fast," Månsson said and returned to his reflections.

The call from Copenhagen came in less than an hour.

Månsson mostly listened. He looked happier and happier.

"Fantastic," he said finally.

"Well?" said Martin Beck.

"Well, the box was with their Technical Squad. At first the guy in Dragør was going to throw it away, but yesterday he put it in a plastic bag and sent it to Copenhagen. We'll get it on the hydrofoil that leaves the Nyhavn canal at eleven."

He glanced at his watch and said to Skacke, "See that a patrol car meets the boat."

"What did he know about Hoff-Jensen?" Martin Beck asked.

"Most everything. Evidently, he's well-known over there. A shady character. But untouchable. He doesn't make his crooked deals in Denmark. Everything he does there is legal."

"Palmgren's crooked deals, in other words."

"Right. And apparently they're big stuff. Mogensen said that both Palmgren's and Hoff-Jensen's names had figured in connection with illegal traffic in weapons and airplanes to countries that are covered by weapon embargoes. He knows that from Interpol. But they can't do anything, either."

"Or maybe don't want to," Martin Beck said.

"Quite likely," Månsson said.

He yawned.

They waited. There wasn't much else to do.

At ten to twelve the box lay on the desk.

They slipped it out of the plastic wrapper. Experience had taught them to handle such things with great care, even though this one had already received rough treatment and clearly had gone through many hands.

Martin Beck lifted the lid, put his fist to his chin and examined the molded sections for the revolver and the extra butt.

"Yes," he said, "you're probably right."

Månsson nodded. He opened and closed the lid several times.

"Opens pretty easily," he said.

They turned the box over and examined it from all angles. It was dry now and reasonably well preserved.

"Can't have been in the water too long," Martin Beck said.

"Five days," Månsson said.

"Here," Martin Beck said, "we've got something here."

He ran his finger over the bottom of the cardboard box, which had obviously been covered with paper. It had been soaked off by now, however, and was completely gone in places.

"Yes," said Månsson. "There was something written on the paper. Probably with a ballpoint pen. Wait a second."

He took a magnifying glass out of one of his desk drawers and handed it to Martin Beck.

"Hmm," Martin Beck said. "The imprint is visible. A 'B' and an 'S.' They show up fairly clearly. Maybe something else."

"Okay," said Månsson, "we have people who work with things a bit more precise than my old magnifying glass. I'll have them take a look at it."

"This revolver is, or rather was, a target weapon," Martin Beck said.

"Yes, I've gone into that. An unusual make, too."

Månsson drummed with his fingers on the table.

"Okay, we'll leave this with the Technical Squad," he said. "We'll have Skacke canvass the rifle clubs. And we'll go out and eat lunch. Not a bad division of labor, uh?"

"Sounds good," Martin Beck said.

"I can show you Malmö at the same time. Have you been in the bar at Översten?"

"No."

"Well, it's about time."

The Restaurant Översten is on the twenty-sixth floor of the Crown Prince Building. Viewing the city from its bar windows far surpassed Martin Beck's memories of similar experiences.

The whole city spread out below them, as if seen from an airplane. They gazed over Öresund, Saltholm and the Danish coast. To the north, Landskrona, Ven and even Helsingborg were visible in the startlingly clear air.

A blond bartender in a blue jacket served them minute steaks and cold Amstel. Månsson ate voraciously, then took all the toothpicks from the condiment rack, stuck one into his mouth and the rest into his pocket.

"Hmm," he said. "As far as I can see, it all fits together."

Martin Beck, who'd been more interested in the view than the food, reluctantly tore his eyes from the panorama.

"Yes," he said, "it looks like it. Maybe you were right all along. Although you were guessing."

"Guessing and guessing," Månsson said.

"Now we just have to guess where he is, too."

"Here somewhere," said Månsson with a leisurely gesture over his city. "But who could have hated Palmgren that much?"

"Thousands of people," said Martin Beck. "Palmgren and his cronies were ruthless. They crushed everyone and everything around them. For example, he ran a whole lot of different companies for longer or shorter periods of time. As long as they were profitable. Then when the profits weren't fat enough, they were simply closed down, and many of the people who worked there were just laid off without a cent. How many people do you suppose have been ruined just by 'legal' loan sharks like Broberg?"

Månsson said nothing.

"But I think you're right," Martin Beck said. "The guy has to be here, provided he hasn't left town."

"Or left town and come back," Månsson said.

"Maybe. Then it must have been unpremeditated. Nobody who'd planned a murder, and above all no hired killer, would ride up on a bicycle one summer evening with a target practice gun in a box on the package rack. Bigger than a shoe box, too."

The tall, blond bartender was standing beside their table.

"Telephone call for you, Inspector," he said to Månsson. "Will there be coffee?"

"It's the guy from the lab," Månsson said. "Coffee? Yes, please. Two calypsos."

Martin Beck caught himself thinking about the fact that Månsson was known at the restaurant. Would *he* be recognized at any restaurant in Stockholm? Maybe, from television and pictures in the newspapers. Then he thought about all the people who'd been mistreated and made to pay through the nose in Palmgren's scandalously bad apartment houses. He should really get a list of the tenants over the last few years.

"Well," Månsson said, "there had been a name on the bottom of the cardboard box. 'B' and 'S,' we could see that ourselves. The rest was hard to decipher. The guy at the lab found that, too. But he claims that there used to be a name there, probably the owner's."

"And what did he make it out to be?"

"B. Svensson."

The man who operated the target range looked thoughtfully at Benny Skacke. Then he said, "Arminius .22? Yeah, there's probably two or three guys around here who use that kind. I can't tell you right off who they are.

"Somebody who was here last Wednesday? I can't possibly keep track of everybody who shoots here. But ask the guy who's standing over there. He's been banging away there for ten days—ever since the beginning of vacation."

As Skacke walked over to the range, the man added, "Ask him how he can afford to buy so much ammunition, too."

The marksman had finished one round, reckoned his points and was in the process of pasting up black and white paper when Skacke approached him.

"Arminius .22?" he said. "Yeah. I know one at least. But he hasn't been here since the middle of last week. Good shot, too. If he'd use one like this instead . . ."

The man weighed his Beretta Jetfire automatic in his hand.

"Do you know his name?"

"Bertil something or other ... Olsson or Svensson, I don't really know. But he works at Kockum's."

"Are you sure of that?"

"Yes. Some real lousy job. A janitor, I think."

"Thanks," Skacke said. "By the way, how can you afford to shoot up so much ammunition?"

"This is the only hobby I've got," the man said and shoved a new magazine into the pistol.

At the manager's cabin he was given a slip of paper with three names on it.

"These are the only Arminius owners I can think of."

Skacke walked back to the police car. Before starting the engine he looked at the list:

Tommy Lind, Kenneth Axelsson, Bertil Svensson

At the police station Månsson put a question to Martin Beck: "What are we going to do with the Broberg and Hansson duo?"

"Send them back to Stockholm. That is, if Åsa's done with her work."

"Yes, I'm done with what I came for," Åsa Torell said and looked at him with clear brown eyes.

The investigation now became routine. Two hours after they'd made inquiries at the police station in Handen the teletype machine spewed out the list of tenants in Palmgren's apartment houses.

It was in alphabetical order, and Martin Beck promptly put his finger on the right line:

Svensson, Bertil Olof Emanuel, lease terminated September 15, 1968.

"In other words, he got evicted," Månsson said.

Martin Beck located the number of Broberg's office in Stockholm. He dialed it, and a woman, who had to be Broberg's secretary, answered. Just in case, he asked, "Is this Mrs. Moberg?"

"Yes."

He told her who he was.

"Well, what can I do for you?" she asked.

"Mrs. Moberg, do you know if Mr. Palmgren closed down or discontinued any of his operations recently?"

"Well, that depends on what you mean by recently. Two years ago he closed down a factory that he had in Solna, if that's what you mean."

"What kind of factory?" Martin Beck asked.

"It was a rather small precision tool factory that made special machine parts. Springs and things like that, I think."

"Why was it closed down?"

"It was running at a loss. The companies that bought the parts must have built their machines or bought new ones, I don't really know. Anyway, there was no market for the products and instead of reorganizing production, they stopped manufacturing and sold the factory."

"And that happened two years ago?"

"Yes. In the fall of '67. I think he had a similar company that was closed down several years earlier, but that was before my time. I know about the other one because Mr. Broberg handled the liquidation of the firm."

"What happened to the employees?"

"They were given notice," Sara Moberg said.

"How many employees were involved?"

"I don't remember. But the papers are here somewhere. I can get them if you want."

"That'd be kind of you. I'd like to have the names of the employees."

"Just a minute," she said.

Martin Beck waited. Several minutes passed before she returned.

"Sorry," she said. "I didn't know exactly where the papers were. Should I read off the names?"

"How many are there?" Martin Beck asked.

"Twenty-eight."

"Did all of them have to quit? Couldn't they be transferred to one of the other companies?"

"No. They were all laid off. Except for one. He was a foreman and became a company janitor, but he quit after six months. Must have found a better job."

Martin Beck had found paper and pencil.

"Okay," he said. "Please read the names now."

He wrote while she read, but when she reached the ninth name, he raised the pencil and said, "Stop. Give me that last one again."

"Bertil Svensson, office worker."

"Is there anything more about him?"

"No, only that."

"Thanks, that's enough," Martin Beck said. "Good-bye and thanks for the help."

He went to see Månsson immediately.

"Here's the name again," he said. "Bertil Svensson. Laid off from a Palmgren company two years ago. He's an office worker."

Månsson turned the toothpick around with his tongue.

"No," he said. "A laborer. I talked to the personnel office at Kockum's."

"Did you get his address?" Martin Beck asked.

"Yes. He lives on Vattenverksvägen."

Martin Beck raised his eyebrows enquiringly.

"In Kirseberg."

Martin Beck shook his head.

"In Öster."

Martin Beck shrugged.

"Hmmph, Stockholmers," Månsson said. "Well, that's where he lives, anyway. But he's on vacation now. Started working at Kockum's in January of this year. Thirty-seven years old. He's divorced, apparently. His wife . . ."

Månsson dug around in his papers and pulled out a slip of paper with some notes scribbled on it.

" . . . His wife lives in Stockholm. The accounts department deducts her alimony from his paycheck every month and sends it to Mrs. Eva Svensson, 23 Norrtullsgatan in Stockholm."

"Hmm," Martin Beck said. "If he's on vacation maybe he isn't in town."

"We'll have to see, " Månsson said. "Maybe we ought to have a talk with his wife somehow. You think Kollberg . . . ?"

Martin Beck looked at his watch. Nearly five-thirty. Kollberg was probably on his way home right now to Gun and Bodil.

"Okay," he said. "Tomorrow."

26

Lennart Kollberg's voice was full of foreboding when Martin Beck called him on Friday morning.

"Just don't tell me it has anything to do with that Palmgren case again," he said.

Martin Beck cleared his throat.

"I'm sorry, Lennart, but I have to ask you for a little help," he said. "I suppose you've got a lot of things ..."

"A lot of things," Kollberg broke in irritatedly. "I'm short of people—like you, for example, and everybody else who ought to be here. I'm swamped with work. It's the same in town. Not even Rönn and Melander are there."

"I understand, Lennart," Martin Beck said softly. "But things have come up that put the case in a new light. You have to get some information on a man who may be the one who shot Palmgren. If worst comes to worst you could ask Gunvald ..."

"Larsson! If the Home Secretary got down on his knees and asked him, he wouldn't be able to persuade him to work on the Palmgren case. He's had a belly full."

Kollberg quietened down and after a short pause he sighed and said, "So who is this guy?"

"Probably the same person we could've picked up at Haga terminal a week ago, if we hadn't screwed up. His name is Bertil Svensson ..."

"Same as about ten thousand people in this country," Kollberg said caustically.

"Probably," Martin Beck said gently. "But we do know this about Bertil Svensson: he worked for a Palmgren company out in Solna, a fairly small precision tool factory, which was closed down in the fall of '67. He lived in one of Palmgren's apartment houses, but was evicted about a year ago. He's a member of a rifle club and, according to witnesses, used to use a gun that could well be the same model as the one Palmgren was murdered with. He got a divorce last fall, and his wife and two children still live in Stockholm. He lives in Malmö and works at Kockum's."

"Hmm," Kollberg said.

"His name is Bertil Olof Emanuel Svensson, born in the parish of Sofia in Stockholm, on May 6, 1932."

"Why don't you arrest him if he lives in Malmö?" Kollberg asked.

"We will, but first we want to find out a little more about him. We thought you could take care of that."

Kollberg sighed resignedly.

"Okay, what do you want me to do?" he said.

"He isn't in the criminal records, but find out if he's ever been picked up. Also find out if the social welfare agencies have had anything to do with him. Ask at the real estate office why he was evicted. And, last but not least, talk to his wife."

"Do you know where she is or shall I hunt for her, too? It only takes several weeks to find the right Mrs. Svensson."

"She lives at 23 Norrtullsgatan. Don't forget to ask her when she saw her husband last. I don't know what kind of a relationship they have, but it's possible he called or went to see her last Thursday. Can you do this as soon as possible?"

"It'll take all day," Kollberg complained. "But I don't really have any choice. I'll call when I'm through."

Kollberg hung up and stared gloomily at his desk, where maps, folders and reports lay every which way. Then he sighed, dug out the telephone directory and started calling.

A couple of hours later he got up, grabbed his jacket, shut his note pad and put it in his pocket. Then went down to the car.

As he drove toward Norrtullsgatan, he went over what he'd learned from his industrious session on the telephone.

Bertil Olof Emanuel Svensson hadn't come to the notice of the police until October '67. Then he'd been taken to Bollmora police station on a charge of intoxication. He'd been picked up in the entrance to the building where he lived and kept in jail for the night. From then until July '68, he'd been taken to the same police station five more times—once on another intoxication charge and four times for causing domestic disturbance, as it's called. That was all. There weren't any entries after July.

The Temperance Board had also been involved. On several occasions they'd been called to his home, by the landlord and by neighbors who claimed they were being disturbed by Svensson's drunken behavior. He'd been under supervision, but besides the two times he'd been held by the police, there'd been no reason to take action against him.

He hadn't been on any drunk and disorderly charges before October '67, and didn't figure in the Temperance Board's records before that date either. He'd got off each time with warnings.

The Svensson family had even come to the attention of the Bureau of Child Welfare. Complaints had been made by tenants in the same building concerning the treatment of the children.

As far as Kollberg could gather, the same neighbor was behind all the complaints to the various officials.

The children, who were then seven and five years old, were considered to have been left "to fend for themselves." They were poorly dressed, and the person who complained claimed he'd heard children screaming in the Svensson family's apartment. The Bureau of Child Welfare had made investigations, first in December '67, then again in May '68. They'd made several house calls, but hadn't found any signs of abuse. The place was not well taken care of, the mother seemed slovenly, the father was unemployed, and the family's finances were in bad shape. Nothing indicated, however, that the children were illtreated. The older one got along well in school, was healthy and of normal intelligence, though somewhat shy and reserved. The younger child was at home with the mother during the day, but was sometimes left with a neighbor when the mother did some temporary job. The neighbor, who had three children of her own, described the child as lively, receptive and sociable and said she'd never shown any sign of poor health. In November of '68 the parents' legal separation had gone into effect. The children were still under supervision.

The Unemployment Office had paid out insurance to

the family during the period from October '67 to April '68. The man had enrolled for job training and during the fall of '68 had gone through a basic course in mechanics at the Vocational Training Board school. In January of '69—the present year—Svensson had found employment as a laborer at Kockum's machine works in Malmö, where he'd then moved.

The Department of Public Health had made noise measurements on the Svensson's apartment in connection with the request for eviction submitted by the real estate agency. The noise—in the form of children screaming, people walking across the floor and water running—was considered above the acceptable norm.

That verdict applied just as well to the entire housing project, but no one seemed to take that into consideration.

In the month of June 1968 the Rent Control Commission reached a decision about the real estate agency's right to terminate the Svenssons' lease. The Svensson family had been forced to leave the apartment on September 1. No alternative housing had been found for them.

Kollberg had talked to the monster at the real estate agency. She was very sorry that they'd had to go as far as evicting the family, but there'd been too many complaints against them. Finally she said, "I think it was best for them, too. They didn't fit here."

"In what way?" Kollberg asked.

"We have a different class of tenants, if you know what I mean. We really aren't used to having, almost every single day, to call in the Temperance Board, the police, the Bureau of Child Welfare and God knows what all ..."

"Then you reported the Svensson family to the authorities, and not the neighbors?" Kollberg had asked.

"Certainly. When you hear that things are not as they should be, it's your duty to investigate. One of the neighbors was very cooperative, of course."

He'd ended the conversation there, feeling almost sick with helplessness and disgust.

Did it really have to be this way? Yes, obviously it did.

Kollberg parked the car on Norrtullsgatan, but didn't get out immediately. He took out his notebook and pencil. With the help of his notes, he made the following list:

1967	Sept.	Laid off
	Oct.	Intoxication (Bollmora Police Station)
	Nov.	Temperance Board
	Dec.	Domestic disturbance. Bureau of Child Welfare
1968	Jan.	Domestic disturbance (Bollm. P.)
	Feb.	Temperance Board
	March	Intoxication (Bollm. P.)
	April	Domestic disturbance (Bollm. P.). Temperance Board
	May	Bureau of Child Welfare
	June	Rent Control Commission's ruling on termination of lease
	July	Decision on eviction. Domestic disturbance (Bollm. P.)
	Aug.	—
	Sept.	Evicted
	Oct.	—
	Nov.	Separation
	Dec.	—
1969	Jan.	Moves to Malmö. Kockum's
	July	Shoots V. Palmgren?

He studied what he'd written for a moment and reflected that this dismal chart almost cried out for a fitting title:

It never rains but it pours.

27

Norrtullsgatan 23 was a seedy old building. After the stifling heat outside, it was surprisingly cool in the stairwell. It felt as though the damp chill of winter lurked in the walls under the flaking plaster.

Mrs. Svensson lived one flight up, and the door with her name, EVA SVENSSON, appeared to be a kitchen entrance.

Kollberg pounded. After a minute he heard steps from within and the rattle of a safety chain being unhooked. The door was opened slightly. Kollberg displayed his identification in the crack of the door. He couldn't see the person who answered, but heard a deep sigh before the door was opened.

Kollberg had guessed right; he stepped straight into a large kitchen. The woman who shut the door behind him was small and thin and had sharp, sad features. Her straggly hair had probably been dyed white some time ago, for the ends were almost white, with darker streaks higher up, changing to brown an inch from her scalp. She was dressed in a striped housecoat of sleazy cotton material with large, dark perspiration stains under the arms. The smell told Kollberg that this wasn't the first time she'd sweated in that coat since it had last been washed. She was bare-legged; her feet were stuck into a pair of terry-cloth slippers of a nondescript color. Kollberg knew that she was twenty-nine, but would have guessed at least thirty-five.

"The police," she said hesitantly. "What's happened now? If you're looking for Bertil he isn't here."

"No," Kollberg said, "I know. I only want to talk to you for a while, if that's all right. May I come in?"

The woman nodded and walked over to the kitchen table, which was by the window. An open magazine and a half-eaten sandwich lay on a flowered plastic tablecloth, and a filter cigarette went on smoking on a blue-flowered saucer, which was already full of filter-tipped butts. Around the table were three chairs. She sat down and picked up the cigarette from the saucer, pointing to the chair across from herself.

"Sit down," she said.

Kollberg sat down and glanced out the window at a dreary back yard, relieved only by a carpet-beating rack and garbage cans.

"What do you want to talk about?" Eva Svensson asked, pertly. "You can't stay too long, because I have to pick up Tomas at the playground soon."

"Tomas," Kollberg said, "is the youngest."

"Yes. He's six. I leave him in the playground behind the School of Economics while I go shopping and do the cleaning."

Kollberg looked around the kitchen.

"You have another one, don't you?" he said.

"Yes, Ursula. She's at camp. On Children's Island."

"How long have you lived here?"

"Since last April," she said and sucked on the cigarette

until only the filter remained. "But I'll only be allowed to stay over the summer. The old lady doesn't like the kids. Damned if I know where to go then."

"Are you working now?" Kollberg asked.

The woman threw the smoldering filter into the saucer.

"Yes. I work for the old lady we live with. That is, I get to live here in return for cleaning and cooking and shopping and washing and waiting on her. She's old and can't go down the steps alone, so I have to help her when she goes out. And other things."

Kollberg nodded toward a door across the room from the outer door.

"Is that where you live?"

"Yeah," the woman said curtly. "We live there."

Kollberg got up and opened the door. The room was approximately twelve feet by sixteen. The window faced the dismal yard. Beds lined two of the walls. Underneath one of them was a low bed that could be pulled out. A chest of drawers, two chairs, a rickety little table and a rag rug completed the furnishings.

"It's not too big," Eva Svensson said from behind him. "But we're allowed to be in the kitchen as much as we want, and the kids can play in the yard."

Kollberg returned to the kitchen table. He looked at the woman, who was now doodling with her index finger on the plastic tablecloth and said, "I'd like you to tell me how it's been for you and your husband during the last few years. I know that you're divorced or separated, but how was it before that? He was unemployed a rather long time, wasn't he?"

"Yes, he got fired almost two years ago. Not because he'd done anything. Everybody got fired because they shut down the company. It must have been losing money. Then he couldn't find a job; there just weren't any. No real job, I mean. He had a pretty good one before that. He was an office worker, but didn't have the proper education, and all the jobs he applied for went to someone who was better qualified."

Kollberg nodded.

"How long was he with this company before it went out of business?"

"Twelve years. And before that he was with another

company with the same boss. Palmgren. Well, maybe he wasn't the boss, but he owned the company. Bertil worked in the warehouse there, and later on he was a delivery boy, but then he was moved to the office of this company that was shut down. The other one must have been shut down, too."

"How long were you married?"

"We got married at Whitsuntide in 1959."

She took a bite from the half-eaten sandwich, looked at it, stood up and walked over to the counter and threw it into the sink.

"So we were married for eight and a half years," she said.

"When did you move out to Bollmora?" Kollberg asked.

The woman remained standing by the sink, picking her teeth with the nail of her little finger.

"In the fall of '67. We lived in a building on Västmannagatan before that. It was company housing, because Mr. Palmgren owned that building, too. Then he was going to repair the building and make offices out of the apartments, I think, and then we got to move into that new building he'd built. It looked a lot nicer, of course, but it was so far outside of town, and the rent was really high. When Bertil got fired I thought we'd have to move, but we didn't have to. At any rate, not until later, and that was because of other things."

"What kind of other things?" asked Kollberg.

"Well, like Bertil drank," she said vaguely. "And the neighbor under us complained because he thought we made too much noise. But we didn't make any more noise than the other people in the building. Sound traveled really well, and you could hear children screaming and dogs barking and record players blaring, even if it was several floors below. We thought they had a piano above us until we learned that the piano was three stories up. And the kids couldn't play inside. Anyway, we were evicted last fall."

The sun had begun to shine into the kitchen, and Kollberg took out his handkerchief and wiped his forehead.

"Did he drink a lot?" he asked.

"Yeah, sometimes."

"What was he like when he was drinking? Aggressive?"

She didn't answer immediately. She walked back and sat down.

"He got angry sometimes. Because he'd lost his job and at the system and things like that. I got pretty tired of hearing that every time he'd had a couple drinks."

"It's claimed there were fights in the apartment sometimes," Kollberg said. "What happened then?"

"Oh, they weren't fights, exactly. We quarreled sometimes, and once the kids woke up and started playing in the middle of the night when we were asleep, and then the patrolmen came. Of course, we might have talked pretty loud once in a while, but we didn't fight or anything like that."

Kollberg nodded.

"Didn't you turn to the Tenants' Association when you were threatened with eviction?" he asked.

She shook her head.

"No, we didn't belong to anything like that. There wasn't anything to do, anyway, so we had to move."

"Where did you live after that?"

"I got hold of a one-room apartment for us to sublet. I lived there until I moved here, but Bertil had to go to a bachelor's hotel when we got divorced. Now he lives in Malmö."

"Hmm," Kollberg said. "When did you see him last?"

Eva Svensson drew her fingers through her hair at the back of her head, reflected a moment and said, "Last Thursday, I think it was. He came here real suddenly, but I made him leave after about an hour, because I had to work. He was on vacation, he said, and was going to be in Stockholm for a few days. I even got a little money from him."

"You haven't heard from him since then?"

"No. He must've gone back to Malmö after that, I suppose. I've seen nothing of him, anyway."

She turned around and glanced at the alarm clock standing on the refrigerator.

"I have to go get Tomas now," she said. "They don't like it if you leave the kids there too long."

She got up and went into her room, but left the door open.

"Why did you get divorced?" Kollberg said, standing up.

"We were tired of each other. Everything was such a mess. We did nothing but quarrel toward the end. And Bertil was home all the time, grumbling and feeling sorry for himself. I couldn't stand to look at him finally."

She came out into the kitchen. She'd combed her hair and put on sandals.

"I really have to go now," she said.

"Just one more question," said Kollberg. "Did your husband know the big boss, Mr. Palmgren?"

"Oh no, I don't even think he'd ever seen him," she said. "Palmgren sat up in an office and managed everything. I don't think he ever went to his companies. They were run by other bosses, sort of managers."

She took a string bag that was hanging on a hook by the stove and opened the kitchen door. Kollberg held the door open and let her walk out into the hall in front of him. Then he closed the door and said, "What newspapers and magazines do you read?"

"*Expressen* sometimes. Especially on Sunday. And *Hennes* and *Hela Världen* every week. Magazines are so expensive, I think. Why'd you ask?"

"I just wondered," Kollberg said.

They parted outside of the door, and he watched her walk away toward Odenplan, small and thin in her sleazy dress.

It was afternoon by the time Kollberg called Malmö to announce the results of his inquiries. During the last half an hour, Martin Beck had been pacing back and forth in the corridor, waiting impatiently for the call, and when it finally came he grabbed the receiver before the first signal had died away.

He started the tape recorder, which was hooked up to the telephone, and let Kollberg talk without interrupting him or making any comments. When Kollberg had finished Martin Beck said, "Good work, Lennart. Now I probably won't have to bother you any more."

"Okay," Kollberg said. "It looks like you've found the

right guy. Now I have to go back to my work, but let me hear from you—to know how it went. Say 'hi' to the people who deserve it. Bye."

Martin Beck took the tape recorder with him to Månsson's room. They listened through the tape together.

"What do you think?" Martin Beck asked.

"Well," said Månsson, "the motive's there. First laid off after more than twelve years with Palmgren's company, then evicted by the same Palmgren and finally divorced into the bargain. And then he had to move away from Stockholm to get a job, a job that's socially and economically worse than the one he had before. All because of Palmgren."

Martin Beck nodded and Månsson continued, "Furthermore, he was in Stockholm last Thursday. I never really did understand why they didn't have time to pick him up at Haga terminal. If they'd just pulled that off, we would've had him when Palmgren passed away. It makes you mad to think about it."

"I know why they didn't make it," Martin Beck said, "but I'll tell you about it some other time. You'll be even madder when you hear it."

"Okay, save it," Månsson said.

Martin Beck lit a cigarette and sat in silence for a while.

Then he said, "There's something rotten about this eviction. It was apparently the real estate agency that put the various authorities onto him."

"With the help of a cooperative neighbor, yes."

"Who was no doubt also employed by Palmgren or Broberg or both. It's a fact that Palmgren wanted him out of the apartment when he didn't employ him any longer. In Stockholm an apartment like that is worth big money. Dirty money."

"You mean to say that Palmgren told his employees in the realty company to find a pretext for evicting him," Månsson said.

"Yeah. I'm convinced of it. Through Broberg, of course. And Bertil Svensson must've understood the connection himself. It's hardly surprising he hated Palmgren."

Månsson scratched the back of his head and pulled a face.

"No, that's true," he said. "But to go so far as to shoot him . . ."

"You have to remember that Svensson had been having a rough time for quite some time. When he began to realize that it wasn't just his own hard luck, but that he was being treated unjustly by one man or perhaps by a social group, his hate must have become an obsession. Practically everything was taken away from him bit by bit."

"And Palmgren represented just that social group," said Månsson and nodded.

Martin Beck stood up and said, "I think the safest thing is to send somebody out who can keep an eye on him for the time being, so we don't miss him again. Somebody who doesn't chase after little piggies on the job."

Månsson stared at him in amazement.

28

The man whose name was Bertil Svensson lived in Kirsebergsstaden, close to the eastern city limit. The area is also called Bulltofta Hills or just the Hills, since, compared to the topography of the rest of the city, there are marked differences in elevation.

Living "out in the Hills" had always been looked down upon by the Malmö bourgeoisie, but many Kirseberg residents were proud of their section and enjoyed living there, even though their homes not infrequently lacked modern conveniences or were in general below average, since no one bothered to maintain or repair them. People who ended up in the poorest apartments either weren't wanted in the smarter residential areas or weren't considered to be in need of a higher standard of living. It was no accident that many of the foreign factory workers who'd come to Malmö during recent years lived in this area.

This was a working-class neighborhood, and few Mal-

mö residents of the category that Viktor Palmgren, for
example, belonged to, had ever set their foot there or
were even aware that the area existed.

It was here that Benny Skacke rode his bicycle on
Friday afternoon. He had instructions from Martin Beck
to find out if Bertil Svensson was at home, and, if that
were the case, to keep watch on him without arousing his
suspicion. Skacke also had to communicate with Månsson
or Martin Beck once every hour.

If all went well they were planning to arrest Svensson
the same night; only a couple details were missing, Martin
Beck had said.

According to what the man had told his employer and
the rifle club, he should live on Vattenverksvägen, a
street that cuts across Kirsebergsstaden from Lundavägen in the west to Simrishamn railroad in the east. From
Lundavägen, the street sloped up to a hill, and Skacke
preferred to get off his bicycle before he came to the
crown. He walked his bicycle past the old, round water
tower, which had been converted many years before into
a residence. Skacke wondered if the apartments inside
looked like pieces of pie. He recalled that he'd read a
newspaper article on the scandalous sanitary conditions
prevalent in the building, and that it was inhabited almost
exclusively by Yugoslavs.

He left his bicycle on Kirseberg Square and hoped it
wouldn't be stolen. He'd used black tape to cover the
word POLICE on the frame, a cautionary measure he
always took when he thought he should remain anony-
mous.

The building he was going to watch was an old two-
story apartment house. He observed it for a moment from
the sidewalk opposite. It had nine windows on the street,
two on each side of the door and five on the floor above.
There were also three attic windows, but the attic didn't
seem to be lived in; the windows were thick with dirt and,
as far as he could see, had no curtains.

Skacke walked rapidly across the street and opened the
door. On the door to the right of the stairs he saw a piece
of cardboard with the name B. SVENSSON printed on it
with a ballpoint pen.

Skacke went back to the square and found a bench

from which he could watch the building. He took out the evening newspaper he'd bought on his way from the police station, opened it to the center spread and pretended to read.

He had to wait only twenty minutes. The door opened, and a man came out on the sidewalk. His appearance fitted the description of the gunman at the Savoy fairly well, though he was shorter than Skacke had imagined. Even his clothes—a dark brown sport coat and lighter brown pants, a beige shirt and a tie with red and brown stripes—seemed to match the description.

Skacke kept his eyes on the man, but took his time. He folded the newspaper, stood up, put it in his pocket and began to follow the man slowly. He turned on a cross street and walked at a fairly brisk pace toward the prison at the bottom of the hill.

Skacke suddenly pitied the man walking ahead of him, wholly ignorant of how close the day was when he would be sent inside the grim walls of that ancient penitentiary. Maybe he was already confident he'd get away with it.

The man turned right by the prison and then left onto Gevaldigergatan, where he stopped beside the fence of the soccer field directly across from the prison walls.

Skacke stopped, too. A match was taking place on the grass field, and Skacke immediately recognized both of the teams—B.K. Flagg in red jerseys and F.K. Balkan in blue. It looked like a lively game was going on, and Skacke had nothing against staying to watch, but the man set off again almost immediately.

They continued out onto Lundavägen, and when they'd passed Dalhem Field the man in brown went into a sandwich shop. Skacke looked sideways through the display window as he walked past and saw the man standing in front of the counter. He waited in a doorway farther down the street. The man came out again after a moment with a box in one hand and a bag in the other and returned the same way he'd come.

Skacke could now afford to keep his distance, since he assumed that the other man was on his way home. As he passed the soccer field Balkan had just scored a goal, and a howl of joy rose in unison from the crowd, which seemed to consist mainly of Balkan supporters. A man with a small child on his shoulders was cheering vociferously, but Skacke didn't understand a word, since the man spoke Yugoslav.

The man he was shadowing went home, as he'd expected.

As Skacke walked past on the sidewalk across the street he could see the man take a can of beer out of the bag.

Skacke took advantage of the moment, went into a phone booth and called the police station. Martin Beck answered.

"Well?"

"He's back home. He went out just now to buy beer and sandwiches."

"Good. Stay there and call if he goes some place."

Skacke went back to his post on the bench. After half an hour he walked to a newsstand in the neighborhood, bought the other evening newspapers and a chocolate bar and returned to the bench.

Now and then he got up and walked up and down the sidewalk, but he didn't dare pass the window too often. It was dark now, and the man inside had turned on the light. He'd taken off his jacket, eaten the sandwiches and drunk two beers, and now he was moving back and forth in the room. Sometimes he sat down at a table by the window.

By ten-twenty Skacke had read the three newspapers several times, eaten four chocolate bars and drunk two bottles of cider; he'd had all he could take and was ready to scream.

Then the light was turned off in the room to the right of the door. Skacke waited five minutes, then called the police station. Neither Månsson nor Martin Beck was there. He called the Savoy. Inspector Beck had gone out. He called Månsson's home. They were there.

"Oh, so you're still out there," Månsson said.

"Of course, I'm still here. Should I have gone home, maybe? Why aren't you coming?"

Skacke sounded as if he were on the verge of tears.

"Oh," said Månsson nonchalantly, "I thought you knew. We're waiting until tomorrow. By the way, what's he doing now?"

Skacke gnashed his teeth.

"He's turned out the light. Probably going to bed."

Månsson didn't answer right away. Skacke heard a suspicious bubbling sound, a soft clinking and someone say, "Ah."

"I think you should do that, too," said Månsson. "Go home to bed. He didn't see you, for God's sake, did he?"

"No," said Skacke curtly, and hung up.

He threw himself on his bicycle and literally flew down the hill toward Lundavägen. Ten minutes later he was standing in the hallway outside of his room, dialing Monica's number.

At five after eight on Saturday morning Martin Beck and Månsson knocked on Bertil Svensson's door.

He answered the door in pyjamas. When he saw their identification cards he just nodded, walked back into the apartment and got dressed.

They didn't find a weapon in the apartment, which consisted of one room and a kitchen.

Bertil Svensson followed them out and got into the car without a word; he was silent the whole way to Davidshall Square.

As they went into Månsson's room he looked at the telephone and spoke for the first time.

"May I call my wife?"

"Later," Martin Beck said. "We're going to have a little talk first."

29

The whole of that morning and a good bit of the afternoon Martin Beck and Månsson sat listening to the history of Bertil Svensson, who was now being held in custody. He seemed glad of the chance to talk, was anxious for them to understand him and looked quite annoyed when he had to take a break for lunch. His story largely confirmed their reconstruction and even their theories about the motive.

After he'd been evicted, forced to move, laid off from

work and finally divorced, he would sit in his lonely room
in Malmö thinking over his situation. It became clearer
and clearer to him who was the cause of all his troubles:
Viktor Palmgren, the bloodsucker, who lined his purse at
the expense of other human beings, the big shot, who
didn't give a damn about the welfare of his employees or
tenants.

He began to hate this man as he'd never thought it
possible to hate any human being.

A couple of times during the interrogation he broke
down and began to cry, but soon pulled himself together
and assured them that he was thankful for the opportunity
to explain himself. He also said several times that he was
glad they'd come to pick him up. If they hadn't found
him, he said, he probably couldn't have held out much
longer, but would have turned himself in.

He didn't regret what he'd done.

It didn't make any difference to him that he would be
sent to prison; his life was ruined, anyway, and he didn't
have the strength to start over.

When they were through, and there was nothing more
to be said he shook hands with Martin Beck and Månsson and thanked them before he was taken to jail.

It was quiet in the room for a long time after the door
closed behind him. At last Månsson stood up, walked
over to the window and gazed out over the yard.

"Goddamn," he mumbled.

"Hope he gets a light sentence," Martin Beck said.

There was a knock on the door and Skacke came in.

"How did it go?" he said.

No one answered for a minute. Then Månsson said,
"Oh, it was about like we thought."

"He must have been a cold-blooded bastard just to
barge in like that and shoot the guy," Skacke said. "Why
did he do it like that? I'd have gone to his house and shot
him through the garden hedge when he was lying out in
the sun or something like that . . ."

"It didn't really happen like that," Martin Beck said.
"You can hear for yourself in a minute."

He wound back the tape on the machine, which had
been running all through the interrogation.

"I think it's here."

He pressed a button, and the spools began to hum.

"But how did you know that Palmgren was at the Savoy at that moment?"

That was Månsson's voice.

"I didn't. I just happened to be passing."

Bertil Svensson.

"Maybe you'd better start from the beginning. Tell us what you did that Wednesday."

That was Martin Beck.

BS: My vacation had begun on Monday, so I was off work. In the morning I didn't do anything much, just messed around at home. Washed out some shirts and underclothes—when it's this hot you have to change pretty often. Then I had a couple fried eggs and some coffee for lunch, washed the dishes and went out shopping. I walked down to Tempo on Värnhem Square; it wasn't the closest store, but I wanted to kill some time. I don't know too many people in Malmö, just a couple guys from work, but it was vacation time, and everybody had left town with their families. After I'd done some shopping I walked back home. It was real hot, and I didn't want to go out again, so I just lay on the bed reading a book I'd bought in Tempo. It was called *Till Death*, by Ed McBain. It got a bit cooler in the evening, and at about six-thirty I rode my bike out to the rifle range.

MB: Which rifle range?

BS: Where I usually shoot. In Limhamn.

PM: Did you have the revolver with you?

BS: Yeah. If you want you can have it locked up in the club house, but I always take it home with me.

PM: Okay, go on.

BS: Then I shot for an hour or so. I can't really afford it. It gets pretty expensive with the ammunition and the membership fee and all, but you gotta have some fun.

PM: How long had you had the revolver?

BS: Oh, some time. I bought it about ten years ago, when I'd won a bit of money on the pools. I always liked the idea of shooting. When I was a kid, I always wanted an air rifle, but my parents were poor and probably couldn't afford one, even if they'd wanted to. But they probably didn't want to, either. The next best thing was going to the fairgrounds and shooting at those metal elks.

MB: Are you a good shot?

BS: Yeah, you could say that. I won a couple of contests.

MB: Well, when you'd finished shooting . . .

BS: When I'd done shooting I rode the bike back into town.

PM: What about the revolver?

BS: It was in the box on the carrier rack. I took the bicycle path along Limhamn's Field, then around the Turbine and past the museum and the courthouse. When I got to the corner of Norra Vallgatan and Hamngatan, I had to stop for a red light, and that was where I caught sight of him.

PM: Of Viktor Palmgren?

BS: Yes. Through the windows at the Savoy. He was standing up, and a whole lot of people were sitting at the table.

PM: You said before that you'd never met Palmgren. How did you know it was him?

BS: I've seen his picture in the newspapers lots of times. And once when I was going past his house he came out of the gate and got into a taxi. Oh yeah, I knew it was him.

MB: What did you do?

BS: In a way I didn't think about what I was doing. At the same time, I knew what I was gonna do. It's hard to explain. I rode past the entrance to the Savoy and left the bike in the rack. I remember I didn't bother to lock it—like it didn't make any difference any more. Then I, uh, took the revolver out of the box and stuck it inside my jacket. Oh, yeah, I loaded it first; nobody walked by, and I stood with my back to the street and sort of left the revolver in the box, while I put a couple cartridges in. Then I walked into the dining room and shot him in the head. He fell down onto the table. Then I noticed that the closest window was open, so I climbed through it and walked back to the bike.

PM: Weren't you afraid of being caught? There were other people in the dining room.

BS: I didn't think that far, only that I was gonna kill that bastard.

MB: Didn't you see that the window was open when you went in?

BS: No, I didn't think about it. I guess I hadn't counted on getting away like I did. It was only after I saw him fall and saw nobody was paying any attention to me that I started thinking about getting outa there.

PM: What did you do then?

BS: I put the revolver back in the box, and then I rode away over Petri Bridge and past the railroad station. I don't know the schedule for the boats, but I did know that the hydrofoils leave every hour, on the hour. It was twenty to nine on the station clock, so I rode over to the Butter Inspection Station and left the bike there. Then I went to buy a ticket for the hydrofoil. I took the revolver box along. I thought it was kinda strange that nobody came after me. When the boat left I stayed out on deck, and the stewardess said I had to go in, but I paid no attention and stayed out there until we were about halfway over the Sound. Then I threw the box with the revolver and the cartridges into the sea and went in and sat down.

MB: Did you know what you were going to do when you got to Copenhagen?

BS: No, not really. I could only sort a think a bit at a time.

MB: What did you do in Copenhagen?

BS: I walked around. And I went some place and drank a beer. Then I got the idea of going up to Stockholm to see my wife.

MB: Did you have any money?

BS: I had a bit over a thousand kronor—my two months' vacation pay.

MB: Okay, go on.

BS: I took the bus out to Kastrup and bought a one-way ticket to Stockholm. They said they'd tell me what plane I gotta fly on. Naturally, I didn't give them my real name.

MB: What time was it then?

BS: It was close to midnight then. I sat there till morning, and then there was a flight—seven-twenty-five, I think it was. When I got to Stockholm I took the bus from Arlanda to Haga terminal and then I walked home to the wife and kids. They live on Norrtullsgatan.

PM: How long did you stay there?

BS: An hour. Maybe two.

PM: When did you come back here?

BS: Last Monday. I got to Malmö last Monday night.

PM: Where did you stay in Stockholm?

BS: At a kind of boardinghouse on Odengatan. I don't remember what the name was.

MB: What did you do when you got back to Malmö?

BS: Nothing much. I couldn't go shooting. I didn't have a revolver any more.

MB: What about the bicycle? Was it still there?

BS: Yeah, I picked it up on the way back from the train.

PM: I've been wondering about something. Before you saw Viktor Palmgren through the window at the Savoy, had you ever thought about shooting him? Or was it an impulse?

BS: I guess I must've thought about it before, but it wasn't like I planned to do it, exactly. But when I saw him standing there and I had the revolver with me, it hit me in a flash that it was the easiest thing in the world just to shoot him. From the moment I decided to do it I didn't worry about what would happen later. Right then it felt like I'd gotten the idea for the first time. But deep down I must've wanted him dead all along.

MB: How did you feel when you read the newspaper? You must have read the newspapers the next day?

BS: Sure.

MB: How did you feel when you realized he might live?

BS: I was mad at myself for making a bad job of it. I thought maybe I should've fired more times, but I didn't want to hurt anyone else, and it looked like he died right then, on the spot.

MB: What about now? How do you feel now?

BS: I'm glad he's dead.

PM: Maybe we should take a break. You need something to eat.

Martin Beck turned off the tape recorder.

"You can hear the rest later, by yourself," he told Skacke. "After I'm gone."

30

Late on Saturday night, July 12 of this warm summer, Martin Beck was sitting alone at a table in the dining room at the Savoy.

He'd packed his suitcase an hour or two earlier and had carried it down himself to the reception desk. Now there was no immediate hurry, and he was considering taking the night train to Stockholm.

He'd talked on the phone to Malm, who'd seemed very pleased and repeated time after time, "No complications, in other words? That's excellent, just excellent."

Just excellent, Martin Beck thought.

The restaurant was comfortable and intimate, but rather splendid at the same time. Flickering candles on the tables were mirrored in the enormous silver tureens. The fitting complement of diners, conversing at a fittingly low level. Not so many as to be intrusive, nor so few as to make one feel lonely.

Waiters in white jackets. The little headwaiter, bowing and eagerly tugging at his cuffs.

Martin Beck had started off with a whisky in the bar and followed it with *Sole Walewska* in the dining room. With his meal he drank the house akvavit, which was flavored with secret ingredients and very good.

Now he was lingering over coffee and a shot of Sève Fournier.

It was all quite superb. Good food, good drink and attentive service. The summer evening outside of the open windows was dense and warm and pleasant.

Morever, a case had been wound up.

He should have felt good, but it didn't look like it.

As it was, he noticed very little of what was going on around him. It was doubtful, in fact, if he was even aware of what he ate and drank.

Viktor Palmgren was dead.

Gone forever and missed by no one, save for a handful

of international swindlers and representatives of suspect regimes in countries far away. They would soon learn to do business with Mats Linder instead, and so things would be, to all intents and purposes, unchanged.

Charlotte Palmgren was now very rich and practically independent, and as far as one could see, Linder and Hoff-Jensen had a brilliant future in store.

Hampus Broberg would probably be able to avoid another arrest, and a staff of well-paid lawyers would show that he hadn't misappropriated or tried to smuggle stocks out of the country or done anything else illegal. His wife and daughter were already in safety in Switzerland or Liechtenstein with fat bank accounts at their disposal. Helena Hansson would presumably receive some sort of sentence, but certainly not so severe that she couldn't set herself up in her former profession within the fairly near future.

There remained a shipyard janitor, who in the course of time would be tried for second-degree, maybe first-degree, murder, and then have to rot away the best years of his life in a prison cell.

Chief Inspector Martin Beck didn't feel good at all.

He paid his bill, picked up his suitcase and walked over Mälar Bridge toward the railway station.

He wondered if he'd be able to sleep on the train.

About the Authors

PER WAHLÖÖ and MAJ SJÖWALL, his wife
and co-author, wrote ten Martin Beck
mysteries. Mr. Wahlöö, who died in 1975,
was a reporter for several Swedish newspapers and magazines and wrote numerous radio and television plays, film scripts,
short stories and novels. Maj Sjöwall is
also a poet.